# CHRISTMAS
# IN CAROL

# CHRISTMAS IN CAROL

•

## Sheila Robins

*AVALON BOOKS*
NEW YORK

Published by Thomas Bouregy & Co., Inc.
160 Madison Avenue, New York, NY 10016

Library of Congress Cataloging-in-Publication Data

Robins, Sheila.
    Christmas in Carol / Sheila Robins.
        p. cm.
    ISBN 0-8034-9804-7 (acid-free paper)
    1. Christmas stories.    I. Title.

PS3568.A235C47 2006
813'.6—dc22

                                            2006024266

PRINTED IN THE UNITED STATES OF AMERICA
ON ACID-FREE PAPER
BY HADDON CRAFTSMEN, BLOOMSBURG, PENNSYLVANIA

For Rose and Robbie

Thanks to Susan Wiggs, Debbie Macomber, and Jill Barnett, my three good fairies who have given me so much good advice and encouragement. Thanks, also, to the Port Orchard Brain Trust: Lois, Kate, Anjali, Krysteen, the two Susans, P. J., and Rose Marie.

## Chapter One

My family is to Christmas what ants are to a picnic. No, that's not strong enough. Let me put it to you this way. Paid assassins couldn't do a better job of killing the holiday than my nearest and dearest.

It's not that they don't celebrate it. They do, by putting their unique Hartwell stamp on it. And that's the problem, because every year that stamp has a new design more horrible than the one before.

One year my Uncle Bob thought it would be cool to help my brother Ben try out his new football inside the house. They broke the pottery masterpiece Aunt Chloe had given Mom and Dad (a vase with graceful but misaligned curves and a glaze that made it look like someone had barfed on it), and that touched off the Christmas equivalent of a dirty bomb. The noise level rose so high, one of the neighbors finally called the police. (There's not a lot of crime in the almost-thriving metropolis of Carol, Washington, and both the neighbors and cops had nothing better to do.) We made the newspaper's police blotter page. No names were mentioned, but people still managed to figure out it was us.

1

Another year my Mom hired a Santa to come to the house and surprise all the kids. But Mom was the one who got the surprise when Santa made a pass at Grandma. Grandma got practically giddy from the experience. Our neighbor, Mr. Harris, was far from giddy when the fake Santa took out his car's rear bumper while driving away.

Then there was the Christmas Dad burned too much wrapping paper in the fireplace and started a chimney fire. Actually, that happened a couple of times. The first time, I was in grade school, and I thought it was exciting standing around outside with coats thrown over our bathrobes and watching the fire truck roar up to the house. But when I was a teenager, the experience was just plain mortifying, especially when I heard one of the neighbors comment, "Hartwell. Who else?" That was mild compared to some of the comments I got when I returned to school after the holidays. We made the police blotter page again that year, and I seriously considered changing my last name. The only thing that stopped me was the realization that I was too late. Everyone already knew who my family was.

I remember thinking, *Why me, God? Why, of all the families in the whole, wide world, did you have to torture me with this one?* Nobody likes a lippy teenager, and God never gave me an answer.

I could cope with little things like chimney fires, family squabbles, and irresponsible Santas. It was the betrayals that finally pushed me to decide I could live (quite happily) without ever spending another Christmas in Carol.

Not that I was bitter. I was simply protective of my heart.

Who could blame me? My first Christmas home from college, I found Gabe Knightly, the one-time love of my life, on my doorstep, mistletoe in hand and looking for my sister, Keira. He had stared at me like I was the Grinch, and stuttered, "Hi, Andie. Merry Christmas."

Yeah, right. Ho, ho, ho.

The next trip home for the holidays, I arrived to find my dad loading his belongings into his Jaguar (the one he'd spent his and Mom's emergency fund on). I guess, when it came to midlife crises, Mom had no patience. The only silver lining to that bleak Christmas was no chimney fires.

By the third Christmas Mom and Dad were divorced and I came back to find Gabe Knightly no longer dating my sister. Now he was seeing my best friend, April White.

Make that former best friend. No, I'm not bitter. I've just been too busy to stay in touch with April. You can't keep up with everyone.

Oh, and the final straw that trip was when Aunt Chloe drank too much eggnog and decided to set Hans, the family parakeet, free. Uncle Bob was coming in the front door at the time, dropping presents, and calling, "Ho, ho, ho. Merry Christmas."

"Shut the door!" we chorused.

He did, right after Hans shot through it. We never saw old Hansy again. I like to think of him in a tree on a tropical beach somewhere, soaking up the rays. It beats thinking of him winding up as Christmas dinner for Lucifer, the neighbor's cat.

My last year of college I got smart and stayed away. I shipped presents to my family, then went with my roommate to her home in Texas and saw how a normal family celebrated the holidays. It was peaceful and quiet. Nobody fought, no one tried to burn down the house, and they all went to Christmas Eve service together. It was deeply soul-satisfying, like living in a Norman Rockwell painting. Much different from my family's Andy Warhol existence.

Then, last year, I was broke and job hunting, and insisted I couldn't come home. I nobly resisted all offers to buy me a plane ticket. And I intended to do the same this year.

Don't get me wrong. I love my family. I really do. And I'd gladly have come home any other time of year to be frustrated, embarrassed, and disappointed. Just not Christmas, at least not my first Christmas in New York. All I wanted was this one nice, normal holiday in my new home.

And I had my excuse ready. I had to work at my new job at Image Makers Advertising Agency clear up until Christmas Eve. That's how it is on Madison Avenue: Busy, busy, busy.

Not that I'm a hot shot. I'm a planner, a fairly new animal in advertising. We take a product brand and project where it's going to go for, say, the next five years. And, of course, do our part to get it there. Sounds exciting, doesn't it? It would have been, if I were the head planner. But I wasn't, which meant my boss got to tap into my genius, suck out all the great ideas, then leave my empty shell to do her grunt work. That supposedly made me a team player. I was fast concluding it made me more of a victim, and with big plans in the works, I was reluctant to leave. Who knew what might happen in my absence or what opportunities I might miss?

"I just can't get away," I said when Mom called.

"You have to come, Andie," she wailed into the phone. "We already paid for your plane ticket."

"Mom. Why didn't you ask me before you did that?"

"Now I need to ask my daughter if she wants to come see her family at Christmas? Especially since she didn't come home last year?" Mom sounded all huffy.

"I have to work." I looked around my cozy living room, funky with old furniture and throw rugs scrounged from flea markets. My roommate, Camilla, and I had already decided where we were going to put the tree.

"Who's your employer, Ebeneezer Scrooge?" Mom demanded. I was still trying to come up with a reply to that when she said, "It just won't feel like Christmas without you." Then she played her trump card. "And it would mean so much to your grandmother. She's not well, Andie."

Oh, no. What was Mom trying to tell to me? "Not well? What do you mean?"

"I mean she's reached an age where you can't take it for granted that she'll be around forever."

Mom was trying to break it to me gently. Something was really wrong with Gram. "Is she . . ." My throat closed up and I couldn't finish my sentence.

"No," said Mom. "But I think you'd better tell your boss to get her priorities straight and let you come home. And tell her you have to stay for New Year's."

There would be fireworks in Carol's town square New Year's Eve. Everyone would be there, including Gabe Knightly. Just the thought of seeing him set off fireworks in my stomach.

New Year's might be a bad idea. Anyway, ever since I hit NYC last August, I'd been looking forward to going to Times Square to see the ball drop. Camilla and I had been talking about it since Thanksgiving.

"We never get to see you now that you're on the east coast," said Mom. "Anyway, you don't want to miss the New Year's Eve celebrations."

Heavens, no! Who wouldn't pick downtown Carol over Times Square?

"So, I'll e-mail the tickets to you. Okay?" Mom asked.

"Let me check with my boss first," I told her. "That way I'll know how long I can stay."

Mom harrumphed at the thought of having to run her holiday plans by another person, but she agreed. "Tell the old Scrooge I already bought the ticket. I'll call you tomorrow at work."

My boss, Beryl Welling (Beryl the Brit behind her back), was our head planner. In her late thirties, she was an elegant and charming barracuda, and office gossip had it that she once dated Hugh Grant. *She* dumped Hugh. Clients ate out of her hand and the owners of the company worshipped at her feet. The only thing her underlings did at her feet was fall down dead from overwork.

There had been plenty of that lately. We were right in the middle of reeling in a big client: Nutri Bread. And I had provided the bait.

I went into Beryl's office, sure that she would make me choose between my job and my family—a terrifying thought because if I didn't come home, Mom would probably FedEx me a spanking.

"Home for Christmas," Beryl said thoughtfully after I'd presented my request.

"If you need me here, I won't go," I said nobly.

I'd call Gram and have a nice, long chat. And I could come back for a few days in the spring, after we had the Nutri Bread campaign up and running. After all, Mom did say Gram wasn't dying. But maybe she was and Mom didn't want to tell me over the phone.

What *was* wrong with Gram? It had to be something serious for Mom to be so insistent that I come home. I wished I'd thought to find out before I went to Beryl's office.

"We are a team, my poppet," Beryl reminded me. "And with so much to do on the Nutri Bread account, you don't see me taking time off." She drummed her perfect, acrylic nails on her desktop. "Our media strategy is complete," she mused.

We'd gone over it only a few days before. I nodded agreement.

"Art proofs?"

"Will be ready by January second."

"Ad copy?"

"Done by the twentieth." I was too efficient for my own good.

I could almost see the wheels turning in her head. "I suppose if your family has already made plans, you must go," she said slowly. "I think we can manage here without you."

I wasn't sure I wanted them to be able to manage without me. "Thanks," I said miserably, and left her office feeling like a gold miner who had just deserted her claim to go have a nice vacation in a mental ward. *You're doing the right thing,* I told myself.

Maybe I would have felt better about doing the right thing if I hadn't been guilted into it. I decided to find out what exactly was going on with my grandmother and e-mailed my sister, Keira. "What's wrong with Gram?"

I got Keira's reply before I left work. "Nothing, other than her usual bad taste in food. She came over for dinner last night and brought prune whip for dessert. Gag. Anyway, where did you get the idea something was wrong with her?"

Where, indeed? I frowned at my computer screen. Leave it to Mom to parlay Gram's never ending intestinal troubles into a coup of motherly manipulation. For that I was supposed to abandon a perfect holiday and, even worse, leave my ideas unguarded and at the mercy of Beryl the Brit.

Of course, advertising execs only steal their underlings' ideas in the movies, so I was being paranoid. Still, I wished I'd checked with Keira before I'd gone to Beryl. I got a sudden visual of Beryl proudly presenting my brilliant media strategy to the client in my absence and taking all the credit.

Actually, brilliant is an understatement. This was ultra brilliant, like those Got Milk ads. With everyone in Western civilization on some form of low-carb diet these days, bread sales are sinking faster than the Titanic. But we still need some carbs. They give us energy and keep our brain functioning. So, what the Nutri Bread people needed to do was remind consumers of those needs and make sure that when they thought of energy and brain food, they thought of Nutri

Bread. To make that happen, I'd proposed we run TV and magazine ads featuring stumbling athletes, students slumped over text books, tired moms leaning against cluttered kitchen counters, worker bees napping on their desks, all in need of rescue. Then we'd ask, "Need a Boost?" The answer to the need, of course, would be Nutri Bread. This was such an incredible idea. I'd projected a double in sales in the first year alone. It would make my career.

If Beryl the Brit didn't start acting like some character in a movie and taking all the credit for it. Did I mention that a lot of the big advertising planners are British?

Well, long live the Queen and all that. I have nothing against imports. It's just the ones who look like Fergie and think like the Antichrist who give me problems. Okay, Beryl wasn't quite that bad. Just almost. Untrustworthy was probably her middle name.

I tried not to think about Beryl's untrustworthiness when I called my mom back. Maybe I could hide the ad copy. And if I got back before the art proofs came in . . .

"I can come, but I have to be home by New Year's Eve," I insisted. "How much will it cost to change . . . ?" I gave up trying to complete the sentence since Mom was already talking over me. I think she stopped listening after the first three words.

"This is wonderful! Everyone's going to be so excited you're coming home. I can hardly wait to see you, sweetie. Bye."

When I got the e-ticket, I learned I was expected to come home a whole week before Christmas. And the return departure date said January 2. Of course, I would change it.

My flight touched down at 8:17 on the nineteenth. By 8:30 I was past security and found Mom, Aunt Chloe, and Keira waiting for me. Mom was holding a WELCOME HOME ANDIE sign like I was a returning soldier, and they were all jumping up and down, waving and calling my name, making me look like a celebrity and themselves look like idiots. Not that it bothered my family what they looked like. It never had.

Keira was très chic in her faux fur coat and black boots, her blonde hair pulled back into a long, fat ponytail.

My hair was just as blond, but short these days, which would make it easy to tell us apart. That and the fact that Keira was still anorexically skinny. I am not fat, but every time I get around my little sister I feel like Miss Piggy.

Next to Keira stood my Aunt Chloe, all decked out to pose for a tacky greeting card, in black stretch pants (stretched to the breaking point) under a huge, red sweatshirt sporting Tweety Bird in a Santa hat. She had topped her boot-black hair with a hat to match Tweety's. Oh, yes. Put Aunt Chloe on the cover of a Christmas card and title it *Want to Trade Relatives This Christmas?* or *Who Says Christmas Cookies Make You Fat? Look at Me.* Hard to believe this woman had gone through two husbands. One died, the other she divorced. Both left her financially well off enough to spend the rest of her life in artistic pursuits and torturing her relatives with the by-products. Everyone in the family had at least one lopsided vase from her pottery phase. And poor Grandma had to hang Aunt Chloe's still life of thawing hamburger on her dining room wall. Mom claims she lost the watercolor Aunt Chloe did of the back yard. I know for a fact she burned it.

Good old Mom. She looked normal—light brown hair cut in a hot new style, slender in jeans, a white tailored shirt, and a cute pink satin jacket. But I knew the moment she turned around I would see some hideous slogan on the back of that jacket, something in truly bad taste.

How did I know this? Because Mom had become a firm believer in self-promotion, and she had a new business to promote: Man Haters, Inc. If you wanted a mug, jacket, tacky wall hanging or T-shirt with some insulting epitaph regarding the male of the species, Mom had it.

Since I hadn't wanted to come home, I was surprised by the wave of emotion that washed over me at the sight of my family as I rushed to hug them. *My family. The people I care about, the people who made up the fabric of my life growing up, the people who helped make me who I am today . . . which is nothing like them,* I hastily added to myself.

And under all that emotion, something else was stirring: curiosity. What was on the back of Mom's jacket? And if it was really bad, was there a way I could pretend I didn't know her, just 'til we got to the car?

"Oh, you look great," Mom gushed. "Like a real New Yorker, all dressed in black." She gave me a mother-smother kind of hug, nearly suffocating me. She was still wearing her favorite perfume that gave off poisonous vanilla-skunk fumes. Maybe that perfume was another reason why Dad left, I thought.

Aunt Chloe regarded me with concern. "You've lost weight."

As a size twelve, I was hardly in danger of getting rushed to the hospital and given an IV drip full of vitamins.

"No, she hasn't," said Keira, not in the least worried about my starving to death. She hooked her arm through mine and started towing me toward the baggage claim, leaving Mom and Aunt Chloe to follow.

"What's on the back of Mom's jacket?" I asked.

"You don't want to know. Ben said sorry he couldn't come to meet you. He had band practice, then he had to hang the Christmas lights for Mom."

Ah, yes. My older brother the musician. By day he could be found at Carol Music, selling bass guitars to rising rock stars. By night he became a star himself, cranking out hot riffs on his guitar. Weekends, he played all over the county with his band, Fish Without Legs. There probably wasn't a church kid within a fifty-mile radius who didn't have one of the band's autographed CDs. The band even had a manager now, which, I guess, finally made them legit for all the adults in the family. What had started out as Ben's folly was now the pride of the Hartwells, and everyone was planning to attend their big concert with two other hot local bands, The Red Sea Pedestrians and Heaven Help Us, at the old Roxy theater.

Now Keira was flashing her left hand in front of my face. "So, is that gorgeous or what?"

I thought the rock on her finger was obscenely huge. I mean, it was so big most people would think it was cubic zirconia.

"Wow," I managed. "That must have set old Spencer back a few pennies."

"He can afford it, believe me." Keira hugged my arm fiercely. "He's such a great guy. I can hardly wait for you to meet him. He's coming with us to Ben's concert tomorrow night. Oh, and tomorrow I want you to go house hunting with me."

"House hunting. You're not getting married until June. Why are you house hunting now?"

"Spencer thinks we should buy now, before interest rates go up. Anyway, it takes time to find a house."

In Carol? Who was she kidding?

"And you have to allow time for the deal to close."

Speaking of closing deals, Keira had sure gotten a ring out of Spencer in a hurry. He went from being her gynecologist to her fiancé in just six months. Marrying your gynecologist. Why did that kind of creep me out?

"So, you'll look at houses with me tomorrow?" Keira pressed.

"Doesn't Spencer want to do that?"

"Oh, I'll send him pics, then bring him back later to see anything I really like."

"Okay then. Why not?" I enjoyed poking around houses, pretending I was rich and could actually afford one. And I *had* come home to see my family.

We were at the baggage claim now, and Mom was turning around to look for my battered Samsonite with the pink ribbon, the ribbon that would match the jacket Mom was wearing with *THE NEW MATH: WOMAN − MAN = NO PROBLEMS* blazing across the back.

"Is that the only jacket she had to wear?" I moaned.

"It's good business," Keira said. She nudged me and nodded at the woman who had just tapped Mom on the shoulder. Now Mom was hauling a business card from her jacket pocket and giving it to the woman. "There. See?"

"And Spencer knows what kind of a family he's marrying into?" I asked.

Keira shrugged. "He knows it's just business, nothing personal. Well, at least not toward him."

"Heaven help him if he does anything to make Mom mad. She could put his face on a T-shirt with bull's-eye rings drawn around it like she did with Dad," I said.

Keira waved that possibility away with a careless flick of her hand. "No, she wouldn't. She knows Spencer would sue her. Oh, look. There's your suitcase."

The ride home was quite chatty as everyone filled me in on the plans for my visit. There was, of course, Ben's concert. And the whole family was planning on attending the Christmas Eve service at New Life Church. This, I learned, was because Ben was going to be singing a solo. And if Ben was singing, Mom said, we were going to be there to support him.

My whole family in church, that would be a new experience. I hoped the members were ready for an entire Hartwell invasion. I wasn't sure I was.

Mom had other plans too. She and Aunt Chloe wanted to take me shopping and show me how well the latest Man Haters item was selling. And Grandma was expecting us for lunch later in the week.

"She wanted to come meet you, but she wasn't feeling good," Mom explained, still playing the ailing grandmother card.

Lunch at Gram's. I couldn't bring myself to think about it.

Aunt Chloe was doing portraits now, and wanted to take some pictures of me so she could start painting mine immediately.

"That way I can have your portrait done in time for Christmas," she promised.

I didn't know you could do a painting in just a couple of days. Aunt Chloe must have really made progress as an artist.

Now Mom was staking a claim on my first morning home. She wanted advertising advice. It seemed to me she was already doing too good of a job promoting her business.

But I said, "Sure," trying to sound as enthusiastic as possible.

"You don't sound very enthusiastic," Mom accused.

"No, I am," I said, trying to pump more energy into my voice.

"You have to give her some time to get used to the idea of your business," Aunt Chloe said.

"Why?" Mom asked.

"Because it's slightly tacky," said Keira the Bold. "I mean, you're building a business on insulting half the human race."

"So? That leaves the whole other half to buy my products," Mom reasoned.

"Mom. Not everyone hates men," Keira said. "In fact, it's

out of style to hate men. Everyone I know is obsessed with finding a good one."

"Which proves how few there are," Mom crowed, making Keira roll her eyes. "Mark my words, girls," Mom continued, "Man Haters, Inc. is going to make all our fortunes."

"I don't need a fortune," Keira said. "I've got Spencer. And Andie's going to be a rich ad exec."

"Well, *I'll* take the money," said Aunt Chloe. "I'm just a starving artist."

That statement was questionable on two counts, but Keira and I kept our mouths shut.

Downtown Carol was dressed for the holidays. Red bows ringed the old fashioned lamp posts, and every storefront window was festooned with swags of greenery entwined with those old-fashioned, fat red Christmas lights. All we needed was some snow. Although the chances of that were rare. We got plenty of rain in Carol during the winter, but the temperatures rarely dipped low enough to turn it into snow.

We moved on and headed for the outskirts where the housing developments lay. All two of them. The newer development consisted of bigger and better houses for bigger and better people. Our development, Pleasant View (which didn't have a view of anything, but oh well), was a mishmash of houses built in the sixties and seventies. Our house was a typical tract rambler, complete with double car garage, one half of which my parents converted to a family room when we were kids. The house sat on a large corner lot, where First and Noel met. Besides the address, the house lent itself well to the holidays, with a huge holly tree in the front yard (great for Christmas, but a prickly pain to get a lawn mower around) and a low roof, perfect for stringing colored lights. At Christmas it always looked cheery and welcoming. Well, except that one Christmas I came home and found Dad moving out. No one had bothered to put up the lights that year.

No lights again this year, I noticed as we drove into the driveway. And, "Where's the holly tree?"

"I had it cut down," Mom said. "I always hated it. I swear, I'm going to strangle your brother with that string of Christmas lights," she added. "He promised he'd come home from band practice in time to get them up for your homecoming."

"He probably lost track of time," I said in Ben's defense.

"He does that a lot," Mom said, "especially when it involves coming over and helping me with something. Men," she added in disgust.

Oh, dear. Maybe Ben would be the next one to end up on a T-shirt with those bull's-eye circles.

"Well, his truck's here," said Keira.

I looked at the dilapidated old Toyota parked by the curb. It looked like a wind-up toy that had been played with one too many times. My brother, the successful musician.

Mom aimed the garage door opener and the door lumbered up to reveal a tall, hunky guy with light brown hair standing in the garage, shielding his eyes from the glare of the headlights. At his feet sat a big box with a snakelike tangle of lights overflowing it.

"Well, I guess I'll have to let him live another day," Mom decided as we got out of the car.

Ben picked up the box and came ambling over to kiss Mom on the cheek. He smiled across the car roof at me. "Hey, Bruno. Welcome home."

Here was another reason not to come home—brothers who refused to abandon insulting childhood nicknames.

"That's Andie to you, Christmas turkey," I told him.

He just chuckled. Typical guy, I thought, clueless and irritating.

Then I realized I was sounding like Mom. I was going to get that departure date changed first thing in the morning.

Ben moved on with the lights, calling over his shoulder, "Save some eggnog for me."

At least the inside of the house looked unchanged. Nostalgia settled over me like a warm blanket as I took in the living room. There was the same burnt-orange couch splattered with flowers that looked like they'd been watered with steroids—and the matching chair. There was the Early American rocking chair, and the coffee table Mom had been threatening to refinish since I was twelve. Beyond the living room, I could see the dining room with its Early American dining table and china hutch. Mom had even put out the old Nativity set on the buffet. It had a cow with a broken horn and only one wise man, who was headless, and the baby Jesus was missing. Leave it to my family to have a Nativity set like that, and display it.

All the other Christmas decorations were in place. The two-foot-tall Santa stood by the fireplace, turning this way and that, looking for good little girls and boys. At this house, he could be looking a long time. Mom's lighted village glowed along the shelf Dad had put up for it years ago. On another wall hung the stocking with the big, Styrofoam candy cane and the scary clown doll sticking out of it. I still remember when Grandma first brought that family heirloom over for Mom.

"Who's Tim?" Ben had asked, looking at the embroidered name running down the stocking.

"Tiny Tim, honey," Grandma had explained.

Ben was still looking confused, so Mom added, "As in, 'God bless us, every one.'"

Ben still looked blank.

"Dickens," Mom elaborated, "*A Christmas Carol*."

"Oh." Then he got it. "The Disney cartoon."

"You're raising Philistines," Grandma had said.

It turned out Mom had married one too. When he came home, Dad looked at the new decoration and asked, "Who's Tim?"

Mom gave up explaining, but she hung the stocking up every year.

"Go ahead and put your things in your room," she said to me as she slipped off her coat. "I've got Christmas cookies and eggnog waiting."

I hoped Aunt Chloe wasn't driving home tonight, not with her history with that particular drink.

By the time I came to the kitchen to help, everything was pretty much done, and Keira and Aunt Chloe were sitting on stools at the counter, watching Mom pour 7-Up into mugs of eggnog.

"I like it better with rum," Aunt Chloe said.

"Well, it likes you better with 7-Up," Mom told her. "This way I know you'll get home in one piece."

Here was a good change, I thought, and took hope that my Christmas in Carol would be nostalgic, peaceful, and uneventful.

That was right before I heard the strangled cry and saw the booted foot crash into the living room window.

## Chapter Two

Aunt Chloe let out a scream that was almost as terrifying as seeing my brother crash into the window like some kind of movie stunt guy. Well, a bad movie stunt guy, because instead of coming all the way through the glass and landing gracefully on the floor, Ben smashed the window to smithereens, then fell backward into the azaleas.

"Someone call 911," Mom cried, and raced for the front door with all of us stampeding behind her in a panic.

We stumbled into each other at the door, then regrouped long enough to get it open and rush outside.

I had visions of finding my brother in the bushes and his severed leg in the flowerbeds. Poor Ben. Could the doctors get him a prosthetic in time for his big concert?

Happily, we found Ben's leg was still attached to the rest of him, but it was a bloody mess.

"Oh, Ben!" Mom cried. She rushed over to him and tried to haul him out of the bushes.

"Don't move him," Aunt Chloe commanded. "He could be in shock. Wait 'til the ambulance gets here."

"Did anyone call 911 yet?" Mom asked.

Of course not. We'd all been busy freaking out.

"I'll call," I said.

As I went in the house I heard Ben moan, "Sorry, Mom. The ladder tipped."

Okay, I told myself. No need to panic anymore. He can talk and his foot is still attached. As I grabbed the phone, I felt a very nippy breeze coming into the house. I didn't know anything about fixing broken windows. Maybe Mom would have to call Dad.

He'd ride to the rescue and make the necessary repairs. Mom would take a look at him in his tool belt and get a zing. Maybe she'd talk to him in something other than a growl, and maybe they'd find their way back to, if not love, at least friendship. And maybe I was dreaming.

I was giving the dispatcher our address when Aunt Chloe rushed into the house. "I need a blanket!"

She disappeared down the hall and came back a moment later, dragging the handmade quilt Grandma gave Mom for Christmas five years ago. Oh, boy. If Ben bled on that and wrecked it, there'd really be trouble. Grandma would let Mom have it for not appreciating a family heirloom, and Mom would blame Aunt Chloe, who would burst into tears and claim that no one appreciated her, and it would all escalate from there.

As soon as I got off the phone, I ran into my old room and snatched the spread off the bed. It was a mauve floral number. The blood would blend right in.

When I got back outside, Ben was crashing out of the bushes and throwing off the quilt Aunt Chloe kept trying to drape over him. Okay, forget the spread. I opened the front door and tossed it inside.

Some of our neighbors had come over to comment on the

broken window, Ben's stupidity, and his state of health. "I've got some plastic," Mr. Winkler from down the street said to Mom. "I'll cover that window for you."

"Thank you, Bill," Mom said. "That's very sweet of you."

"You know why he's doing that, don't you?" Aunt Chloe said as Mr. Winkler walked back across the street.

"Don't go there," Mom warned.

Bill Winkler—Aunt Chloe referred to him as Wee Willie Winkler—was single. He had the hots for Mom, and ever since Dad left he'd been trying to find ways to get into her good graces. He was a skinny, bow-legged chain-smoker who looked like a Marlboro Man reject, and Mom never did anything to encourage him, which, according to Aunt Chloe, was why he was so hot for her. "Bake him cookies," Aunt Chloe advised. "That'll make him think you're husband hunting and scare him off."

I was glad Mom hadn't gotten around to scaring him off yet. At least it meant tonight we'd be warm.

Two aid cars and a fire engine pulled up at our curb, their lights circling the neighborhood, sporadically bathing everything and everyone in red light.

The EMTs put Ben on a gurney, and one examined his leg.

"Oh, I think I'm going to faint," Aunt Chloe whimpered, clutching Grandma's quilt.

Keira put a hand on her head and bent her in half. "Put your head between your legs, Auntie."

That made quite a picture. Now I was going to faint.

"Hanging Christmas lights, huh?" guessed the older EMT as they worked on Ben.

"How'd you know?" he asked.

Well, duh. There was the tipped ladder and the dangling string of lights.

The guy shrugged. "It happens a lot this time of year. Usually not this close to Christmas, though."

"It would have happened sooner if he'd done this when I first asked him," Mom said, giving Ben one of those looks moms use on their kids when they're bad. Now that the crisis was over, Ben had been taken off Mom's critical list and moved to her doo-doo list. He'd have gotten a lot more sympathy if he'd chopped off his leg.

"I think you're probably going to need a few stitches," said the EMT.

Mom let out a faint moan at that.

"It's okay, Mom," Ben said.

Okay or not, we all trooped down to the hospital to wait while Ben got his leg stitched. Everyone had a reason why she needed to tag along. Aunt Chloe brought the quilt. After all, it was cold in those emergency operating rooms, and besides, something homemade would bring him comfort. Mom knew her son would need her by his side to comfort him with questions like, "How could the ladder have tipped?" and "You should have done this when it was daylight so you could see what you were doing."

Keira was the bearer of the clean jeans and tennis shoes. "They'll probably have to cut his pants and boot off," she predicted as she got into the car.

And me, well, I thought maybe my brother would like someone who could hold his hand and keep her mouth shut.

The doctor wouldn't let us keep Ben company while he got his leg stitched, though, so the only thing that went into the nether regions of the hospital with him was his pants. And the shoes. We, his ministering angels, sat in the emergency room waiting area, the quilt keeping us company.

As we waited, I drummed my fingers on the arm of the chair and tried to stave off boredom by people-watching.

An old couple huddled together in one corner. I couldn't tell which one was supposed to be sick. They both looked bad: pale, frail, and red-eyed. The man didn't say anything, but every once in a while, the woman spoke. Loudly. Either he was deaf, or she was. Having to listen to her was enough to make the rest of us wish *we* were.

"I just can't do it this year. I don't feel good, and I don't want all the kids over."

Hmmm. A mother-of-the-year award nominee.

Her husband nodded but didn't say anything. Maybe he figured she wouldn't hear. Maybe he'd given up talking to her years ago.

"I just wanted a quiet Christmas," she said after a minute.

And I just wanted to stay in New York, I thought. We don't always get what we want, although it seemed by the time a person got to be that woman's age, they ought to.

"Wendy never watches the kids," the woman said after another minute of silence. "She lets them run everywhere. My nerves can't take it. You're going to have to call them, tell them I'm sick."

So, that was why they were in the emergency room. This woman was faking illness to get out of seeing her obnoxious family. Why hadn't I thought of that?

I checked out the other occupants of the waiting area. A few chairs down, a woman sat trying to quiet a fussy baby. I hated to assume the man next to her reading the paper was her husband, but he probably was.

A guy about my age sat slumped in the row of chairs across from us. He wore glasses and was overweight. Or maybe it was the heavy jacket and the sweats that made him look big. He wore a muffler around his neck, even though it was plenty warm inside, and he was sniffling like he had a cold. I guessed he had no medical insurance, which would explain why he was hanging around the emergency room. He eyed Keira for a long time until she finally glared at him. Then he opted for watching his toes.

These were our companions in misery. I sighed. What

would I be doing right now if I was still in New York? Having dinner at Sardi's? Seeing a Broadway play? Who was I kidding? I'd be in bed by now, snoring with a half-digested mystery lying across my chest.

"So," Aunt Chloe asked me. "Have you met anyone special in New York yet?"

Oh, great. The third degree on my love life was starting already. Why do people always have to pump you to see if you've found anyone? It's as if there's nothing more to life than men.

Not that I had no men in my life. I'd had dates, just not with anyone I felt a connection with.

Mom jumped in to explain my manless state. "Andie's busy with her career. She doesn't have time for men. She could barely schedule in a trip home for Christmas."

"A woman can always find time for men," put in Keira. "New York's a huge city. There's got to be tons of available guys there." Underlying message: *So what was taking me so long?*

Okay, so I'm picky. There's nothing wrong with that. "I've met a few people," I said.

"Anyone rich?" Aunt Chloe wanted to know.

"If they are, they haven't told me yet," I said.

"So, are you hitting the singles bars?" Keira asked.

"Of course she's not," Aunt Chloe said. "She'll probably meet her dream man in an art museum."

"I bet you can find a lot of cute guys to get close to on the subway," Keira mused.

Oh, yeah, sure. The subway is one big speed-dating sardine can. "Be my guest," I said.

"I've already got mine," she said back.

"Lots of creative people in New York," Aunt Chloe observed. "Of course, it's so big, so impersonal, so far from your family. You must get lonesome."

"Lonesome," I repeated, and nodded. I tried not to wonder what my friends were doing right now.

I picked up a worn copy of *People* to distract myself and started thumbing through it. I was just starting a juicy tidbit on Orlando Bloom when a middle-aged man with silver hair, a worn pea coat, tattered jeans, and dirty tennis shoes sat down next to me.

"Home for Christmas," he muttered.

It almost sounded like a question, but not quite. Because I couldn't tell if he was telling me his story or asking mine, I just nodded politely.

"Hate coming home for Christmas." He hacked out a nasty cough, the kind that gives you images of yourself keeling over from SARS or Bubonic plague or that flesh-eating disease.

I gave him another nod, from one sufferer to another, and leaned away from him, hoping the germs would float the opposite direction.

"Things got broken," he said in a gravelly voice.

I thought of the living room window.

On the other side of me, Aunt Chloe was getting protective and giving him a scowl that looked about as threatening as something from the Pillsbury Dough Boy.

The man didn't see. He was too busy making eye contact with me. He had the most intense blue eyes I had ever seen. "Got to mend them, you know," he said. "If you don't pull down the walls you can't build something better." The expression in those eyes was suddenly probing. I felt the hair at the back of my neck start doing the wave. What kind of woo-woo thing was going on here?

Just as I began squirming in my seat, he looked away. I decided I'd been imagining things. The poor man was simply talking to himself. Maybe there was no one in his life to listen.

Ben came out, wearing the jeans and shoes Keira had brought for him and limping. We all rose like a chorus of handmaidens.

I hated to leave the poor, muttering man with no words of cheer, so I wished him Merry Christmas.

"It is what you make it," he said as I hurried after my family.

Mom was at Ben's side now, an arm around him for support.

"I've got to stop by the pharmacy and get some pain medicine," he told her.

She nodded. "Then we'll go home and wash it down with eggnog. Do you want to sleep at the house tonight?"

He shook his head. "I'll be fine."

As we left the waiting room, I took one last glance around. Good-bye, germ-breeding ground. Good-bye, grumpy old lady. Good-bye poor, stressed-out mom with the jerk for a husband. Good-bye lonely guy with no insurance, good-bye . . . where was the crazy man? I stared at the empty seat where, only a moment ago, he had sat muttering.

He must have decided that he wouldn't find what he needed at the emergency room. I hoped he found it somewhere.

We got Ben his pain meds, then drove back to the house. It was raining now. Big surprise. It rained a lot in Carol.

"Oh, look," said Aunt Chloe as we pulled into the driveway, "Wee Willie fixed the window."

It was all covered with heavy plastic now, and the Christmas lights were up. Home, sweet home.

"I'm sorry, Mom," Ben said. "I'll pay for the repair."

"Don't worry about it," Mom told him.

"Speaking of paying, I bet Mr. Winkler's going to expect Mom to go out with him," Keira said as we climbed out of the car.

"Does he know about her business?" I asked.

"Oh, yeah. He thinks she's an astute businesswoman."

"But her business . . ."

"I know," Keira said. "Maybe he's a masochist."

Inside, we settled in the living room with the plate of cookies and fresh eggnog.

The plate was filled with my favorites: sugar cookies rolled out in the shape of trees and Santas, chocolate fat bombs with gobs of frosting, and gumdrop cookies.

I took a Christmas tree. Just one. I wanted to go home with my clothes still fitting.

I still had eggnog left after I ate it, though, so I took one more just to balance things out.

Ben appeared to be fully recovered now. At least his appetite was coming back, I noted, watching him vacuum the cookies off the plate with his mouth. And now, Aunt Chloe was going for the last Christmas tree.

I beat her to it. *Great, Andie. Eat a million cookies right before bed.* At this rate, by New Year's I'd look like Aunt Chloe's twin.

Speaking of bed, I sneaked a look at my watch. It was one in the morning back in New York, and I would be well into my beauty sleep. But the sugar was starting to kick in now, so who cared? Anyway, there was no one I needed to be beautiful for in Carol. That was for sure.

"I think I'll get some more eggnog," Aunt Chloe said and launched herself from the couch.

I knew she was going to raid the Tupperware container on the counter and stuff another Christmas tree cookie in her mouth while she was at it. At this rate there'd be nothing left by Christmas Eve. Oh, well. We could always bake more.

*No. No more cookies.*

Mom pushed the plate my way. It held one solitary gumdrop cookie. "Have the last one, Andie."

"No, that's okay," I said. "I've had enough."

"Are you sure?" Mom asked.

"Mom, maybe she's trying to diet," Keira said, and lifted the cookie from the plate.

"It's the holidays. You don't diet at the holidays," Ben said. "So, you coming to my concert tomorrow night?"

"Of course."

"You should cancel," Mom said. "How will you be able to play with stitches in your leg?"

"Better than I'd play if I didn't have a leg."

"You're liable to get a blood clot."

"Mom. It'll be okay."

The phone rang. It was Dad, looking for me.

"You're finally home," he said. "I've been calling for an hour."

"We were at the hospital," I said.

"What?" Dad sounded panicked.

"Ben put his foot through the window hanging the Christmas lights."

Dad let loose with his favorite four-letter word, then asked, "Is he okay?"

"He's fine."

"Well. I'll be right over to cover the window."

"No need. Mr. Winkler covered it with plastic."

"Winkler," Dad said in disgust.

Dad had never really liked Mr. Winkler. Maybe that was because Mr. Winkler had always liked Mom.

We had a moment of silence while Dad digested the happenings of the evening and the news that some other man was doing repairs on what used to be his home. Then he said, "So, you going to have time for your old man while you're in town?"

"Just you and me?" I asked. *Oh, please don't let him want me to hang out with the twenty-nine-year-old girlfriend.*

"How about lunch tomorrow?" Dad suggested, avoiding

the question. "I'll take you to the Steak 'N' Bake by the mall, then we can go shopping for your Christmas present."

I was surprised Dad had any money for Christmas shopping with the way he'd been going through it since he and Mom split. "I can't tomorrow. How about the day after?"

"Okay. It's a deal," he said, and we set a time.

"I hope he's not planning on monopolizing your time," Mom called from the living room as I hung up.

"It's just lunch," I said.

"Well, tell him that's all he gets. He wasn't the one who paid for your airline ticket."

I made a mental note to myself: call the airline first thing in the morning and reserve an earlier flight out.

## Chapter Three

Everyone would have happily talked until midnight, but the sugar was wearing off and I was turning into a zombie. Trying to convince both my family and myself that my life was totally glam and completely fulfilled was exhausting work. Finally, I quit stifling my yawns.

After my third, Mom got the idea. "We need to let Andie get to bed," she announced.

Ben eased himself to a standing position. "I should get going, anyway."

Mom pointed a finger at him. "You are not going anywhere. You're taking narcotics. You can't drive."

"Aw, Mom. I'll be fine," Ben protested.

"You're right you will, because you'll be sleeping in your old room."

Which was now the sewing room, and so full of fabric and craft projects there was barely room for the day bed Mom had stuffed in there.

Ben grimaced. "All those dried flowers make me sneeze."

"Better to be safe and sneezing than driving and dead."

"I only live a mile away!"

"Most accidents happen within a mile of home."

I didn't know why Ben was bothering. He was going to lose his argument with Mom. He knew it. We all knew it.

And since I knew the end of the story . . . I retrieved my bedspread, waved at my bro and sis, and said, "Goodnight guys. I've got to crash right now. My head's feeling fuzzy."

"Mine isn't," said Aunt Chloe. "The eggnog would have been better with rum," she added as she kissed me goodnight.

"Well, you wouldn't have been better," Mom retorted, and hugged me. "Sleep well, sweetie," she said, and kissed my cheek.

It made me feel like a kid again, in a good sort of way.

As I went down the hall, I could hear Aunt Chloe say, "I'm too tired to drive home. I think I'll sleep here."

"All the beds are full," Mom replied. *No room at the inn.*

"That's okay," Aunt Chloe said. "I'll share yours."

Ah, sisters. Would that be Keira and me someday? Another reason to stay on the east coast.

My body was on New York time, so I heard Keira leave the house at the crack of dawn the next morning for her early shift at The Coffee Break. She'd worked at the popular downtown coffee shop since her freshman year of college, serving donuts and cookies to Carol's worker bees along with their drug of choice: caffeine. She claimed she was still there to earn money for the wedding. At the rate she was spending money on the big event, she'd be at The Coffee Break until she was 642. Well, it was a job. And what else could you do with a degree in literature? Except write a book, which she claimed she was doing. It was going to be about a woman who worked in a coffee shop. She'd already e-mailed me some of her musings, along with the title: *A Cup of Crazy*. So far the best thing she had was the title.

I suspected once she was married, she'd forget the book.

What Keira really wanted to do was plunge headlong into happily-ever-after in Carol. She liked being the big Beta fish in the small pond.

Not me. I wanted to be something more in some place bigger and better, far from my embarrassing family and my not-so-good hometown friends. Which would explain why I was in New York clinging to the bottom rung of the ladder of success at Image Makers.

Come to think of it, I wasn't much more successful than Keira. At least she had a fiancé and a cubic zirconia ring to show for her post-college endeavors. What did I have? Well, I had New York. And that should be enough for any woman.

I thought longingly of acting on my resolve of the night before and calling the airline. But that would be . . .

Tacky. I could tough it out, and there would be other chances to ring in the New Year in Times Square.

Maybe not so many chances to land a great job. I got out my BlackBerry and shot off a bunch of messages, putting out fires before there were any.

I was thoroughly awake now. I decided to go for a morning run, and slipped into my running sweats and my tennies.

Nothing had changed, I thought as I jogged around the old neighborhood. It looked like the Blackmans had a new car. Big surprise there. They got a new one every year.

Lights were on inside the Harrises' house. Mr. Harris, the hot shot executive (a legend in his own mind) was up and getting ready to go to work. He still had the most anally perfect lawn on the block. In fact, everything about his life was as perfect as he could get it. Probably the only thing that made it not perfect was having to live in the same neighborhood as my family. The Harrises spoke to us as little as possible and steered clear of our neighborhood barbecues. Maybe those Christmas chimney fires had made them leery of getting too near Dad and his grill.

I remembered a conversation I overheard between Mom and Mrs. Claussen about the Harrises back when I was in middle school. "They never entertain," Mom had said.

"They do," said Mrs. Claussen. "They take their friends out to dinner. Lani hates to cook."

"I think they just don't want the hoi polloi tracking dirt on their carpet," Mom decided.

Judging from the *For Sale* sign on their front lawn, it looked like the Harrises were ready to end their years of living under house arrest. Maybe they'd move to the bigger and better housing development. Probably no hoi polloi there. No Hartwells, anyway.

The Olsens and the Baileys were still competing for the honor of the most decorated house in town, with almost every square inch of yard and roof occupied by Santas, snowmen, reindeer, candy canes, and enough lights to fill an entire warehouse.

After my run I went home to make some coffee and prepare for my morning of torture, talking about Mom's business. As far as I was concerned, the first order of business should be to discuss changing the name of her company.

By the time I'd showered and made coffee, Mom was up. "Bacon and eggs for breakfast?" she suggested, giving me a doting smile.

Breakfast for me was usually a bottled nutri-drink. Bacon and eggs sounded like a luxury. "Sure," I said.

"Go knock on your brother's door and tell him breakfast will be ready in five minutes," Mom said, opening the fridge door.

Ben was out ten minutes later, looking sleepy-eyed and scruffy-chinned. "I've got to go," he told Mom, and kissed her cheek. "I need to shower and shave before I open the store."

"This is done," Mom protested, shoving a plate at him.

She hated it when any of her kids denied her the chance to feed them.

Ben wasn't one to turn down free food. He took the plate and plopped down at the table.

Now Aunt Chloe made her entrance. "I thought I smelled something good. She poured herself a cup of coffee, then went to hover over the stove and watch Mom work. "Are we having pancakes, too? In honor of Andie's return," she added. "You really need to put some more meat on your bones," she told me.

"The one you should tell that to is Keira, not me," I said.

Aunt Chloe shrugged. "She's anorexic."

"She is not," Mom snapped.

After all the cookies I'd seen Keira put away the night before, I had to agree with Mom.

"Bulimic, then," Aunt Chloe decided. "Have you shown Andie any of our new projects yet?" she asked Mom.

So much for Keira's possible eating disorder.

"I haven't had time," Mom said. "Why don't you get them?"

Aunt Chloe nodded eagerly and lumbered out of the room.

"So, you're expanding," I said, trying not to sound terrified.

Mom nodded. "Just a couple things."

Aunt Chloe returned with a cardboard box. She set it on the kitchen table.

I have to admit, I was curious. I left my stool at the counter and went to stand next to her. Peering into the box, I saw a small plaque, a mug, several sheets of paper with indecipherable pencil sketches, and a couple of T-shirts.

Aunt Chloe pulled out the mug. "I did the art work for this," she said proudly.

It was kind of cute, actually. A string of simply-drawn gingerbread boys held hands around the circumference of the mug.

"I came up with the saying," Mom added as she lay a plate of eggs in front of me.

Aunt Chloe snagged it.

Ben read, "The only good men are made of gingerbread." He frowned. "Thanks, Mom."

"Not you, dear," she said to him. "Just men in general."

"I am a man in general," he reminded her, and gnawed off a bite of bacon.

"Actually, this has been selling pretty well, hasn't it?" Aunt Chloe said, looking to Mom for confirmation. Mom nodded, and Aunt Chloe reached into the box and pulled out the plaque. Now she was frowning. "Your mother had someone else do the art work for this."

"You didn't capture what I was looking for," Mom said defensively.

Ben shook his head. "Somebody should capture that and give it a death sentence."

It was truly horrible. There stood Elmer Fudd's mother, clad in a frumpy dress and old army boots, frowning and pointing a rifle. Underneath her, in fuchsia letters, were the words *Put the toilet seat down. Now!*

"It's to hang in the bathroom," Mom explained, and set down another plate of eggs.

I wasn't feeling too hungry anymore.

Out came more merchandise. There was a T-shirt picturing the contents of a sporting good store—fishing gear, bowling balls, football and baseball equipment—and under it sat the words *Little Shop of Horrors*. Another shirt proclaimed *I Stopped Having Nightmares When I Got Rid of the Man of My Dreams*.

Ben was really scowling now. "Who buys this stuff?"

"Bitter women." Oh, no. Had I actually said that out loud?

A deafening silence descended on the room. I scrambled around my brain in a panic, looking for some diplomatic words to give my mother before she whanged me on the head with the frying pan. Why is it you never can find things when you need them most?

Aunt Chloe stepped into the breach. "That's a big market, hon."

"That's a sick market," Ben said. "I mean, yeah, some of this is funny, I guess. But why don't you do some stuff that's not so, I don't know, mean?"

"Because this is Man Haters, Inc.," Mom informed him.

He made a face, then stuffed the last piece of his bacon in his mouth and pushed away from the table. "I'm out of here." He pointed a finger at me. "See you at the concert tonight."

"I'll be there," I promised.

"We'll all be there," Mom said as he kissed her cheek. "And stay off your foot at work today," she called after him. She sat down at the table with her own plate of fried eggs and glared at it. I was surprised the eggs didn't start to bubble.

Great. My first day home and I had a major toxic spill to clean.

I took a deep breath. "Mom, I know you have a market," I said gently. "but it's limited. You're so clever. Why not come up with some cute ideas for things you could sell to men and happily married women, too?"

"No man is going to buy from a company called Man Haters," Mom said testily.

*What the heck. Wade neck deep into the spill.* "You could change the name."

Mom looked at me like I'd suggested she grab a bread knife and saw out her heart. "And just what would I change it to?" she demanded, daring me to come up with something better.

' I shrugged. "I don't know. Maybe 'A Good Laugh, Inc.' or 'Make Me Laugh.' " I shrugged. "If you appeal to a broader customer base, you'll make more money." Now there was some sound business advice that should appeal to any businesswoman.

"I'm not doing this just for the money."

Okay, so much for that strategy.

"I'm doing it for the personal satisfaction."

In other words, revenge on Dad. I thought of the T-shirt with the bull's-eye.

"You did ask her for advice," Aunt Chloe reminded Mom.

"I wanted advertising advice, not. . . . this," Mom finished in disgust.

I pushed away my plate. I was definitely not hungry. "I'm sorry, Mom. I didn't mean to insult you. I think the business is a great idea." Well, somewhere in there was a great idea.

Mom wasn't fooled. "I can see that. You love everything about it but its name and what I sell."

"Some of it's cute," I said. Okay, the bathroom plaque wasn't all that bad.

Mom sniffed.

"Make Me Laugh is kind of clever," Aunt Chloe ventured.

Mom gave a snort of disgust. "Don't make me laugh."

"Actually, that wouldn't be a good name for your company," I said, back-pedaling. It was just something I'd thrown out off the top of my head. I mean, that's what you do when you brainstorm. I could do better.

"My company already has a good name," Mom insisted. She bit down on a piece of toast and ground it between her molars.

"Why isn't Make Me Laugh a good name?" Aunt Chloe asked.

"It doesn't really tell you what the company is. You could be anything from clowns to stand-up comics. You want a name that not only says you're special, but that lets people know what you're selling, also. Like . . . Great Goodies."

"Yuck," said Mom.

Aunt Chloe was nodding. "I see. How about something like . . . Jazzy Junk?"

"I don't sell junk," Mom snarled.

"Sooorry," said Aunt Chloe.

"Well, it was just something to think about," I added.

"I like my company name just fine," Mom insisted. "What I wanted you to do was help me think up ways to promote it."

Just what I always wanted to do, help my mother unleash more of her anger on the world. A slow throb began to march across my forehead.

"Okay," I said. "But you might want to at least *consider* changing it. I really think you could come up with something equally clever that would get you more customers."

"Then I'd have to change my product line," Mom said.

And that would be a bad thing? I thought. But I didn't say it. My bulb may not be the brightest on the tree, but it does get some electricity.

"Not necessarily," I said. "You'd just expand it."

Mom was still not looking happy, so I moved on. "Okay, let's talk about marketing. Have you got a Web site yet?"

Mom shook her head. "So far I've just been selling on consignment to Gifts 'N' Gags in the mall."

"You need a Web presence."

Mom nodded. "I figured as much."

"I know a couple of guys who do Web design. I can give you their numbers."

That made her smile. "Great."

I started poking around in the box again. "So, what's going on the shelves for Valentine's Day?"

"Valentine's Day!" Mom made it sound like a dirty word.

"That's a huge day for merchandisers," I said.

"See, I told you," Aunt Chloe said.

Mom glared at her, then said, "I don't think my products lend themselves to Valentine's Day."

"You could do something that has nothing to do with men," I suggested.

"Like what?" Mom looked at me suspiciously.

*Okay, brain. Wake up.* "How about a mug?" I began.

"Everybody likes mugs," put in Aunt Chloe.

"Yeah?" Mom prompted.

"Showing a box of chocolates or, better yet, an entire table filled with everything chocolate from candy to cake. You could caption it: *How Do I Love Thee? Let Me Count the Ways.*"

"Ooh, I like that!" Aunt Chloe cried.

Mom grinned. "Me too."

"We could fill this whole table with chocolate stuff, then take a digital picture," Aunt Chloe said.

"If I got going right now, I could still get something to the store in time for Valentine's Day," Mom said. She nodded. "I'll call Clarissa this morning." She grabbed my head and kissed me. "My daughter the genius!"

From doo-doo to darling in five minutes. Not bad. I went to the kitchen and dumped the cold eggs into the garbage, then put the plate in the dishwasher. Then I got out of the kitchen before I could lose my improved status. You know what they say, if you can't stand the heat, get out of the kitchen.

I was standing in front of the bathroom sink brushing my teeth when Aunt Chloe snuck up on me with her camera. "There. Now I can go home and start working on your Christmas present."

"You're going to paint me brushing my teeth?" Great. Where was I supposed to hang that? In the bathroom, I guessed, right next to the Elmira Fudd plaque.

"Don't worry. I'll take the toothbrush out of your hands," Aunt Chloe promised. "Or maybe I'll put you in a field of daisies." She gave me an impish grin. "Or maybe I'll paint you like Saint George, slaying a dragon."

I played dumb. Mom was not a dragon lady, only when it came to her business. And Dad.

Aunt Chloe went home to start painting, and Mom got busy making phone calls.

I had a call of my own to make, back to Image Makers. It was about 11:30 New York time, and I figured I should be able to catch Beryl between meetings.

"Hi, Andie," said Iris the secretary. "Ready to come back yet?"

"I was ready to do that before I left. I've been in touch with the rest of the team on the Nutri Bread campaign. I thought I'd check in with Beryl, see if we've had any new developments. Is she in?"

"She is, but she's in a meeting."

Was she really or had she just told Iris to say that? Was she avoiding me? Was I paranoid?

"Okay," I said, "I'll call later."

"You might be able to catch her right before noon," Iris suggested.

"Thanks," I said, and hung up, unable to shake the feeling that Beryl was putting me off.

I had a sudden unpleasant thought. If she was putting me off, it could only mean one thing: she'd gone behind my back and gotten the big boss, Mr. Phelps, to set up a meeting with the Nutri Bread people while I was out of town.

I tried to forget about my worries by burying myself in a book. It was an unsuccessful burial. I couldn't stop thinking about what might be happening back at Image Makers.

I pulled out my BlackBerry and shot off communiqués until I was in danger of getting BlackBerry thumb. The replies I got seemed vague. Don't worry. Everything's under control The last one I got from my co-worker Amanda made my blood freeze: *Will run by The Brit if there's time. She's killing us.*

Killing them? Killing them doing what?

I called the office again at 5 minutes to noon, New York time.

"Oh, you just missed her," said Iris.

"She never goes to lunch this early," I protested.

"Sorry. I did tell her you called, though."

"And she's got my cell number, right?" Like she'd use it. Why bother to call her assistant planner, who was supposed to be happily vacationing with her family?

"Oh, yes," Iris said airily, which meant she really didn't know.

"Who's she having lunch with?" I demanded.

Iris spoke so fast I couldn't quite catch what she said. It sounded like, "Nutrd."

"What?"

"Nuterrrid. Oh, I've got another call coming in."

"Iris. Did you say Nutri Bread?"

"I've really got to go, Andie," Iris said, and hung up.

It was a bad connection. I'd misheard, that was it. Iris wasn't trying to spare me from a miserable holiday by hiding the fact that Beryl was planning to meet with the Nutri Bread people in my absence.

Right.

Okay, so what? Beryl was probably busy charming Mr. Nutri Bread, priming the pump. She wouldn't run with this and leave me at the starting block. I was part of the team.

I was the water girl.

I called back again. I barely gave Iris time to say hello. "Tell Beryl I need her to call me. It's an emergency."

"Oh, no. Andie, what's happened?"

"Just tell her to call me," I said, and disconnected. There.

If Beryl was sneaking in a meeting behind my back, she'd have to tell me to my face.

I opened my book again. I was worrying for nothing. We didn't even have the art proofs yet. She couldn't do anything.

Oh, yes, she could.

I called the office once more. "Iris, have we gotten the art proofs for the Nutri Bread account yet?"

"Art department sent them over today," Iris said. "Beryl put a rush on them. Andie, are you all right?"

"Just make sure Beryl calls me," I said through gritted teeth. I practically strangled my phone as I disconnected. I knew I should have stayed in New York. I knew it.

Keira came home to find me on my bed, hunched over my laptop and glaring. "Are you ready to go?" she asked. "The real estate agent will be here in ten minutes."

I shrugged. "Okay," I said, still typing. "Let me know when she gets here."

Keira frowned. "You don't even have your makeup on. And is that what you're going to wear?"

I looked down at my sweatshirt and jeans. "What's wrong with it?"

"It's . . . sloppy."

"I'm in Carol, not New York. There's no one here I need to impress."

"Well, there's no one here you need to embarrass, either," Keira retorted. Baby of the family. Spoiled rotten.

But I was a middle child and, basically, a peacemaker. "Okay, okay," I muttered.

She left happy and I exchanged the sweatshirt for a black sweater from my suitcase. What was the big deal, anyway?

I found out what the big deal was a few minutes later.

"We're ready," Keira called from down the hall.

I checked my makeup, then slipped into a blazer and

threw a teal scarf around my neck. I slapped a hat over my head and stepped into the hallway.

I could hear voices drifting toward me: Mom's, Keira's, and a low, masculine one. It figured that Keira would pick a man to be her real estate agent. Knowing her, he was probably cute. His voice sounded familiar.

When I reached the living room, I knew why. There he stood, all six feet of him, looking like Mr. J. Crew: gray slacks and a white shirt under a Christmas sweater, a navy sports coat, penny loafers. His hair was still blond and his eyes were still blue, and his mouth just as kissable. Was I hallucinating?

"Hi Andie," said Gabe Knightly. "Good to see you."

Hallucinations didn't speak. So that could mean only one thing: I was having a nightmare.

## Chapter Four

I quickly checked to make sure I was dressed. My clothes were still on, which meant this couldn't be a nightmare. But maybe it was the kind of nightmare where you were dressed. I crossed my arms and gave myself a quick pinch. It hurt.

Okay. I was really seeing Gabe Knightly, the same Gabe Knightly I'd once fantasized over marrying, the president of the student body, king of the basketball court, wolf in sheep's clothing who had ruined my senior year and left me without a date for the senior prom (did I fail to mention that?), then humiliated me by dating my sister and my best friend. This wasn't happening. Couldn't be happening. I'd ruled out hallucination and nightmare. What else could it be? Whatever it was it was giving me butterflies in my stomach.

"Gabe's my real estate agent," Keira said blithely.

I looked at him and tried for a smile, but it felt more like I was baring my teeth. Still looking at Gabe, I said to Keira, "You didn't tell me." And we both knew why. No way would I have consented to this stupidity if I'd known.

Gabe's smile was looking a little tentative, but he managed a hale and hearty "So, let's get going."

43

I took a step back. "Actually, I'm expecting a call."

"Bring your cell," said Keira. "You got it?"

It was still lying on my bed. I wanted to join it. I shook my head.

Keira rolled her eyes. "I'll get it."

She skipped off to the bedroom and I followed her and shut the door after us.

"What were you thinking?" I demanded.

She picked the phone off the bed. "What do you mean? I'll bet you don't have any calls. What's your code?"

I snatched the phone away from her. "I can check myself." I did. No one had called.

"Told you," Keira said, looking over my shoulder.

I glared at her. "You should have told me Gabe was your agent. That was just plain sneaky."

"No, it wasn't. It was manipulative."

"It was bad."

Keira held a hand in front of her and slapped it. "Bad Keira. Okay. You feel better?"

"I'll feel better after you're both gone."

"Oh, come on. Don't be small."

"I'm not being small," I informed her. "I just don't want to spend the day with Gabe Knightly."

"You're still mad, after all this time, that I went out with him."

"I am not," I lied. "I just think he's a twit."

Keira went on as if I hadn't spoken. "I can't believe it. I told you nothing happened. We never, like, slept together or anything."

Neither did we, I thought, but it wasn't for lack of trying on Gabe's part. I'm sure he got what he wanted from Ashleigh Horne after he took her to the prom.

Well, senior proms are overrated. Anyway, I could have gone if I'd wanted. Andy Klein asked me. He's now president of Computech Software, and a multimillionaire. I hear he married Ashleigh. Life is strange, isn't it?

Keira was in my face now. "So, what is your problem, Andie?"

"I told you. I just don't want to spend the day with Gabe Knightly."

Keira grabbed my arm. "Well, get over it. You promised to spend the day with me."

She began to tug. I dug in my heels and gritted my teeth.

Someone cleared their throat. I looked up to find the door open and Gabe standing in the doorway, one eyebrow raised. "Ready?"

He said it like a challenge. What did he think, I was afraid to be with him?

I stuffed my cell phone in my purse and raised my chin. "Any time you are."

He smiled. That smile hadn't lost its golden glow. In fact, if anything, it was brighter.

Well, all that glittered wasn't gold. I followed Keira out of the bedroom and brushed past Mr. Date Every Chick in Town. There was a time when even standing near him practically gave me an electric shock. No shocks now, just an angry flare like what you get when you catch something greasy on fire.

Keira hurried across the lawn to Gabe's Acura, anxious to spend Spencer's money. Before either of us got there, she'd opened the backseat door and climbed in.

Oh, cute. I supposed she thought that meant I'd have to take the front seat. I went around to the other side and got in back.

Gabe got into the driver's seat and Keira glared at me like I was a stupid thirteen-year-old who had foiled a big, romantic plan.

"I guess I'm chauffeur today," Gabe said lightly.

"Home, James," quipped Keira. "Or in this case, homes. What have you got for me?"

"I've got a Dutch Colonial, a Greek Revival, a Victorian . . ."

*And a partridge in a pear tree.* Good grief, I thought. We'd be out playing house all day at this rate.

". . . a rambler, and a split level in Carol Estates," Gabe finished.

"Forget the rambler," Keira said.

"Okay, scratch the rambler."

Good, I thought. One less house to wander through. That whittled down the torture by at least half an hour.

"What else?"

"Got a couple of really nice places in the new development."

"Oooh, Dream Land," Keira said. "That's almost as good as getting something out on Lake Carol."

"There's at least one you can probably swing," he told her. "Not at the lake, but in the development," he added quickly.

"There's a new development?" I asked.

Gabe shrugged. "It's not New York, but the town is growing."

"It's called Fairhaven," added Keira. They're putting in a golf course there."

"Golf club membership comes with the deal," Gabe informed her.

"Spencer would like that," Keira said. "Let's go there first. We may as well start at the top."

Gabe nodded and turned the car west. "So, how do you like New York?" he asked me.

"I love it," I said. "Museums, fabulous restaurants, the theater."

"Got somebody to go with to the theater?" he asked. He

made it sound casual, like he didn't really care. Maybe he didn't. I didn't care if he cared or not.

"You can always find somebody to go places with," I said. No need to tell him I didn't happen to have anyone to go with at the moment. I caught sight of his eyes studying me in the rear view mirror. I raised my eyebrows. *So what do you think of that?*

"A lot of crime in that city," he observed.

I shrugged. "There's crime in every city."

"Not Carol."

"Carol doesn't qualify as a city," I said. "It doesn't qualify as exciting, either."

"Oh, I don't know. It can get pretty exciting around here sometimes, can't it, Keira?"

"There's plenty of excitement here," my sister agreed.

Yeah, and my family created half of it. I looked out the window and watched as houses with quiet lawns slipped by. It was like getting stuck in a time warp and finding yourself on Beaver Cleaver's street.

Rain began to spatter the car, and Gabe flipped on his windshield wipers. Watching the rain sluice down my window, I could almost imagine myself in a car wash, going nowhere slowly.

I thought of New York, its press of people pumping along its streets like blood through an artery. The place was alive, full of energy. Carol was a town of sleepwalkers, and even the New Year's Eve fireworks couldn't wake it up. I was glad I'd left. I wanted to live, really live, do something exciting with my life, make an impact.

Like anyone could make an impact on New York? Well, if they were mayor. The rest of us just kept rushing around the streets, pumping, pumping, keeping the city alive. I frowned. That didn't quite sound right.

Now we were going through downtown again. I watched

out the window. No human corpuscles here. Just people strolling along under umbrellas. No one strolled along in New York. No one had time. That was because they had a purpose. Here people only marked time. I looked at a trio of residents standing in front of Handy's Hardware—a couple and a man, decked out in Eddie Bauer specials. The woman had on a knitted cap, probably handmade. She stood with her arm linked through her man's. The other man said something and she laughed.

Further down, two women walked side by side, talking animatedly as they ducked inside Flora's Flower Shoppe. The bakery was full of morning customers, its tables along the front window crowded with people chatting, sipping lattes and mochas and downing Mrs. Swenson's Christmas scones.

It was like looking at one of those lighted Christmas villages, suddenly come to life. It gave me an odd and unexpected tightness deep in my chest. I closed my eyes and thought of skating at Rockefeller Center, of shopping at Macy's. Ah, that was better. *Those little town blues are drizzling away . . .* or however that old song went.

Keira already had her cell phone out and was reporting in to Spencer on our destination. Or, at least to his receptionist. "Tell him we're on our way to Fairhaven. I'll call him when we get there."

I thought of the cell phone sitting inside my purse and willed it to ring. Here was Keira, blabbing away about nothing while I, who had something vital and urgent to discuss, sat with a stubbornly silent phone in my purse. It would be a miracle if I heard from Beryl.

"You enjoying your stay so far?" Gabe asked me.

A visit to the emergency room, a breakfast business consultation with Lucy and Ethel, the Next Generation, and now a ride around town with an old boyfriend courtesy of my meddling sister. What was there not to enjoy?

"Oh, yeah," I lied.

"A lot slower pace here," he said.

*Not so far.* "Mmm hmmm."

"Lots of movers and shakers in New York," he observed. "Are you one of them?"

That sounded like a dare. *Go ahead, Andie, just try to prove that you're better than the rest of us.*

I wasn't out to prove I was better. I was just out to do something with my life. There was nothing wrong with that.

And I was doing something with my life. I was about to help promote a really nutritious bread and help people get over their carb fear. That was a good thing. Did it count as moving and shaking?

"I don't know," I said honestly. Sometimes there were a lot of things I didn't know. This morning was shaping up to be one of those times. "So, how did you end up in real estate?" I asked.

It was all I could do not to add, "What happened?" Everyone assumed Gabe Knightly, man most likely to succeed, would go on to do great things: become president (if not of the country, at least of a major corporation), end world hunger, turn himself into a millionaire overnight. But here he was, a small-town real estate agent. Not that there was anything wrong with being a small-town real estate agent. It just didn't match my expectations for Gabe. And he appeared perfectly content with it. Somehow, it just didn't seem right, like he'd set out on the road to success and had taken a wrong turn somewhere. Probably dating every woman in town had gotten him sidetracked.

"Real estate looked like a good thing to do with a business degree," he said. "I guess you could say I'm playing my own version of Monopoly. Of course, I'm no Donald Trump," he added modestly.

"Good grief, I hope not," Keira said in disgust. "That man has the worst hair."

"His record with women isn't real good, either," I observed.

"With hair like that maybe he thinks he needs to prove he's sexy," said Keira.

"Yeah, I've known guys like that," I said.

A slightly uncomfortable silence took over. Oops, I thought. Oh, well, if the heel, er, shoe fits.

We were now in the 'burbs of Carol. Actually, all of Carol looked a little like the 'burbs, but that was beside the point.

"There it is," Keira said, pointing to a massive gated entrance. Etched into one of the brick walls in a barely legible script was the word *Fairhaven*. Translation: *Snob haven*. Behind it rose the kingdom of Self-Importance, still under construction.

Since when did we need a gated community in Carol? I wondered. Obviously, since now.

The gate wasn't up yet, and we drove right through. "Oooh," said Keira. If drool had a sound, her voice was it.

I felt a little drooly, myself. Many of the houses were still only framed-in shells, waiting to be completed, but even in their unfinished state they were impressive. These weren't houses we were rolling past, they were mansions. You could probably fit three families in each one and still have room for servants. Even though they were big, it was still a housing development, I told myself. Tract mansions, I added scornfully.

*The likes of which you'll never live in.*

True. If I stayed in New York, I'd probably spend the rest of my days in an apartment. Well, there was nothing wrong with that. Less to clean.

"Here we are," Gabe said, and pulled up in front of one of the smaller mammoth structures. It was two stories, with a three-car garage. Brick trim everywhere, huge brick porch running along the front of the house with fat brick steps layering up to it. A double-door entry. Enough windows to suck in every ounce of sunlight the Carol sky could produce. And, speaking of sunlight, the rain had already stopped and a burst of winter sun was now making the structure glow like a prize in some gigantic cosmic Happy Meal. The house had no landscaping yet, but the yard was the size of Texas.

Tara, I thought, and the theme from the old movie *Gone With the Wind* started running through my head.

Keira got out of the car, staring at the house like she was Dorothy seeing Oz for the first time. *We're not in Kansas anymore, Toto.*

I didn't feel like we were in Carol anymore either.

Keira started up the walkway, awed reverence in every step.

*Good grief*, I thought, *it's just a house.*

"Nice, isn't it?" Gabe said at my elbow.

I told myself the zing that just shot through my chest had nothing to do with chemistry. He'd startled me, that was all. "If you like overblown and pretentious," I said.

"So, you wouldn't want to live here?"

I supposed most people would want to live in a gorgeous, huge, new house. But . . . "Not in a housing development," I said. "I'd want a place with some land, woods, and maybe . . ."

"A pond," he finished with me.

That jerked my head around to stare at him. I loved New York, but sometimes I still had visions of an old, rambling house on a wooded chunk of land.

"We talked about what kind of place we'd want to live in once," Gabe said softly. "Before you broke up with me," he added, putting teeth into the reminiscence.

Oh, no. We weren't going to play Blame Andie. He hadn't mourned all that long after we broke up. In fact, he hadn't even given me time to reconsider before he went out and found a new woman. And he hadn't exactly pined away for me after I went to college either.

I scowled at him. "Do you really want to go down that road? If you do, I could refresh your memory on a few things."

He sighed. "Andie . . ."

He didn't get to finish his sentence. Keira was already at the front door and complaining. "Hey, there's a lock box on it."

"That's to keep the riffraff out," I informed her, and stepped away from Gabe.

"Ha, ha. Come on, Gabe. Open this. I'm dying to go inside."

He remembered he was supposed to be working, not thrashing around in the stickers of Memory Lane, and went to unlock the front door. I followed at a leisurely pace, feeling the kind of righteous satisfaction you can suck out of verbal one-upmanship.

Gabe opened the door, then stepped aside to let us enter. My jaw dropped as we walked in. Slate entryway. Oak stairs with a carpet runner leading to the second story, off to the right the living room. I leaned against the archway and took it in. You could probably fit the entire Mormon Tabernacle Choir in there, and with those vaulted ceilings I supposed the acoustics would be great. (Not that I knew anything about acoustics, or even music. My brother got all the talent in that area.) I looked lustfully at the huge fireplace with its elaborate mantel and the built-in bookcases flanking it. Oh, I could have fun filling those with books and pictures and cut-glass vases with dried flowers. (They'd have to be dried. I'm not much of a gardener.)

"Ooh, this is gorgeous," breathed Keira. She whipped out

her cell and took a picture. "Look at that fireplace. I can already see the mantel with candles and holly and stockings hanging from it."

It wasn't hard to imagine. Someone had hidden a Glade plug-in somewhere, and the scent of bayberry danced around us.

Keira walked into the center of the room. The walls were a light peach color, the carpet beige. The room was filling with sunlight. Standing in the middle of all the light, Keira looked like she should be in an Impressionist painting. Maybe Aunt Chloe would come here and paint her picture. She could call it: Young Woman With Everything.

Oh, dear. This was not a nice way to feel. *Don't get jealous, Andie.*

Who was I kidding? I already was. My sister was going to have a big fat house to go with her big fat ring. Just for a moment, I felt like a big fat failure.

I went up the stairs and entered one of the bedrooms. It had a walk-in closet, naturally. I walked into it. My kitchen wasn't as large as this.

"Lots of closet space," Gabe said behind me.

The closet suddenly shrank. What after shave was he wearing? It had been bad enough in the car, but here it was taking over. He was taking over. And I was zinging again.

"You're selling the wrong woman," I said. "My sister's the one with the money." Well, she would be once she was married.

I slipped past Gabe, making sure not to breathe through my nose as I passed. Too many more of those aftershave fumes and I was liable to get a hormone high. I got out just in time to see my sister scurrying from the bedroom, obviously hoping not to interrupt what she thought might be a potentially romantic moment.

Cupid Keira. How very convenient that she had picked

Gabe Knightly to be the real estate agent to squire us around today. So, what was that about, really? Maybe she was assuaging her guilt over dating Gabe after I went away to college. Not that it mattered anymore. What did I care who dated him after I was done with him?

My cell phone rang. Gratefully, I pulled it from my purse. "Hello."

Keira walked back into the room, frowning. "Who is that?" she demanded.

Whoever it was, they were breaking up. I pressed the phone closer, put a finger in my other ear, and strained to hear. "Hello?"

It sounded like Beryl. "Andie? Can . . . *zwiittt, err*?"

"Just a minute," I said, and rushed from the room.

"Tell them you're on vacation," Keira shouted after me.

Of course, I lost Beryl. I went outside and walked to the center of the Texas yard plot where I'd get good reception, then I called back.

"Oh, there you are," she said cheerily. "Are you having a perfectly splendid time with your family?" She might just as well have asked, "Are you enjoying the Mad Hatter's tea party?"

"I'm having quite a time," I said, trying to be truthful, loyal and diplomatic all at once. "What's going on with the Nutri Bread people? Have you been talking to them?" Hmm. That might not have been quite the way to phrase my question. After all, Beryl was The Planner. I was just the assistant planner. With the ideas!

"Not to worry, my poppet," Beryl said. "Everything is going swimmingly here. There will be plenty to do when you come back."

Not to worry? I had just gotten the most evasive answer since "Am I my brother's keeper?" and she was telling me not to worry?

"Beryl," I began.

"Now, I have to run, so you have a wonderful time there in Clairol."

"It's Carol," I said. I was gritting my teeth. I would probably be doing that in my sleep tonight. By the time the holidays were over I'd have TMJ.

"Yes. Well, ta ta."

And then she was gone. Ta ta? Surely no self-respecting English person would ever say that. And surely no self-respecting English person would try to keep a member of her team out of the loop.

Ha! I called back, this time zeroing in on Iris the secretary. "Iris, what's going on with the Nutri Bread account?"

"What do you mean?" she asked. She sounded evasive, like she was trying to spare me some sort of grief. Or maybe it was just a simple question and I was becoming the most paranoid woman on the planet.

"I mean what is Beryl up to? She hasn't scheduled a meeting with the Nutri Bread people, has she?" Not the week before Christmas. The bread people would all be heading home to their families to eat bread pudding. And surely even Mr. Phelps would have plans this close to Christmas.

"If there is a meeting, Beryl hasn't told me yet," said Iris.

That didn't mean a thing. "Well, when she does will you tell me?"

"Sure, but Mr. Phelps isn't going to schedule anything until after the holidays. Everybody's busy with office Christmas parties and shopping. Anyway, you won't be back until after the first, and I'm sure Beryl will want you there. Oh, just a minute, Andie. she's buzzing me.

The just a minute felt like a millennium. Finally Iris returned. "That's odd. She wants me to get Mr. Margolin on the phone."

Mr. Nutri Bread, himself. My molars crunched against each other. "Keep me in the loop, Iris."

"Okay," Iris said and hung up.

I snapped my cell shut with a growl. *Not to worry, my poppet*. Right.

Keira was coming out of the house now, her cell phone to her ear. "No, we're not done looking, but I don't need to look anymore. This house is the one. I'm sending you a picture. It's absolutely incredible and worth every penny."

Easy for Keira to say, I thought, considering who was coughing up most of the pennies.

"All right, I'll keep you posted. We're going to go have coffee, then look at some more."

Going out for coffee? Since when was that part of the house-hunting ritual?

I frowned and marched to the car. I was going to go have coffee with Gabe Knightly and Cupid Keira while, back in New York, Opportunity said, "Oh, it looks like Andie's not home," and moved off to knock on other doors. *Ta ta, Andie.*

Could this day get any worse?

## Chapter Five

We picked up eggnog lattes at The Coffee Break, then, with me grinding my teeth and text-messaging all the way, moved on to the next house: a split level in Carol Estates. The candy cane stencils and home drawn art displayed in the front windows announced, "Kids live here."

Gabe almost stumbled over a pile of shoes in the entryway.

I watched as he pushed aside the small tennies and rain boots with his foot. A vision of a couple of kids who looked like me (not Gabe. There was no resemblance to him!) flashed through my mind. They splashed through a mud puddle in bright yellow rain slickers and little rubber boots and laughed. The background scenery in my vision looked more like Carol than New York, and that was all wrong.

"The carpet's worn," Keira observed as she went up the stairs.

I followed her to the first level. The living room looked tiny compared to the one in the previous house. But it was cozy. Someone was into knitting, and a half-finished blanket dangled from one arm of the couch.

"This isn't bad," I said.

Keira looked over her shoulder at me and raised an eyebrow.

I shrugged and followed her into the kitchen. It looked like it had been completely overhauled. The cupboards practically smelled new.

"I like this," said Keira, Queen of Take Out.

Those same little kids I'd seen splashing in the puddle now joined me in the kitchen. We were making cookies. Peanut butter. My mouth started to water.

Keira moved on and Gabe moved next to me.

"You looked a million miles away just now. What were you thinking?" he asked.

"I just had the best fantasy."

He edged closer, an expectant smile on his face. Here was where I was supposed to share my deepest yearning: barefoot, pregnant (by him, of course), and happily baking Christmas cookies.

"Yeah?" he prompted.

"I was thinking about peanut butter cookies. I can't remember the last time I had a peanut butter cookie."

He frowned and followed Keira down the hall to the bedrooms.

"What? You don't like cookies?"

No answer.

I smirked and followed after them.

"This place isn't doing it for me," Keira was saying. "Let's go to the next one."

"Okay. How about the Victorian? I bet you'll like this one, Andie," he added.

I shrugged. "Too bad I'm not in the market."

"You never know," Keira said from in back of me. Short-term memory loss. She'd forgotten which one of us was getting married.

I took her left hand and held it in front of her face. "You're the one who's looking. Remember?"

"I'm multitasking. I'm looking for both of us."

"Real estate's always a good investment," Gabe added. "You could buy something and rent it. Let the renters make your house payments."

Why did it feel like Gabe Knightly was always trying to sell me on something? In high school it was sex. Now it was real estate.

"I'll have to keep that in mind," I said diplomatically.

The Victorian was adorable, baby blue with white trim. The house had it all: patterned shingles, cornice trim, shuttered windows, and a charming front porch.

"It's gorgeous," I breathed.

"Too old-fashioned for me," Keira said.

The house was calling to me. "Let's look inside."

Inside was even better than outside: hardwood floors, a staircase with a banister and a newel post, a grandfather clock standing sentinel at the foot of the stairs. The living room wasn't as big as the one in the first house, but it was the perfect size to hold an intimate collection of friends at a holiday party. I took in the floral sofa and matching wing-back chairs and the Oriental rug and imagined a group of women sitting around visiting in front of the fireplace, drinking vanilla tea. This fireplace wasn't as big as the one in the first house, but large enough to accommodate Santa . . . if he went on a diet. As if the house itself wasn't enough to lust over, someone had used a scented plug-in to fill the place with the scent of cinnamon.

"I'm going upstairs," Keira announced.

I tore myself away from the living room and followed her up the hardwood stairs. The owners had put a carpet runner on them and we went up as soundlessly as burglars, the only noise in the place the slow ticking of the grandfather clock.

I tried not to drool as we drifted in and out of bedrooms. The two kids' bedrooms were obviously occupied by girls, with canopy beds and walls painted pastel pink and lavender. The rooms were relatively neat, with only a couple of books or ballet shoes on the floor, the beds occupied by dolls and stuffed animals. The master bedroom offered a walk-in closet, lots of light from the windows, and thick beige carpet. I looked at the sleigh bed piled high with pillows and imagined myself snuggled under the Chinese red comforter and propped up against those pillows, reading. And next to me . . .

*Don't go there,* I scolded myself, erasing the Gabe Knightly look-alike from the vision.

"Nice, isn't it?" said Gabe at my elbow.

Glue Guy. It seemed I couldn't shake him. "You think April would like it?" I asked sweetly.

The mention of my former best friend and his ex-girlfriend swiped the smile from his face. "We haven't been together in over a year."

I looked at him in disgust. "You really have commitment issues, don't you?"

"Actually, I don't. And that's been the problem," he added.

*Oh, yeah. Try to suck me into asking all about your love life.*

"Whoa, come look at this master bath," Keira called.

I looked. And wanted. If we got bathrooms in heaven, this was what they'd look like, all blinding-white tile and soft beige carpet.

"The Incredible Hulk would get lost in that tub," Gabe said.

Keira opened the glass shower door and looked in. "Two of them could fit in here."

"What do you think so far, Keira?" Gabe asked, looking at me.

"It's not me," she said. "This looks more like Andie."

Yeah, I could see myself in this place, dressing it all up, entertaining, eventually raising kids. "It's nice," I admitted.

"Something like this on that half-acre with a pond?" Gabe guessed.

"Something like that," I admitted. "In the Hamptons," I added, and he frowned.

We checked out a couple more houses, then Gabe took us to The Salad Bowl, one of Carol's newer restaurants, for lunch. As we parked in front of the squat brick building I tried not to compare it to all the great restaurants I'd been trying in New York: Jia Xiang Lo's for a Chinese breakfast of deep-fried Crullers and sweet soybean milk, The Candle Cafe for Veggie Hero Reubens, or the Original New York Milkshake Company where I always got good-natured harassment along with my grilled cheese sandwich and cherry vanilla shake. I didn't even have to set foot in this restaurant to know it couldn't measure up.

"Good choice," Keira approved. "I love this place."

"I figured you would," Gabe said, and opened the door for us.

He knew my sister's tastes so well. It irked me. And the fact that it irked me, well, that irked me. What did I care, anyway?

We entered and were overwhelmed by the smell of garlic and freshly baked bread. The place was painted a pale green, and it held so many plants I felt like I was in a salad bowl. Maybe that was what the owners were going for. Maybe they wanted us to be one with our food.

It was doing a brisk business, with almost every table full. We got the last booth and settled in, surrounded by planters full of exotic greens. The one in back of me brushed hungrily at my skin, making me feel like a fly on a Venus fly-trap. This plant obviously preferred humans. I leaned forward and drummed my fingers on the table. What was Beryl the Brit saying to Mr. Margolin over lunch? One thing I knew for sure. My name wouldn't come up.

"Nervous?" asked Gabe, nodding at my tapping fingers.

I stopped drumming. "No."

"You never used to do that," he said.

"I never used to be in business." And living in New York City, where life moved faster than the speed of light and no one cared that the meek would inherit the earth. There the meek couldn't even inherit attention from a store clerk. You had to be aggressive in New York. Who wouldn't drum their fingers?

"If it's making you that uptight maybe you're in the wrong business," Gabe suggested. "Or the wrong city."

What was he thinking? New York was the most exciting city in the world. Of course I was in the right city. It was a perfect fit for me. It just took some getting used to after growing up in a small town, that was all.

"She's not uptight," Keira said before I could formulate the perfect reply. "She's probably bored. She's used to eating at Sardi's." The way she said it made eating at Sardi's sound like a crime.

Gabe cocked his head. "Is that it? Is it boring here?"

"With my family? You've got to be kidding." But there were different kinds of excitement, and I preferred New York's with its fabulous nightlife and unlimited opportunity.

"We're not so bad," Keira said.

"We're certainly not boring," I said diplomatically.

"Your family's great," Gabe said.

"Is that why you dated half of us?" I asked.

Keira disappeared behind her menu.

Gabe looked irritated, but he recovered quickly. "Rejected by two Hartwell women. Pretty sad."

"To get rejected by somebody you have to first want them," Keira said from behind her menu.

There was a cryptic remark. What did it mean?

Nobody explained. Instead, Keira announced, "I'm going to have the Hail Caesar Salad. What about you guys?"

"I guess I'll have the Toss Your Tacos," Gabe said. "It's the only meat I'm going to get here."

"You could have the Curried Clucker," Keira suggested. "That's got chicken."

Gabe made a face. "Yeah, but it's also got curry and green olives. And apples."

I read down the menu: Leaf Me Alone, We Cantaloupe Fruit Lovers Salad, and the Berry Pleasing Northwest Mix, which was basically a tossed salad with blackberries and walnuts and a berry vinaigrette dressing. The soup names were just as bad. In the Spuds Potato Soup? Was that supposed to make me want to order? Whoever had come up with these names should have been drowned in Thousand Island Dressing. I mean, I like cute, but this wasn't Disneyland. It was an upscale restaurant. Supposedly. I wondered who did their advertising.

And speaking of advertising. *No, don't go there.*

Our waitress arrived, resplendent in black pants and a green polo shirt. She was wearing a white apron printed with vegetables and a cap on her head that I guessed was supposed to look like a tomato. Sadly, it looked more like the world's largest Superball.

"We need to leave her a really big tip," I said after she took our orders and hustled off.

Gabe raised both eyebrows. "She hasn't even served us yet."

"She deserves a reward just for being willing to wear that getup in public," I said.

Gabe gave the woman an assessing look. "It's not so bad."

"Andie doesn't like Mom's jacket, either," Keira explained.

"Well, who would?" I protested.

Gabe came to Mom's defense. "It's just in fun."

I pointed a finger at him. "You should be offended. You're a man."

One side of his mouth lifted in a half-grin. "You noticed."

I shook my head in disgust.

"She doesn't mean anything by it," Gabe said. "Anyway, it's probably good therapy or something."

"Or something," I muttered.

Gabe changed the subject. "So Keira, which house did you like the best?"

"The first one. It's got to be the first one."

"It's a great house," Gabe agreed. "And the value can only go up."

Like Spencer's blood pressure when he found out how much money his future wife was committing them to spending.

"I just have to convince Spencer it's worth it. We may have to be DINKs for a while."

Double Income, No Kids. I doubted Keira's salary at The Coffee Break was large enough to make her and Spencer a double-income couple. How would you describe them? As an INK? An INK and a half?

And what was I? One Income, No Kids. Hmmm. That made me an OINK.

"Are you okay?" Keira asked suddenly.

"Yeah. I'm fine. Why?"

"You looked like you were in pain just now."

"No pain here." I was perfectly happy being an OINK.

My phone rang just as the waitress showed up with our salads: one Toss Your Tacos, One Hail Caesar, and one Curried Clucker.

"I hate it when people have to talk on their cell phones every minute of the day," Keira grumbled.

I ignored her and answered it.

It was Iris. "Beryl's meeting with the Nutri Bread people next Wednesday. She said to let you know."

"Next Wednesday?" I had to have misheard.

"What's next Wednesday?" Keira demanded.

I turned away from her, getting snapped by the Venus humantrap plant in the process. "But Beryl knows I'm not going to be back until after New Year's." Which was, of course, why she'd done this. "What's the meeting about?" Dumb question, of course. It was about Beryl holding center stage, hogging the glory and presenting our media strategy for the next five years *sans* me. "Never mind."

"So, should I tell her you won't be able to make it back in time?" Iris asked.

I'd have done Christmas with the family. It was all I'd really committed to, anyway. I made a quick, decisive decision. The Carol fireworks would have to take place without me. I suffered a moment of guilt, knowing my family (well, mostly Mom and Grandma and Aunt Chloe) would be disappointed in me. But a career girl had to do what a career girl had to do. They'd simply have to accept that fact.

"I'll be there," I said.

"Okay, I'll tell her," said Iris, and hung up.

Good. This was working out perfectly. I wouldn't miss the action at work and I'd make it back to New York in time to see the ball drop. And I'd have done my duty and had Christmas with my family.

Keira barged into my thoughts. "You'll be where?"

"I've got a big meeting with the Nutri Bread people next week."

"Next week! You're supposed to stay through New Year's."

"Well, I'll be here through Christmas."

"But Spencer and I are having a party for you before the fireworks."

That was my sister. She lived for parties.

"Everyone's going to be there, and they're all looking forward to seeing you."

She made it sound like I was running out on her wedding. We needed to put this in perspective. "Who's everyone?" I asked.

"Me, for one," Gabe said.

"I'm already seeing you. Right now."

"And doesn't it make you want to see me more?"

I gave him a get-a-grip look and he shrugged and dug into his salad.

Keira was scowling at me. "I'd think being with your family for the first time in two years would rate higher than some dumb meeting about bread."

I didn't need a second mom for Christmas. "Not all of us are marrying a sugar daddy." I was sorry the minute I said it.

"I love Spencer," Keira said, stung.

I sighed. "I'm sorry."

"You should be. And I've gone to a lot of trouble to plan this party. We're having it at Spencer's. And it's catered."

*Oh, boy.*

"Mom's not going to like this."

I was barely home and we were already falling into old patterns. Keira should just as well have said, "I'm telling."

"Look. Let's not spoil Christmas. Okay?" I pleaded. "And you can still have your New Year's Eve party."

"It won't be the same without you."

I suddenly remembered how Keira had always wanted me at her parties when we were kids and how she tried to horn in when my friends and I sprawled around my bedroom and talked about boys. She was my little sister, and she'd looked up to me.

And I loved her. So to prove it, I was escaping back to NYC as quickly as possible. I felt like a rat.

Until I remembered about my sister dating Gabe. Then I felt justified in ducking out on her party. Anyway, she hadn't said anything about it until now, so it wasn't like I was deliberately ditching her.

I pointed that out.

"I didn't see any need to put it in your Palm Pilot since you were supposed to be here."

"Well, I was planning on it."

"And now you're not." She looked at me in disgust. "What if a big meeting comes up on my wedding day? Will you bug out on being my maid of honor?"

"I wouldn't have a meeting on a weekend."

"Well, you shouldn't have a meeting during the holidays, either."

"Hey, you two. The blood's starting to splash everywhere and you're ruining my appetite," said Gabe.

Keira shut up and glared at her salad.

I stabbed a piece of Curried Clucker, then put it in my mouth and chomped down hard. *Are we having fun yet?*

## Chapter Six

Keira didn't speak to me for the rest of the afternoon. I could live with that. Happily. What I didn't want was for her to start talking when we got home. To Mom.

Thankfully, she didn't rat me out when we got back. This was because Mom was having a teleshrink session with Dr. Phil and wouldn't have heard the ratting.

Mom's obsession with Dr. Phil. Now, there was an interesting phenomenon. I watched her staring at the TV while he counseled a couple in crisis and thought of that old saying about shutting the barn door after the horse was already gone. In Mom's case it was more like shutting the garage door after the Jag had vroomed off.

Keira found the Tupperware container of Christmas cookies and pulled out a couple, then set to work heating a mug of water for tea.

My salad had long worn off. I wandered out to the kitchen for a sugar fix and opened the container. I stared in disbelief. Empty, bare, nada, zip. I looked up and saw my sister quickly stuffing the last frosted tree in her mouth.

"You ate the last one," I accused.

"There'll be more at the New Year's Eve party," she said, shooting crumbs at me. Then she made a so-there face.

I glared at her and pulled a mixing bowl out of the cupboard. "Never mind. I'll make more."

She swallowed the last of her cookie. "I helped pay for that ticket, you know."

"I'll pay you back your share. With interest."

Keira frowned and turned to go.

"Come on, Keir. Try to understand," I pleaded.

"Oh, I already understand," she said. "I understand more than you think."

"What's that supposed to mean?" I demanded.

She shook her head, the picture of disgust, then took her mug of tea and left.

Of course she couldn't answer me. She had no idea what she was talking about. She was just trying to sound dramatic and mysterious. It was all those plays she'd done in high school. If she wasn't so invaluable at the coffee shop, she could have become the next Julia Roberts.

I looked to where Mom sat in front of the TV. What was the big deal, anyway? I wasn't leaving until after Christmas. And I'd told Mom I couldn't stay more than a week. It wasn't my fault she hadn't listened. Nobody in my family listened. Ears were wasted on them.

Of course, I should have let my sister's pettiness go. But I didn't. Instead, I fumed as I flattened and cut dough, generating enough heat to bake cookies without the oven.

Dr. Phil finally finished giving Mom her daily dose of relationship advice, and she joined me in the kitchen. "More cookies?"

"Keira ate the last of the rolled ones," I said as I slipped another tree on the baking sheet. I sounded whiny. Well, a little sugar would fix that.

Mom didn't ask if I wanted help. She just got out powdered sugar, butter, and milk and started making frosting. I watched as she dribbled in a couple drops of rose extract. Mom's secret ingredient for great frosting. I remembered all the times as a kid when we had helped her frost cookies, piling on mountains of sprinkles, sampling so many trees and Santas that we buzzed for hours after.

She smiled at me over her shoulder. "Do you do much baking in New York?"

"No time."

"You like to bake," Mom reminded me.

"No, I like to eat what I bake."

Mom grinned. "You've always been big into treats." She reached out and patted my arm. "Speaking of, it's a real treat to have you home."

I almost felt a tiny Keira dancing up and down on my shoulder, screeching, "See? See? You need to stay."

I gave her a mental swat and sent her flying. I didn't need to stay. I was already staying through Christmas and that was enough.

"It was really sweet of you to buy the ticket," I said.

"Your sister and brother chipped in. And Aunt Chloe. We all wanted to see you."

"Remember, Mom, I told you I couldn't stay all that long."

Mom turned her attention back to the frosting bowl. "I know. But we figured it was the holidays, and you wouldn't be all that busy. Anyway, who knows when you'll make it home again."

*Probably not for another decade.* I opened my mouth to explain about the important upcoming meeting at Image Makers, but got cut off by Aunt Chloe's grand entrance.

"I'm here," she announced, lumbering into the kitchen. She held a bulging bag. "Brought dinner from the deli," she said, unloading imitation KFC. "Ooh, cookies." She dipped a pudgy finger in the mixing bowl, dredged up a wad of dough, and popped it in her mouth.

"Will we have time to frost them before the concert?" she asked, removing more dough from the bowl.

I sighed inwardly. Now that Aunt Chloe was here any chance of getting my fill of frosted trees was officially gone. Like my chance of breaking the news of my early departure to Mom.

I guess I could have told both her and Aunt Chloe right then and there in the kitchen that I would not be here come New Year's, but they were both smiling, looking so pleased; with life, with me, with the cookie dough. It seemed a shame to spoil such a happy, not to mention normal, moment. I opened the deli bag and took out a chicken leg to munch, then tried not to feel like a cannibal as I bit into one of my own kind. *Cluck, cluck, cluck.*

"It's way too quiet in here," Aunt Chloe decided. "We need some Christmas music." She flipped on the stereo in the living room to the local station and the voice of Burl Ives started to wish us a holly jolly Christmas. She turned around and held out both hands. I half expected her to take a bow. "There. How's that?"

"It beats 'The Little Drummer Boy,'" Mom said. Then added, "Barely."

We had started frosting the cookies when Keira returned. I was sure her nose had led her. The kitchen smelled like a bakery early in the morning.

"Well, we're all here," said Aunt Chloe around a mouthful of chicken. "I guess we can eat."

We settled down at the kitchen table with Aunt Chloe's take out offering. I tried to enjoy the food, but dread that Keira would announce my early departure did bad things for my appetite.

"So, how did the house-hunting go?" Mom asked her.

A distraction. Thank God.

She set down her chicken. "I found the most amazing house." She bobbed her open hands up and down in a stop-and-listen-to-this-incredible-news motion. "It's in Fairhaven, and it is fabulous." She grabbed her purse from the counter, took out her cell phone, and brought up the pictures she'd taken.

"Wow," said Aunt Chloe. "Is that the new housing development?"

Keira nodded.

"You'll have to mortgage your firstborn to get into it," Mom predicted. "Oh, my. Look at that living room."

"It is a little pricey," Keira admitted, "but Gabe thinks we can swing it."

"Gabe isn't the one who has to live with the house payments," Mom said.

Keira frowned. "Whose side are you on?"

"Yours, of course. I just don't want to see you get in over your head. Nothing strains a marriage more than financial problems."

"Don't worry," Keira assured her. "Anyway, I'll do without something else if I have to. Food, clothes, furniture . . . I don't care. I must have this house."

I flashed on an image of a starved and naked Keira, sitting on the floor of her unfurnished new house, and moved my plate away. In the background, some woman sang "Santa, Baby."

"We'll bring you care packages of Christmas cookies," Aunt Chloe promised. She pushed away from the table and headed for the counter where the newly-frosted batch sat, defenseless.

The doorbell rang. "That's probably Spencer," Keira said, and hurried out of the room.

"I hope they know what they're doing," Mom said.

"Don't worry," said Aunt Chloe. "As long as women need pelvic exams your daughter will have a roof over her head."

Keira returned, towing Spencer behind her. "Spencer, this is Andie."

Spencer was a hunk. If you crossed Johnny Depp with Brad Pitt you would have Spencer. *Johnny Pitt.* With money. *Johnny Pitt Trump.*

"I'm glad to finally meet you," he said. He took my hand and I let him shake it around a little bit.

"Same here," I said."

Spencer was giving me a brotherly smile now. "I feel like I already know you. Keira talks about you all the time."

Keira frowned. "Oh, I do not."

I could just imagine what she'd have to say to him about me tonight.

"So, you're in advertising," he said.

I nodded.

Keira had had enough of sharing the spotlight. "Gabe said he'd show us the house before the concert, which means we should go right now." She tried to turn Spencer around to leave, but with his gaze fastened on the table, he was hard to turn.

"Have you eaten yet, Spencer?" Mom asked.

"Actually, no."

"We can fix that," Keira said. She grabbed the bag with the leftover chicken. "Come on. You can eat in the car."

He looked horrified.

"I'll feed you," she said, and started pushing him. "See you guys there," she called over her shoulder.

Mom shook her head as they exited. "Poor Spencer. He has no idea what he's getting into."

*If he doesn't, his brains have been sucked out by aliens,* I thought.

"Well, we'd better get this mess cleaned up and get ready

to go," Mom said. She picked up her plate and Keira's and stood.

"I'll put the cookies away," Aunt Chloe offered.

Good thing she hadn't been specific about where she was putting them, I thought as Mom and I loaded the dishwasher. My aunt had a system: one cookie for the container, one for her. I felt like a troll watching someone make off with his treasure. *Never mind, you've had enough,* I told myself firmly.

And by the time next Wednesday came, I'd have had enough of my family too. I knew that as surely as I knew Aunt Chloe was going to wolf down at least four more frosted Christmas trees before we could get her out the door for the concert.

We got to the auditorium and found good seats right in the middle. Mom dug some tissue out of her purse, pulled off a couple of pieces, and stuffed them in her ear. "There, I'm ready," she said to Aunt Chloe.

Aunt Chloe shook her head. "You've gotten old."

"So have you," Mom retorted. "You just don't know it yet."

Keira and Spencer joined us.

"So how was the house?" Mom asked.

"He loves it," Keira said.

"What?" Mom took the tissue out of one ear.

"He loves it," Keira repeated.

"Yeah, but it's out of our price range," Spencer added.

"Gabe can make a lower offer," Keira said.

"I don't think there's an offer low enough that we can afford," Spencer said. "I'm afraid . . ."

Keira cut him off. "Hey, they're starting." She let out a whistle and started clapping.

*Oh, Spencer,* I thought. *Be afraid. Be very afraid. My sister is going to blow your piggy bank to smithereens.*

Ben's band was halfway through their first song when I

caught sight of Dad slipping into a row at the back and felt my throat suddenly tighten. We should all have been sitting together as a family for this, and the fact that we weren't made me mad.

I know. People get divorced all the time. But how many log in thirty-some years and build a false sense of security in their family before they do it? What kind of a dirty trick is that to pull on your grown children? My parents probably had scarred us for life.

Not all of us, I decided as I watched Keira hit the mosh pit and get instantly surrounded by zit-faced fourteen-year-old boys. She was engaged, happy, and in control of her life.

I was in control of my life too, I consoled myself, except for when I had to leave it to come home.

The band really ramped up and, next to me, Aunt Chloe started getting into the concert, calling things like, "Go, Ben!" and "Yow!"

I tuned her out and watched my brother with growing admiration. You'd never have known he'd almost severed his foot from his leg the night before. He was great on the guitar. Better than Phil Keaggy or Eddie Van Halen. He burned up the stage, and all the thirteen-year-old girls in the audience (actually, most of the audience was thirteen-year-old girls) went crazy when he played his screaming riffs.

Me, I was going crazy for the bass player. His hair was blond as a California beach bum's, and he had a gorgeous, chiseled chin that could have qualified for space on Mount Rushmore. He was singing with that pained expression musicians get when they're really into the music. I couldn't understand the words, but I'm sure whatever he and my brother were singing together was profound. A man who was both profound and cute. He had the whole package. Was the package tied up with a girlfriend?

After the concert I ambled down to congratulate my

brother. Yes, and to meet the bass player. Since I was hip deep in thirteen-year-olds, I resigned myself to a long wait.

But Ben spotted me and called me over, and the girls eyed me jealously. Ben hauled me up on the stage, then slung an arm over my shoulder and pointed me at his bass player, who had been talking to a crowd of tweenies.

"James, this is my hotshot New York sister, Andie. Sis, James Fender."

James was still wearing his bass, fingering the frets. He smiled at me and Greg Kinnear dimples popped out on his cheeks. "Hi."

"You guys were good," I said.

"Just good?" Mr. Fish Without Legs was angling for a better compliment.

"Okay, you were great."

"You play music too?" he asked.

I shook my head. "Ben got all the musical talent in the family."

James nodded. "Well, you got the looks."

James Fender was a very astute man.

"And the brains, from what Ben tells me," James added.

I tried to look modest.

"I suppose you're busy seeing all your friends," he ventured.

I shrugged. "Not that busy."

"Got time for dinner?"

"Great job, man," I heard a familiar voice behind me saying.

Oh, no. Not Gabe. Not now.

No time for coy replies. "When?" I said.

"Tomorrow?" he suggested.

My brother is the only man I know who can multitask. He stopped in midconversation with Gabe to insert, "She can't tomorrow. Mom's got us going to get the Christmas tree."

"Day after tomorrow," I said quickly. If anyone had family bonding plans for me, too bad. I should at least be allowed one night off for good behavior.

"Great," said James. "How about I pick you up?"

"You know where I live."

"Around seven?"

"Sure."

Behind me, Aunt Chloe's voice boomed. "Has anyone ever told you that you look just like Paul Revere? Only with blond hair."

My aunt was comparing the bass player in my brother's band to a guy from the Revolutionary War? Great. I could already see my date getting canceled on grounds of insanity.

James stared at her blankly.

"You know," she prompted. "Paul Revere and the Raiders. The band. He was a hunk."

Near-recognition dawned in his eyes, and he nodded politely.

"Have you met my niece?" she asked.

He smiled at me. "Just did."

"She's only in town for a little while."

"Thank you for sharing that," I said, trying to keep it light. I made an attempt to move her away.

Aunt Chloe planted her feet. "I wouldn't wait too long to call her. You don't have a girlfriend, do you? Or an ex-wife?"

My whole face felt like a stove burner on high. "We'd better let him get back to signing CDs," I said quickly. I put my shoulder into it and turned her around. Then I started us marching the opposite direction, shooting an apologetic look over my shoulder as we went.

James Fender was wearing one of those quizzical smiles you always read about characters in books wearing. I'm sure it got even more quizzical when I marched right into someone.

I started to apologize, then realized who I'd bumped into.

Gabe nodded the direction I'd just come. "I see you have time in your schedule for making new friends. Maybe you could fit in dinner with an old one."

"Well, I'll just leave you two," said Aunt Chloe, Mistress of Subtle. She gave me a pat on the shoulder, then practically skipped off.

I was zinging again. I neutralized it by looking over to where James stood, still strapped into his bass and scribbling on CDs. "My schedule's going to be full."

Who was I kidding? Aunt Chloe's romantic assistance had probably scared off James. Heck, she'd scared me. I'm trapped in a sitcom, I thought miserably.

No, not trapped. I would be going back to New York. And soon. First thing tomorrow I was calling the airline.

## Chapter Seven

Gabe didn't take my rejection too hard. Maybe that was because he wasn't taking the hint. "Oh, well. I'll be over at your place off and on," he said. "So I'll see you around."

"What do you mean you'll be over?" Since when was Gabe Knightly a fixture at the Hartwell house? "For what?"

He shrugged. "This and that. Might have to take Keira house hunting some more if she can't convince Spencer to make an offer on that one place she wants."

That would put Gabe in our front room a grand total of five minutes. I could stay in my room.

"Your mom has me over for dinner sometimes," he added.

I stared at him, sure I'd misheard. The founder of Man Haters, Inc. was feeding the man who had betrayed both her daughters? If it wasn't for the fact that I didn't want to go on national television with my entire family, I would have written Dr. Phil. *Dear Dr. Phil, My mom's a great fan of yours. Maybe she'll listen to you.*

"Did Keira ever tell you why we broke up?" Gabe asked suddenly.

"No. Why did you break up?"

79

"Why don't you ask her sometime?"

*Because I've got better things to do.* "I'll have to put that at the top of my list of New Year's resolutions," I said and walked away.

I suddenly wished I had one of those Advent calendars my mom used to get us when we were kids, the ones that gave you the countdown to Christmas by letting you open a little door each day and get a piece of chocolate. It would have made me feel better to have a visual aid as I did the how-soon-can-I-split countdown. The daily dose of chocolate wouldn't have hurt either.

Aunt Chloe didn't hang around long after the concert. She was anxious to get home and listen to her old Paul Revere records. We left shortly after her. By eleven it was just Mom and me, seated at the kitchen table and nursing cups of hot chocolate. This would be the perfect time to tell her I wasn't sticking around for New Year's Eve.

It would also be the perfect time to enjoy a cup of cocoa together, I decided.

Mom talked about Ben's career in the band. Where was it going? He'd never make a living as a musician, especially if all he played were churches and old theaters.

I assured Mom that, if the band took off, Ben would probably make a very good living. And while I explained the success of bands like Mercy Me to her, I had a little conversation with myself. *Coward. Gutless Wonder. You have to tell her. Okay. I will, I will.*

But I didn't. And then Keira came home, earlier than anticipated, so there went my chance.

"You're back early."

Keira threw down her purse. "Yeah."

*Uh-oh,* I thought.

"Did you two have a fight?" Mom asked.

"That man is stubborn and selfish." Keira joined us at the kitchen table, plopping onto the nearest chair.

"He's not going for the Barbie Dream House, huh?" I guessed.

"Ha, ha," Keira practically snarled at me. She turned to Mom. "You know, one minute it's, 'I just want you to be happy, baby. Whatever house you want, it's yours.' The next minute he's saying, 'Not that one.'"

"Didn't he also say the house had to be within a certain price range?" Mom reminded her.

"I'm working too. We can afford this."

*As long as you sit on the floor naked,* I thought. Math had never been Keira's strong suit.

"Maybe, if you look at some more houses," Mom ventured.

"I am not looking at any more houses," Keira vowed, "not when I've already found the one that is perfect, the one I really want."

That meant I wouldn't have to see Gabe. Every cloud has a silver lining.

I listened to Keira sputter for another ten minutes, then claimed I still had jet lag and left Mom to listen to her. Poor Mom. My sister could be such a whiny brat sometimes.

And poor Spencer. At this rate, he wouldn't have to worry about financing any house. He'd be history by next year. My sister had never had much patience for dream men who liked to drift into reality.

Why had she and Gabe broken up?

I didn't sleep well that night. I kept having these weird dreams. In one of them my family was gathered at Keira's too-expensive new place for a housewarming party. There was no furniture anywhere, only flimsy wooden crates that broke when people tried to sit on them. Keira couldn't afford clothes in this dream, and she was wearing an old dress of Aunt Chloe's that made her look like a five-year-old playing dress-up. She kept tripping on the skirt, spilling red punch from her cup.

"You'll never get that stain out of the carpet," Mom predicted.

"If I hadn't kicked in for Andie's plane ticket I could have had a new dress," Keira said.

That was when I ran screaming into the night. Next scene I was on an airplane, watching from a tiny window as Gabe Knightly chased the plane down the tarmac, while over the speaker Beryl the Brit's voice announced, "Andie Hartwell, please put your seat in an upright position. You are in for a bumpy ride when you return to New York." Then she started laughing maniacally.

I woke up to the sound of the shower running: Keira getting ready for work. I would write her a check and leave it on her dresser, maybe with a note that said, *Buy yourself some new clothes.*

After she was out the door, I went to the kitchen and dug the phone book out of the junk drawer. I looked up the phone number for Great Bargain Airlines and called.

A woman with a thick accent I couldn't identify answered. I think she said, "Welcome to Great Bargain Airlines," although it sounded like "Veelcoo to Greet R.E. Eelees."

I checked to make sure I'd dialed the right number. I had. Oh, greet.

"Eese is Dearie," said the woman.

*Dearie?* That didn't sound right. *Darla? Dede? Deirdre?* Pick a name, any name.

"Hee mee Eee help you?"

"I need to change my departure date," I told Dearie.

"Theer veel be een tee heendred deeler fee to cheenge yeer fleet."

"Eeen tee heendred deeler fee?" I repeated. Was she saying two or three hundred? For all I knew she could be saying five. What did it matter? I had to get back.

"Yeees, ees de heeledays."

"Okay," I said. I could put it on Meester Card.

We went through the rigamarole of name, flight number, departure date, etcetera. Then Dearie informed me that the only time I could get out was on a flight that left at 10 P.M.

Better to arrive in New York with red eyes than not arrive on time. "I'll take it," I told her and gave her my charge card number.

"Theenk yew," she said when we were finished. "Meery Chreestees."

"Meery Chreestees to you too," I said and hung up.

"So, you're leaving early," said a voice tinged with motherly rebuke.

*Meery Chreestees*, I thought, and took a deep breath.

I turned around, looking as sorrowful as I could. "I'm sorry. I have got to get back. My boss has scheduled an important client meeting that I just can't miss."

Mom scowled. "Who does any business the week between Christmas and New Year's?"

"My company," I said. "It's important, Mom."

The scowl shrank to a frown.

"If it wasn't, you know I wouldn't go." That was the truth. If I hadn't felt like my job was on the line, I'd have sucked it up and stuck it out until the bitter end.

Now Mom just looked regretful. She nodded. "I know." She gave a one-shouldered shrug. "I'd just hoped we'd get to have you for a little longer."

"At least I'll be here for Christmas," I reminded her.

She nodded like a true good sport and turned her attention to the coffeemaker. I'd started coffee and Mom got busy pouring herself a mug. With her back to me. I knew what that meant. She was trying to hide the fact that she was upset.

And I was the rat who had upset her. *Queen Ratisha.*

I tried to make it up to her. "How about I make breakfast this morning?"

"Actually, I'm not very hungry," she said. "I'm going to go take a quick shower. Go ahead and make whatever you want. We've got waffles in the freezer."

She left and I opened the freezer. There they were, blueberry waffles, my favorite. Mom had probably stocked up, just for me.

I wasn't very hungry either. Guilt and waffles don't go well together. I settled for a mug of coffee.

Mom hid in her craft room for the first part of the morning, but by about 10:30, she had recovered from the shock of having her plans for me rearranged and was up to speaking to me again.

"So, what would you like to do today?" she asked.

"I'm having lunch with Dad," I reminded her and braced myself. First I change my flight plans, then I spend an afternoon in the enemy camp. This would go over well.

Mom frowned. "I forgot. Well, please don't make any other arrangements with your father until you talk to me first. Okay? Remember, Grandma is expecting us to come over for lunch tomorrow, and we're going shopping with Aunt Chloe."

Tuna Torture Casserole and Gram's special, Prune Whip, followed by fun with Mom and Aunt Chloe. There was an indigestion combo.

"And don't forget we're going to put up the tree tonight," Mom added.

"Ben already told me," I said. "I'm planning on it."

Mom was almost smiling now. She loved decorating for the holidays, and tree trimming had always been an important Hartwell holiday ritual.

So had knocking over furniture with a too-tall tree and having said tree fall down at least once during the stand-fitting process. So was breaking ornaments, which always brought a howl out of someone, usually Mom. Tree trimming, I decided, must be a little like childbirth. Once you see the lovely thing, you forget all the misery and hassle it caused you while you were in the process of giving it life.

I flashed on a sudden image of Dad and Mom, standing with their arms around each other, enjoying the sight of the decorated tree, and felt homesick, even though I was here in the same house where I grew up. Mom and Dad might never stand in our living room with their arms around each other again, but maybe they could stand in the same room and smile at each other. I fervently hoped The Girlfriend would not be joining Dad and me for lunch.

The Steak 'N' Bake was just a block away from the North Center Mall, which serviced Carol as well as nearby Cedarwood. This time of year, I knew the mall would be a mob scene. Maybe I could talk Dad into going to the Barnes and Noble down the street instead. We could get me a good mystery and him a book on how to have a successful relationship—with someone his own age.

I saw Dad waiting alone in the steakhouse lobby and nearly burst into the Hallelujah chorus. It looked like it would be just the two of us.

He beamed at the sight of me and held out his arms. "Hello there, New York, New York."

I walked over to him and let myself get crushed in a big Michael Hartwell bear hug.

He held me at arm's length and inspected me. "You look great."

"Thanks," I said. "You look great yourself."

"Your old man's holding up pretty good," he told me.

"I wouldn't have believed it if I hadn't seen it for myself," I teased.

He frowned. "Your Mom should have told me what she was planning. I'd have paid for your airline ticket."

Oh, goody. Only together one minute and already the parent rivalry was beginning.

"So, do we have a table?" I asked.

Dad nodded. "Oh, yeah."

"Maybe we'd better get started. Unless the bank is now giving their collections managers longer lunch hours."

"I took the afternoon off," Dad said. "Wanted to have plenty of time to spend with my girl."

Girl. Singular. That confirmed it. I wouldn't have to deal with The Girlfriend.

Dad looked over my shoulder and his smile got wider. "Great. We're all here now."

*Uh-oh.* I turned and saw a woman with pencil legs in tight jeans and a long coat coming our way. Her haircut looked expensive. I couldn't say the same for the dye job. She looked like a rooster.

"Brittany," Dad called as if she couldn't see us standing there. To me he said, "At last, my girls get to meet."

Brittany had a self-assured stride. She was still coming at me when she stuck out her hand to shake. "Andie. Your dad has told me so much about you."

I forced a smile. "Brittany," I said, and left it at that. I'm never at a loss for words, but I guess there's a first time for everything.

The hostess led us to a table, and Brittany dropped onto a

chair. "I had a terrible time getting away," she confessed. "This is our busiest time of year."

"Where do you work?" I asked politely.

"Chez Rory's."

"Brittany's a hair stylist," Dad added.

And right now she was looking speculatively at my hair. *Don't even think about it.* I nodded.

"Everyone's trying to get ready for holiday parties," Brittany explained. "And next week will be even crazier."

Words. I dealt in words. Why was I having trouble accessing any?

Actually, I'm working on my master's in psychology," Brittany explained. "But before I went back to school I went to beauty school. I figured it would be a good way to pay the bills."

I nodded politely. "There's probably no better place to study the human mind than a beauty salon."

I could almost see her psychoanalyzing dad. *It's natural to feel unsettled at your age, Mike. Don't worry. I can help you through your midlife crisis.*

Our waitress appeared. "Can I start you folks out with a drink?"

If ever I was going to become a drinking woman, it would be now. "No, thanks," I said quickly before I could change my mind. *Just pound me over the head with a hammer until I see stars.* Anything would be better than having to sit at this table for an hour and look at Brittany. And Dad. Together.

"I don't drink," Brittany said primly.

I could understand that. A woman had to keep her wits about her when she was seducing a middle-aged man.

"I'll have a beer," said Dad.

The waitress left. Words were finally forming in my mind.

"So, how did you and Dad meet?" Dumb question. I had already figured out the answer.

Sure enough, Brittany smiled at Dad like he was Santa and said, "Mikey came in for a haircut."

Mikey? I could feel my facial muscles balking at donning an isn't-that-sweet expression. I tried to force my mouth up at the corners. It felt like some little elf had hung a fifty-pound weight on each corner of my lips.

Fortunately for my lips, Brittany wasn't looking at me for approval. She was gazing at Dad. She stretched a hand out to him, and he took it and looked at her like a puppy who had just been promised a lifetime supply of slippers to chew.

A waitress hurried past with a plate holding a steak and a sizzling pile of fried onions. I told myself it was the smell of grease and onion that was making me sick, not the sight of my father looking googly-eyed at a woman my age. After all, this sort of thing happens. Men date younger women, women date younger men. Anything goes these days. Whatever rings your bells.

But what about everybody else's bells? My Dad was holding hands with a woman my age. She could be my step-mom. I had a sudden vision of myself at Hallmark, trying to pick out a Mother's Day card for my new mommy. Then I had a vision of Mom coming in the store and catching me at it.

I stood up and started backing away from the table. "Would you excuse me for a minute? I need to . . ." *Throw up.*

"Look out," cried Brittany, just as I turned to run for the ladies' room and a paper-towel cold compress.

Too late. I collided with a waiter bearing a tray full of steak-laden plates and a condiment server of sour cream, green onions, and bacon bits.

The plates jumped off the tray, the tray did a somersault,

and the condiment server took a bow, dumping sour cream on my black turtleneck.

The waiter looked mournfully at the scattered plates and food, then at me. "Are you all right?"

I scooped a blob of sour cream from my chest. It was dotted with brown bacon bits. "I'm fine." I held up my palm full of sour cream and said to my dad and Brittany, "I'll be right back."

I stepped past the waiter, who was now kneeling over the mess, and beat feet to the bathroom. Thankfully, I had the place all to myself.

I dumped my handful of sour cream down the sink and scowled at the messy blonde in the mirror. "You've got to get a grip," I told her. "You're too old to be indulging in *Parent Trap* fantasies." Anyway, Brittany wasn't that bad. Looking on the bright side, I'd probably get free haircuts for life.

Except that I was going to remain on the east coast, far from my family. And my future stepmom.

The bathroom door opened and Brittany slipped in. "I thought you might like some help."

*How many women does it take to clean up a sour cream spill?* "That's okay. I think I can get it," I said and reached for a paper towel.

She stood there, gnawing her lip and watching me work. "I guess it seems kind of strange to see me with your dad," she finally said. "With our age difference and all."

I shrugged. "It's nothing personal. I'm just used to thinking of him with my mom."

She nodded. "Most guys my age are so shallow. Your dad, he's different."

I wasn't so sure about that. I'd observed some of my dad's midlife behavior.

"When we first met, I felt like I could talk to him forever."

About what? I wondered. Hair? Sports cars? The repo business? I suppose someone could find what my dad does for a living interesting. He can sure make it sound good. He thinks of himself as James Bond, the bank version. That's probably because he has an alias he uses to call and harass people who tend to forget minor details like paying bills. And he has been known to be involved in sneaking out at night and repossessing cars. As a matter of fact, I think his jag was a bank repo bargain. It was still expensive, though, so Mom never quite got the bargain concept.

"I'd broken up with my boyfriend," Brittany started explaining. "I was drifting, confused. Your father's been a real anchor for me."

Well, anchors aweigh, I thought. I nodded and started to work on the sour cream spill.

"Of course, I know that sounds like I just dated your dad on the rebound. But it wasn't like that."

"Ummm," I said politely, and waited for her to tell me what it was like.

She didn't. Instead, she switched gears. "So, you're in advertising."

"Yes, I am."

"Do you like it?"

"Yes, I do." Part of me chided myself over my refusal to properly hold up my end of the conversation. But another part of me insisted I would be disloyal to Mom if I did. I felt like I was in middle school again, in the lunchroom getting pressured to choose whose table to sit at.

Meanwhile, Brittany stood there, half smiling and nodding like a bobblehead Barbie. I supposed she was going to stay here with me until I was completely done. Female bonding in the bathroom. So far the glue wasn't taking.

Brittany didn't seem to realize that. She just kept looking at me expectantly. I searched my brain for something polite and noncommittal to say. "You've got a pretty full schedule, going to school and working." *Are you sure you have time for my dad?*

"I like to keep busy." Now she was looking at my hair again. "That's a great cut," she told me.

For what I paid for it, it should be, I thought. The sour cream was now a damp, gray blob on my chest. A damp, gray blob with paper-towel lint embedded in it.

I realized the mess wasn't going to get better, so I gave up and tossed the towel. "I guess we'd better go order." I wished I had an excuse to order something to go. The thought of lunch with Dad and Brittany was not pleasant. Maybe, if I were lucky, she'd have some hairy clients waiting for her and she'd have to hurry off after we ate.

No such luck. After she'd consumed a fortune in steak, side orders, and dessert, she was ready to hit the mall. We stood and she linked her arm through Dad's. He offered me his other arm, and we all strolled out of the restaurant.

"Oh, look," said an old woman as we passed. "What a nice dad, taking his daughters out to lunch."

Dad's cheeks suddenly looked sunburned.

I sneaked a peek at Brittany. That should be enough to tell her she needed to find someone her own age to play with. Her chin had shot up another notch, and I noticed she now had Dad's arm in a death grip.

"So," Dad said once we'd hit the parking lot. "Where would you ladies like to start?"

"Nordstrom," said Brittany.

Dad smiled at me. "You fancy some new duds for Christmas?"

What I fancied was some time alone with my dad, but I obviously wasn't going to get that.

"We should get her a new top," Brittany said. "She'll feel a lot more like shopping if she can lose that one."

"Good idea," Dad agreed.

So I got a new top for Christmas. Dad paid.

Brittany got a new top too, and some perfume and a cashmere sweater. Dad paid some more.

"Oh, Mikey," she gushed. "You're going to spoil me."

"He's good at that. Just ask Mom," I cracked.

Brittany lost her smile and Dad looked like he'd like to send me to my room without supper.

No one gets my sense of humor. I decided to inspect a nearby display of scarves.

"Would you like one of those?" Dad asked.

Was he offering me a present or a bribe to shut up?

"I've got plenty of scarves," I assured him.

"A top isn't much to get you for Christmas, Princess. What else would you like?"

*For life to be a video you could rewind and edit.* I shook my head. "Nothing. I'm fine." What a liar I was!

We window shopped a little more, making our way past piles of fake snow and phony snowmen with plastic carrot noses and stick arms dangling signs pointing the way to Santa's workshop. "I Saw Mommy Kissing Santa Claus" blared at us as we passed a maternity shop. This was a nightmare, like the one I had about Keira in her too-expensive new house. I surreptitiously pinched myself, but I didn't wake up.

Dad asked about my job and my car, and gave me a pop quiz on the security at my apartment. Once I'd passed those tests, he seemed to run out of steam.

I was feeling a little steamless myself. Brittany was still going strong, though. They had to be missing her over at Chez Rory's by now. Maybe she was just hanging around to make sure I didn't get a chance to bad-mouth her to Dad when she was gone.

There wasn't anything to bad-mouth, really. She was nice

enough, just not old enough. I have to admit, I was hoping she'd get a sudden urge to return to her scissors and hair gel so I could ask Dad if he was suffering from some kind of reverse Oedipus complex, but she stuck with us.

I finally gave up trying to outlast her. "I'd better get going," I told Dad.

"Oh, look," she said, pointing to the plastic shack where a tired-looking Santa was jiggling a howling two-year-old on his knee. "We should get our picture taken with Santa first."

There would be a charming memento: me, Dad, and The Girlfriend. My luck, he'd put it on Christmas cards and one would somehow get back to Mom.

The line for Santa wasn't too long, but long enough. "Sorry, I really have to get going," I told her. "Maybe next year." Maybe by next year there would be no girlfriend in the picture.

"This was way too short," Dad said as I hugged him. "You ought to let me take you out to dinner."

"Oh, good idea!" said Brittany. Did she come by that perky voice naturally, or did she practice it?

Another threesome, I thought. *What fun!* "I'm afraid Mom's got me pretty busy," I said. "Did Ben invite you to the Christmas Eve service?" I asked Dad.

He nodded.

"I hope you'll come," I said.

"For another chance to see my girl? I'll be there." He hugged me again. "See if you can sneak away from your mother one more time. I won't tell."

"Me either," said Brittany.

I didn't say anything, just smiled in a noncommittal kind of way. I wished Brittany a merry Christmas (and a new boyfriend, I added mentally), told Dad I'd see him Christmas Eve, then hurried away, relieved to have the torture session over.

As I left the mall all I could think about was getting back to the house, shutting myself in my room for an hour and recharging my Miss Manners batteries. Dad and his hair stylist had drained what little was left of them.

"Andie?"

Oh, no. There was nothing left in my batteries. This was not a good time for holiday chitchat. I hurried on, pretending deafness.

"Andie, wait!"

What does a girl do when her Miss Manners batteries have run out of juice and she meets her former best friend at the mall? I was about to find out.

## Chapter Eight

I squeezed the last little bit of juice out of my drained batteries and turned to smile at April White, who was closing the gap between us in one final, perky bound. April had been in gymnastics when we were in high school. She was a human spring. A short spring, with long brown hair, a round face, bee-stung lips, and a button nose. Half of the guys in our class at Carol High had lusted after her, except Gabe, of course, who had lusted after me. April and I and the rest of our gang had spent our summers out at nearby Lake Carol, reading *Seventeen* and *People*. During the school year we had been inseparable, each other's fashion police when shopping at the mall, each other's brain when doing homework. April was one of those people who actually got math, and she helped me through Algebra I and II, and Geometry. Words were my specialty, and I fed her ideas for all of her English papers. In fact, I wound up writing most of the papers while she sat beside me, offering comments like, "Oh, I like that," or "Yeah, that sounds good."

We had vowed to be friends forever. I guess forever sort of fizzled after she started dating Gabe.

Judging from the eager smile on April's face, it looked like she was hoping to find it again. "I heard you were coming home for Christmas." She looked at me admiringly. "You look great—so sophisticated, so New York."

"Thanks," I said. "And you haven't changed a bit." *Other than the fact that you lost your scruples somewhere along the way.* I mean, how tacky is that, to start dating your best friend's old boyfriend, the same boyfriend you knew your friend wanted to get back together with. Once.

All right, so the once had been in high school. Ancient history. Maybe I was overreacting, but what can I say? That's how I felt.

"We have to get together," April informed me.

*No we don't.* "Gosh, I'm not sure I'm going to have time," I said. "You would not believe how busy my family has me."

"Oh, yeah. I would. I hope you can fit me in, though." She looked a little shy now. "I know we kind of went through a period where . . . well, I hope we can put that behind us. I'd really like to be friends again."

Judas had wanted to turn back the clock too. It didn't always work that way.

"So, what are you doing these days?" I asked, dancing around the subject.

April lit up like a state fair midway at night. "I got a job at Meister Bookkeepers. I'm an accountant now."

I nodded, all the while counting the seconds until I could scram. My fake smile was making my cheeks ache. "That's great."

"So, check your calendar and let's get together," April said, refusing to let me sidetrack her. "I have tons to tell you. Any night you can fit me in. Or we can do lunch. I really want to hear about your life in New York. It sounds so glam."

I could certainly make it sound that way if she wanted.

After all, that was what I did for a living, make things sound great.

Not that it would be hard. I was happy with my life in the Big Apple.

"I'll sure try," I said. That was a big, fat lie. But hey, I told myself, social lies to make people feel good aren't as bad as mean lies.

"I'd better get going," I said. "Good to see you," I added and felt my nose start to grow.

We hugged. "Call me," April urged.

I just smiled, then pulled away.


Back home Mom was burning holiday candles, and the house smelled like Christmas trees and sugar cookies. It was a comforting fragrance. Some aromatherapy combined with a little couch time and a mug of instant cocoa was just what my drained batteries needed.

I heard voices coming from the kitchen and went to investigate.

"It smells good in here," I said as a I wandered in.

A new scent hit me. *Chocolate.* I looked over to the kitchen table and saw Mom and Aunt Chloe hovering over enough goodies to give me psychosomatic insulin shock.

"Hi, Hon," Mom called. "We're working on our display for the Valentine mug."

Aunt Chloe didn't say anything. She had her mouth full and was chewing as she wove pink netting around two different chocolate cakes, platters of chocolate chip cookies and brownies, and chocolate-covered donuts. I saw they had artfully spilled a couple boxes' worth of truffles and bon bons across the table also. They even had a chocolate cream pie, with a piece removed to reveal the chocolate filling. No need to wonder where that piece of pie had gone.

"Whoa," I said, edging closer for a better look.

Aunt Chloe had finally swallowed. "Do you think it's enough?"

"You could give a sugar buzz to the entire town of Carol with what's on this table," I said.

"Well, we want the picture to be good," Aunt Chloe said. "You would not believe how long it took us to get all this," she added. "Retail is hard work."

"I think we'll just have frozen pizza for dinner tonight," Mom said. "I'm not going to want to cook."

I wasn't sure I was going to want to eat. Just looking at all that junk food was making me slightly nauseated.

I decided against the cocoa, and went in search of my BlackBerry and laptop.

An hour later, Mom and Aunt Chloe were finished, declaring their chocolate photo shoot a success. Aunt Chloe waddled out the door, carrying a bakery box topped by a plate of cookies in one hand and a bag of donuts in the other. Her purse strap was slipping off her shoulder.

"Andie, Hon, could you get the door for me?" she asked around a mouthful of food.

"Sure."

I hopped up and opened the door, and she gave me a chocolate kiss on the cheek. "See you tomorrow," she said.

Tomorrow. Oh, yes. Lunch at Gram's and the mall expedition. At least I had my date with James Fender to look forward to.

Mom came out into the living room a few minutes later and flopped down on the couch. "That was exhausting, but we got a great picture."

"It'll be cute," I said. And certainly not as tacky as her normal merchandise. There was a step in the right direction.

"So, how was lunch with your father?" She asked it casually, but her body looked like a stretched rubber band, waiting to shoot someone.

"It was okay," I said. "We ate at the Steak 'N' Bake."

Mom studied her fingernails. "Just you and Dad?"

"Pretty much." Now I was probably looking like a stretched rubber band.

"Pretty much. What does that mean?"

"Um, Dad's friend was there."

Mom scowled. "You mean his girlfriend. Just say it. I can take it."

I sighed, feeling like an accomplice to a crime. "I'm sorry, Mom. I didn't know she was going to be there."

Mom managed a tiny smile. "It's not your fault your father's an idiot."

"I just don't know what he's doing with her," I blurted. "Well, I mean I knew, but I still couldn't wrap my mind around it. Other people's dads took up with younger women, not mine.

"He's trying to recapture his youth," Mom said in disgust. "I think your father's going for the record for the world's longest midlife crisis." She grabbed a sofa pillow and hugged it. "I'm sorry I was such a pill about you seeing him. Even if he is an idiot, he is your father. Guess I didn't want to share."

It had to be hard being my mom these days, trying to go about the business of living while her ex-husband ran around town with a woman young enough to be their daughter. Riding a wave of sudden respect and tenderness for her, I reached over and gave her a hug.

"I know," I said. "But you always told us kids we had to share."

"Yeah, well, do what I say, not what I do."

"Very profound."

"I thought so. In fact, that calls for a drink. I stocked up on sugar plum tea. Want a cup?"

I nodded. She started to get up, but I said, "You stay put. I'll get it."

"Oh, nonsense," Mom said.

I pushed her back. "You've had a hard day photographing fat in the larvae stage. I'll get it."

As I went to the kitchen I pondered the significance of my conversation with Mom. Maybe I could mine some gold out of this visit home and act as a peacemaker for my parents.

I thought of the events and outings that lay ahead. Helping Mom and Dad reach a domestic peace accord would be my consolation for the myriad of trials and embarrassments that were a natural part of a Hartwell holiday.

We were still sitting on the couch when Keira popped in, laden with shopping bags. "This is it," she announced. "All my Christmas shopping is now officially done."

"And with three days to spare," Mom teased. "What a woman."

Just then my brother came in behind her. "I'm doing better than Ben," she said, nodding in his direction. "I don't think he's even started."

"Started and finished," he retorted, shrugging out of his coat. "I shopped on the Internet."

Keira looked scornful. "Boring."

"Easy."

"You miss all the smells and sounds of Christmas," Keira said.

"Yeah, and the crowds."

She shrugged. You couldn't argue with that.

"So, what's for dinner?" Ben asked.

"Chocolate," said Mom.

Half his upper lip rose in disgust the same way it used to

when we were kids and Mom announced spinach was on the menu. "Chocolate!"

"Mom and Aunt Chloe are working on their gift line for Valentine's Day," I explained.

"You're buying chocolate for that now? Does it last that long?" he asked.

"We only needed it for the picture that's going on our new mug," Mom explained. "I'm too tired to cook. I'm just going to take a pizza out of the freezer."

Ben whipped out his cell phone. "I'll do better than that. I'll order us one."

"Bennett Hartwell, that's a complete waste of money when I have a perfectly good pizza in the freezer," Mom said. But she said it half-heartedly.

"The stuff you get from Amore Italiano is always better," Ben said.

"No pepperoni," Keira reminded him.

"I know, I know."

An hour later, we lay around the living room, the nearly empty cardboard delivery box out on the dining room table.

"I should have made a salad," Mom said.

"Pizza doesn't need anything but Pepsi," Ben told her, raising his can. He took a big swig, then let out a belch.

"If all your screaming fans could see you now," I told him.

"Guys gotta be guys," Ben said and upended the can over his mouth.

Mom just shook her head. "Before you get any more comfortable, you'd better go get our tree. I heard on the radio that it's supposed to snow tonight, and the tires on your truck are practically bald."

"They've been predicting snow all week," Ben scoffed.

I noticed he didn't argue about the tires, which didn't exactly make me excited to go tree shopping in the snow with him.

"It hardly ever snows in Carol," he said. "At least not enough to stick."

"It's supposed to this time," Mom said.

"Okay, okay." Ben stood up. "Come on, girls. Let's go cut us a tree."

"Maybe we should go to the Boy Scouts' tree lot," Keira suggested. "That way we'd be sure to beat the snow. Anyway, I heard some of my customers at the coffee shop talking this morning. People at that end of town have been seeing a cougar."

"Don't be dumb," Ben told her.

"I'd rather be dumb than dead," she retorted.

"Something from the Boy Scouts' tree lot would be fine," put in Mom.

Ben favored us all with one of those looks men give women when they think we're acting like an inferior species. "No self-respecting cougar is going to hang around Grandma's Tree Farm and risk having Ned Tuttle take after it with his rifle. Anyway, they avoid humans, and this time of year there'll be all kinds of humans running around Grandma's. Most of them will probably be a lot scarier than any cougar."

Keira headed down the hall.

"Where are you going?" Ben called after her.

"To get my pepper spray."

"Oh, brother," he said in disgust. "I'll meet you guys at the truck."

Ben went to the garage to scrounge an ax while Keira got her weapon and I got my jacket.

"Here, take a scarf," Mom said, draping a tatty old knitted number over my neck. "Have you got mittens?"

I held up my black leather gloves.

"You'll ruin those if you get pitch on them," Mom cautioned.

"I don't plan on touching the tree," I said. "That's what we've got Ben for."

Keira was back now, bundled up in a baby blue ski jacket, a gray felted hat on her head.

"Be careful," Mom said, like we were soldiers going off to war.

Keira held up her can of pepper spray. "Don't worry. We'll be fine."

"You aren't planning on getting close enough to anything to use that, are you?" I asked.

She shrugged. "No, but I like to be prepared. Anyway, if something jumps at us, get behind me."

"Okay, Davy Crockett," I teased.

Ben was already in the truck and gunning the engine. We piled in, Keira first.

She wrinkled her nose. "This truck stinks."

She had that right. It smelled like a cross between a prison and a barnyard. "What have you been doing in here," I asked, "butchering hogs?"

"Just farting," Ben said amiably.

"I'm buying you an air freshener for Christmas," Keira said.

"Thought you were done with your shopping," he teased.

"For you I'll make an exception and buy one more thing. Roll down your window, Andie."

"I wouldn't roll it down very far," Ben cautioned. "The heater's broke."

"I think I prefer to freeze," I decided, and let down the window.

Keira rolled her eyes. "We should have taken my car. We could have strapped the tree on the top."

"This is easier. We can throw it in the pickup bed."

"I think we should get a blue spruce this year," Keira said. "Or a pine. Something different."

"We always get noble fir," I said, surprising myself that I had an opinion. What did I care what kind of tree we got?

"Noble fir it is, then," Ben said, "in honor of Andie's return." He looked past Keira and shot a smile at me. "Kind of like killing the fatted calf."

"Except I'm not a prodigal son," I reminded him.

"Nope, you're a chick. Same principle."

I didn't think it was the same at all, but I kept my mouth shut.

Grandma's Tree Farm was a mile outside the city limits. We followed Main and were there in under fifteen minutes.

It was getting colder, and the air smelled like snow. We hadn't had a decent snowfall in Carol in years, and, for some weird reason, I found myself wishing we would get one.

A smattering of cars dotted the parking lot. Ned Tuttle, the owner of Grandma's, was posted next to a shed at the entrance, which was marked by a couple of giant crossed candy canes. Beyond that stretched the tree farm itself, a manicured forest of trees raised and carefully groomed for holiday star performances in living rooms all over Carol.

I caught sight of a couple of kids wearing bright parkas darting in and out among the rows, followed by a man who was probably their father, and remembered trips out here when we were kids. Going to Grandma's had always been an adventure, filled with high excitement as we cut the tree and even more excitement when we got home and realized it was too big to fit through the front door.

"Evening," said Ned as we approached. He nodded approvingly at Ben. "I see you remembered your ax."

"We're ready," Ben assured him.

Ned stuffed a wad of tobacco into his cheek. "Got some oversized trees toward the back. If you take one off my hands, I'll give you a deal on it."

"Sounds good," Ben said.

" 'Don't worry, Mom,' " Keira taunted as we trooped toward the back of the tree farm. " 'I'll pay for the tree this year.' "

"Hey, I'm going to pay," Ben said.

"You're going to get something cheap and awful," Keira predicted. Not such a far-off prediction, since Ben was a typical broke musician and on a budget.

"There's nothing wrong with looking at the bigger trees," Ben told her.

"I've got some money," I offered.

"Ben's paying," Keira said. "We settled this before you came."

"That's right," Ben said. "So give it a rest, Keir."

She sighed dramatically and trooped after him, and I fell in step behind her. Something wet landed on my nose. And then another something, a delicate, white something.

"It's starting to snow," I announced. Cutting down a tree in a snow-speckled tree farm—it sounded romantic, and I couldn't help feeling a little excited by the prospect (as long as we got back before the roads got too slick for Ben's bald tires).

"Great," Keira muttered. "If the cougar doesn't get us, we'll freeze to death. "Come on, Ben. Any one of these trees would be great."

"Quit whining," he told her. "We're almost there."

It wasn't hard to tell when we'd reached the bargain tree section. They were all hugely oversized.

"These aren't Christmas trees," Keira said in scorn, "they're mutants."

"I think they're kind of cool," Ben said. "One of these babies would really fill up the living room. What do you think, Andie?"

I thought it would not only fill up the living room, but after that it would go on to take over the world. "I don't know," I said.

Keira shook her head. "It's too big."

"Hey, we can always cut it down to fit," Ben said.

I studied the tree. "You could be cutting till midnight."

He grinned and elbowed me. "Come on. Side with me. Don't let the baby push us around."

"Oh, ha, ha. Like anyone ever listens to me," Keira complained, and Ben and I grinned. She was grinning now too, until she got a sudden look of fear on her face. "What was that?" She pointed into the darkness.

Ben looked over his shoulder. "What was what?"

Keira jiggled her finger. "Over there. I saw something."

"I suppose you saw a cougar."

"It could have been. It had four legs and a long tail, and it was big."

"A dog," Ben said in disgust and went to work with his ax.

Keira didn't say anything, but she moved closer to me and took out her can of pepper spray.

"Put that away," I said. "You're liable to spray us by accident."

"We need some protection."

"No, we don't. We've got Ben and his ax."

"I'm not going to let anything happen to you," Ben said, chopping away at the tree trunk.

"You wouldn't see anything happen to us," Keira argued. "And by the time you got the ax out of the tree it would be too late. We'd be torn to shreds."

"No you wouldn't. You'd be rolling around on the ground with the cougar chewing your arm, just like in the movies."

"But she'd be spraying it with pepper spray," I teased.

"Spraying herself, more likely," Ben muttered.

"I really saw something, you guys," Keira insisted.

"It's okay," Ben said calmingly. "Anyway, we're done." He gave the tree a push and it toppled. "You guys grab the top and the middle. I'll take the base."

I realized I should have taken those mittens Mom offered. I might have known Ben would pick a tree no man (except maybe Paul Bunyan) could carry single-handed. I stripped off my gloves, stepped behind my brother, and shouldered a chunk of tree.

Keira pocketed her weapon and gingerly picked up the tippy-top, and we set off with our find.

We took up all available space as we made our way through the tree farm, forcing other customers to dive for safety. If we were crowded out here in the open air, I hated to think what would it be like back at the house.

"That's some tree," called a man stationed a few feet away by a cute little blue spruce.

"Trade you," Keira called back.

"No, thanks."

"That's the tree I wanted," she grumbled.

"This one's bigger," Ben said, stating the obvious.

"Bigger isn't always better," Keira informed him.

"That's a nice tree you found," approved Ned Tuttle when we got back to his shed. He turned and shot a stream of tobacco into the bushes.

"Eew," Keira said under her breath.

"Yeah, we got a good one," Ben said. "How much do I owe you?"

Ned eyed the tree and named a bargain price.

"Great," Ben said gleefully.

While he was digging in his wallet, Ned asked, "Didn't see any cougar out there, did ya?"

"I think I did," Keira said.

Ned shook his head. "Population's growing. We're gonna have to do something pretty soon."

We knew what that meant. Right now cougars were a protected species in our part of the world. But if they became a danger to the citizens, that could change. Ned sent a loving look to where his rifle leaned against the shed. He would probably be the first to sign up to hunt cougar.

"I think so far we're safe," Ben said. "Come on, girls."

We left Ned Tuttle to watch for predators and headed for the parking lot.

It took all three of us to get the tree in the truck. Ben stood inside the bed and dragged, and Keira and I pushed from the outside. With one final heave, we got it in. Green branches overflowed everywhere. It was like a scene from that old sci-fi movie, *The Blob*. *The Christmas Blob*. The tree had just gotten the truck. Next it would reach out and eat us. Even in the dimly lit parking lot it was plain to see we had gotten more tree than Ben had bargained for.

"Oh, boy," I said.

Keira wiped her brow and leaned against the side of the truck.

Suddenly her eyes got big as an owl's, and she screamed. "Look out!"

Before I knew what was happening, she had me by the arm and was turning me toward the truck cab. "What?" I demanded.

"Cougar!" she cried and yanked open the door.

## Chapter Nine

"Oh, for Pete's sake," I began, but that was all I got out before she shoved me into the truck. I lost my balance and landed on my nose on the seat.

Keira didn't even wait for me to straighten or slide over. She piled in on top of me and shut the cab door, screaming, "Get in, Ben!"

"Get off me!" I demanded.

She got up enough for me to pull my torso free.

I sat up, holding my nose. It felt like a punching bag with Muhammad Ali, George Foreman, and Evander Holyfield all pounding on it at once. "You broke my nose."

"Better a broken nose than getting your body torn from limb to limb."

I looked past her, out the truck window. "I don't see anything." My sister had just broken my nose for the sake of an imaginary cougar.

"It's out there," she said and began scrabbling in her pocket.

I grabbed her arm. "Touch that pepper spray and you die. We're safe in the truck now."

"But Ben's not."

"And he's not even worried. That should tell you something. You broke my nose for nothing more than a runaway imagination."

She looked at my face. "It's not even bleeding." Then she turned back to scanning the horizon for predators.

Her lack of sympathy inspired me with an uncivilized urge to mash her face into the cab window and see if her nose would bleed. "Thanks for the sympathy," I grumbled.

"I saved your life."

Ben climbed into the cab. "What was all that about?"

"I saw a cougar," Keira told him. "Didn't you hear me screaming for you to get in the truck?"

"Yeah, but since there wasn't anything around but a mongrel dog, I wasn't too worried."

"Dog?" she repeated weakly, and I glared at her.

Ben shook his head and started the engine. "I'm out with Dumb and Dumber."

"Not funny," I said, insulted.

Keira was still peering out the window. "Are you sure?"

"Yes, Keir, I'm sure. I saw it too."

"Well, you might have said something before she trampled me," I complained.

He shrugged. "She wouldn't have listened."

"Just like you didn't listen about the tree," Keira said. "We're going to have to saw half the thing off just to get it in the house."

"It'll look great once it's up," Ben said.

*That's my story and I'm stickin' to it,* I thought.

We went down the road like a street sweeper, the dangling branches brushing the dusting of snow from the pavement. Passing cars hugged the curb or swerved and honked.

Keira looked out the back window. "We look like a float."

We looked like something, that was for sure.

Ben went down the middle of our street in an effort not to hit any of the neighbors' cars parked along the curb.

At one point we heard a yelp and saw a fuzzy four-legged ball doing a backward somersault.

"Oh, no! Stop the car!" Keira commanded. "Your tree just drop-kicked the Baileys' dog."

"Is it okay?" Ben asked. He didn't stop, but he checked his side mirror.

I looked over my shoulder. Mrs. Bailey had come out and was cradling her cockapoo. The dog was wriggling and licking her face, probably thankful to be alive. *I'll never complain about my humans again.*

"Looks like you dodged that bullet," I said.

Keira pointed to the left and cried, "Look out!"

"What!" Ben swerved and the truck skidded, making the monster tree in back do the hula.

We skated sideways on Ben's bald tires and heard scraping as the tree ran woody fingers along the side of a car parked in front of the Harrises' house. This was followed by a distinctive *thwunk* that proclaimed something got broken.

"Oh, no," Keira moaned. "Your tree just attacked that car. Looks like it took off the side mirror."

"Great," Ben said. He scowled at Keira. "What were you yelling about, anyway?"

"A cat. You were going to hit it."

"Better a cat than the Harrises' car," Ben said.

"That's a terrible thing to say," Keira scolded. "Anyway, that's not their car. They keep both theirs in the garage."

Ben sighed. He stopped the truck, leaving it in the middle of the road, and got out.

Right on cue, the Harrises' front door opened to reveal Mr. and Mrs. Harris and three other people—a couple and a man. Mr. Harris and the two men were just shaking hands when Mr. Harris saw Ben walking toward him. His easy smile melted into a frown.

"Roll down the window some more," Keira commanded. "I want to hear."

I complied, deciding if anything bad were going to happen, Keira and I should be prepared.

"Good grief," Mr. Harris was saying in disgust. "Why'd you bring home such a monstrosity, anyway? What were you thinking?"

One of the men in the visiting trio said, "That's okay. The streets are slick. It could have happened to anyone."

"Not necessarily," said Mr. Harris. Implied message: only a Hartwell could manage to sideswipe a car with a Christmas tree.

I felt my face start sizzling. I wanted to call out, "I'm just a passenger, a visitor." No, make that "I don't know these people. They kidnapped me."

"I'm really sorry," Ben said to the owner of the damaged car. "I'll be happy to pay for a new side mirror. And a new paint job," he added.

"Don't want to report it to your insurance?" goaded Mr. Harris.

"Well, it's a small enough thing," said the other man amiably. "What's your phone number, son?"

While Ben and the other man exchanged phone numbers, I heard the third man ask Mr. Harris, "Are these people neighbors?" He was looking at us like we'd stepped out of the pages of *The Grapes of Wrath.*

"They live down the street," Mr. Harris said evasively and made a wave with his hand that implied we were clear at the end of the block.

Two whole houses down, I thought.

"The neighbors on both sides of us are great," Mr. Harris continued.

The man looked at us thoughtfully. Keira tilted her head and looked cross-eyed at him, and I slumped down in the seat.

"What are you doing?" I hissed.

"Just giving them something to look at," she said loudly enough for the entire neighborhood to hear.

Ben skidded back to the truck and got in, and I put the window back up.

"It looks like Mr. Harris had a fish on the line to buy his house," I said. "I think we scared him away."

Keira chuckled. "Merry Christmas, Mr. Harris."

Poor Mr. Harris. I really couldn't blame him for wanting to get away.


We took out the mailbox turning into the driveway.

Mom came to stand in the doorway and looked to where the truck was hiding under our evergreen. "That looks awfully big," she called.

"That's what I told him," Keira said as she came up the walk, "but he wouldn't listen."

"It'll be fine," Ben muttered and set to work turning the tree loose.

As Keira had predicted, it was too big. We couldn't even get it into the house, so Ben was banished to outer darkness to chop off limbs while we stayed warm inside and helped Mom untangle strings of lights to the accompaniment of Christmas music on the radio.

"We Need a Little Christmas" had just begun to play when the door opened and two sets of legs began marching in under the flopping boughs of the tree. Maybe James the bass player had stopped by, I thought hopefully.

"We're putting it in the usual spot by the window," Ben said.

James didn't know the usual spot for the Hartwell Christmas tree. Come to think of it, that body looked awfully familiar. I looked again and got the now familiar zing.

The tree started to rise to its majestic height, scraping the paint off the ceiling in the process. "Looks like we'll have to trim the top some more," said Gabe.

Keira shot me a mischievous glance. Had she known he was coming over?

"Gabe, what a nice surprise!" Mom chimed.

Behind her a new song began, a choir singing "The Twelve Days of Christmas."

"On the first day of Christmas, my true love gave to me . . ."

*A pest to match my oversized tree,* I thought.

"By the way, the snow is really sticking now," Gabe announced as he and Ben dragged the tree out, scraping off more ceiling paint in the process.

"Maybe you should go home before the streets get undrivable," I suggested.

"I have four-wheel drive and all-weather tires," he called back.

Mom stood looking at the ceiling. "Looks like I'll be ringing in the new year repainting," she said.

"Did you know Gabe was coming over?" I asked her.

Mom shook her head. "No."

My sister had taken advantage of Mom's little speech and retreated to the kitchen, where she was now hiding behind the fridge door. "Anyone want some cranberry juice?" she called.

"Keira, did you know Gabe was coming over?"

She didn't answer me.

I marched into the kitchen. "Did you, by any chance, tell him we were putting up our tree tonight?"

She was now much too busy filling her glass to look at

me. "I was talking to him about houses earlier. I might have mentioned it."

"You *might* have mentioned it."

"Well, okay, so I did. So what?"

"So stop it already. I didn't come home to see Gabe."

Keira put the juice container back in the fridge and shoved the door shut. "You know, we've all stayed friends, so there's no reason why he shouldn't come by to visit if he wants to." She grabbed her glass and sauntered back into the living room.

That was beside the point. "I know what you're doing," I said. "You're trying to match us up, probably as a sop to your conscience. And I don't need to be matched. I can get my own man."

"Yeah? Who've you gotten so far?" Keira taunted.

"That's enough, you two," Mom said just as the door opened again.

"Okay," Ben said, "this time it should fit."

The Christmas tree might fit, but Gabe sure wouldn't. In fact, he was going to be a complete damper on the evening. He had a home of his own. He should be in it. Who asked him to keep popping up here like one of Scrooge's ghosts?

The guys had the tree secured in the tree stand now. It took up a quarter of the living room.

Ben stepped back and admired his handiwork. "Looks great," he approved.

It'll take two weeks to decorate, I thought.

"It looks a little tippy," Mom said.

"Oh, it's in there good and solid," Ben assured her. "So, where's the lights?"

"You guys'll have to put them up," Keira said. "There's no way we'll be able to reach around your monster tree to do it."

Ben scowled.

"No problem," Gabe said cheerily. He smiled at me.

I turned my back and headed for the kitchen. "Anyone want some eggnog?"

"Sure," Gabe said. "Thanks, Andie," he added, like I'd really meant that offer for him.

"I'll take some too," Ben said, shrugging out of his coat.

I fetched eggnog, and Mom put out cookies and yogurt-coated pretzels, and somewhere along the way I forgot I was ticked with Keira and Gabe and got into the ritual of hanging ornaments.

"Oh, I remember these," I said, pulling out the box with the hand-blown Italian balls. There were only three left now in a box that had once held six.

Mom took the box from me and looked at it wistfully. "Your father and I got those the first year we were married."

I wished I hadn't said anything.

"Look," Keira cried, pulling out a white bird of paradise with a long, sweeping tail. "The bird Gabe gave you." That made me think of the fun times we'd had that Christmas we were together, and I found myself smiling in spite of feeling badly about Mom and Dad.

My smile fell away as I pulled out a bell made of spun acrylic. I held it on my palm. "I think this is something he gave you." I looked at him, daring him to deny it.

His cheeks suddenly looked like he'd swallowed a red tree light. He looked at me helplessly and shrugged.

The phone rang and Mom snagged it. "Well, April. We haven't heard from you in ages. How are you?"

I cocked an eyebrow at Gabe and his cheeks got redder.

"Should I ask her why you broke up too?" I said to him under my breath.

"I could tell you. If you'd listen."

"Telephone, Andie," Mom called.

Saved by the bell. "I'm sure it's a fascinating story, but

some other time," I said. I didn't want to talk to April any more than I wanted to talk to Gabe. Surely it was enough for me to come home and deal with my nutsy family without having to add old boyfriends and false girlfriends to the list.

I took the receiver from Mom and injected politeness into my vocal cords before saying hello.

"So, did you get a chance to check your schedule?" she asked.

"I haven't even had a chance to check my makeup," I said. No lie. My family had me on the fast track. "We just got back with the tree, and now we're putting it up. Gabe's over," I added, just to see what she'd say.

"Oh, wow. Are you guys getting back together?"

She sounded so genuinely interested and caring. What a fake!

"No," I said firmly.

"You need to know something," April said, "even if you can't fit in getting together this week. Gabe was still hooked on you when he was dating me."

"Right," I scoffed.

"No, it's true. I could tell it wasn't working between us, and I finally pinned him down. I thought you two were long over. I mean, it had been years." April made a sound of disgust. "When he admitted he still had it bad for you I told him to take a hike. Anyway, it was all for the best. I'm with a really hot guy now. He's an accountant too."

A hot accountant. I guess numbers could be exciting.

"So, maybe we could all go out together," she suggested.

"I'll be coming back to visit again," I said. *In a millennium or two.* "How about next time?"

There was a silence on the phone. I could almost hear the wheels in April's mind turning while she tried to decide if I was ditching her or planning for the future.

"Okay," she said at last. "Let's not lose touch like we did before."

Lose touch. There was an interesting expression. It always made it sound accidental when people decided a relationship wasn't worth the trouble.

"Not a good thing," I agreed vaguely.

It seemed to satisfy her. "I guess I'd better let you get back to the tree trimming," she said.

I looked to where the others were happily hanging ornaments. A real, live, Norman Rockwell moment. I should take advantage of it while it lasted. I said good-bye to April and returned to the tree.

"So, are you girls going to get together?" Mom asked.

"Probably not this trip," I said. "There's already a lot on the calendar."

Mom's smile soured a little. "Yes, and less time to do it all now that you're leaving early."

"I thought you were staying through New Year's." Ben sounded shocked.

"Oh, yeah. The meeting," Gabe said.

"Business emergency," I reminded him.

"I still don't see why you have to go back early," Keira said in disgust. "It's not like you're a doctor. Who's going to die if you stay with us a little longer?"

"My career," I said as I pulled a golden ball out of the ornament box.

"Your career sounds like a pain in the butt," said Ben. "Whoa, look at that snow coming down now." He nodded to the whitening scenery outside the window. "It's got to be at least three inches."

He was right. The grass had gotten buried under a fat carpet of white, and the tree boughs and bushes wore lacy coats.

Mom stopped her decorating to gaze out the window. "It's gorgeous."

"You know what this means," Keira said to Ben.

He exchanged grins with Gabe. "I suppose you want to do something dumb like boys against girls."

"We can take you easy," she taunted.

That was it. War had been declared. Within the hour I knew we'd all be outside hurling snowballs at each other.

Unless Mom prevailed. "Bennett Hartwell, you've already gotten hurt once this season."

"I think I can manage to throw a snowball without killing myself," he retorted.

"You'll break open your stitches."

"Mom, I only had three."

"Three is enough."

He just smiled and shook his head, brushing off her concern like snowflakes from a jacket. "I'll be fine."

She frowned in disapproval, but Ben cheerfully ignored her.

The tree still seemed unbalanced to me, and it wobbled a little when Keira leaned into it to hang a little plastic snowman.

"Are you sure this thing is steady?" I asked Ben.

"Sure it is," he assured me.

"We could wire it to the wall," Mom suggested. "We still have that little nail in the corner from three years ago."

"Nah," said Ben. "It'll be fine. Trust me. I know what I'm doing."

"Your father used to say that." Mom bit her lower lip and studied the tree.

I was with Mom and said so. A tree this big, if it fell into the window . . .

"Guys, give it a rest. This thing is perfectly balanced," Ben said. He reached through the bows, grabbed the trunk in a one handed stranglehold, and gave the tree a shake. It jiggled back and forth, making the ornaments swing and tinkle. I could almost hear it choke.

Mom held out a hand, ready to catch it. "Okay. I believe you. Stop already."

I noticed Ben was very careful taking his hand away. If this tipped and broke any of my childhood ornaments, I was going to get a stranglehold on him.

Another few minutes, and we were done. "There," said Keira as she hung a final red ball. "That's the last of them."

Mom was already stuffing tissue back in the big cardboard boxes. "I guess you guys better go pulverize each other with snowballs then."

It was all the permission we needed. We forgot to be responsible adults and help clean up the post-trimming mess. Instead, we scattered to find coats and mittens.

"Take some mittens out of the winter clothes box in the craft room, Andie," Mom called after me. Then I could hear her asking, "Gabe, do you need some gloves?"

"I'll be fine," he assured her.

*You've been fine since the seventh grade.* Where had that thought come from? I had no idea, but I hoped it didn't have any siblings ready to pop out unexpectedly at me.

I followed the others outside. A quiet, winter stillness hung over the night. Somewhere down the street, a child whooped in excitement. The snow was coming down fast and furious now, and the lawn stretched out in white perfection, like a mountain meadow in winter.

I hated to step on it. A front yard thick with snow and unpolluted with footprints is one of life's small, often unappreciated beauties.

Any more philosophical reflection was aborted by a handful of snow down my back, followed by an uproar of laughter from my brother. "That'll teach you to bail out on us early."

Forgetting the snowy meadow thing, I took off after him.

We tore up the yard, screeching and hurling snowballs at each other, intermittently switching from the winter version of dodgeball to football, where the guys would come after us and take us down in a tackle.

Gabe was an expert tackler, and, covered in snow, looking up into his smiling eyes, I remembered the last winter it snowed like this. A similar snowball fight had found us both side by side on the ground, sharing a kiss that should have melted every flake within a ten-mile radius.

He remembered it too. I could tell by the way his expression changed from teasing to serious. "Andie."

"Get off me," I growled. "I'm freezing." What a big fat lie, I thought as I scrambled to my feet. I was burning up.

"Hey, you women need help?" called Kenny Mason, a neighbor from down the street.

Kenny had grown since I last saw him. He was tall and wore a parka that made his chest look like Arnold Schwarzenegger's. Under it protruded long, skinny legs wrapped in jeans that were sopped at the cuff. His feet were probably already wet in those tennis shoes, but he didn't seem to care. He had a friend with him who was almost as skinny, and they were armed with snowballs.

"Take 'em out," I said, nodding at Gabe.

Then the war began in earnest. Next thing I knew, Mom was out there too.

"Hey, Mrs. H!" Gabe called approvingly.

"You boys need help," she informed him.

We tore all over the neighborhood, jumping over neighbor's juniper bushes, scraping snow off car hoods and roofs, sneaking around house corners.

Just when Gabe looked like his fingers were getting frostbitten, Mom declared a truce and insisted everyone come in and begin the peace process over hot cocoa.

"Good idea," said Gabe, who was now standing next to me. "My hands are getting cold." He plunged them inside my collar, making me screech.

Everyone laughed, and as we trooped inside I felt like I'd gotten into a time machine and traveled back to my senior year in high school. *You can't go back,* I told myself firmly.

"Just dump your coats in the entryway," Mom instructed as she headed for the kitchen. "Kenny, why don't you call your mom and tell her we've kidnapped you for a game of Spoons."

Spoons was a family favorite involving a mad sorting through cards for the right combination that would entitle the holder to start a group dive for a spoon from a pile of several. With one less spoon at the table than there were players, this game always got wild. People lost fingernails, got gouged, and sprained wrists, all in an effort to come out with a trophy utensil. But that never stopped anyone from coming back for more. We'd introduced Kenny to the game when he was twelve.

He was already grinning in anticipation. "Your family is so cool," he said to me.

My family as cool. Now, there was an unusual concept, and one I knew was completely erroneous. Okay, so we could have fun. What did that mean, really?

I thought of my torturous afternoon with Dad and The Girlfriend. Oh, yeah. That had been cool. Kenny should walk a day in my snowshoes. He'd change his mind in a hurry.

## Chapter Ten

Kenny's mom finally called, insisting her son and his sidekick had been in our hair long enough and that they be sent back out into the cold. Gabe too decided he'd better slide on home.

As I stood by the front door watching our drop-in guests shrug on their coats, I caught a glimpse of myself in the mirror that hung on the entryway wall. I was smiling.

And I wasn't faking it. I'd had fun. I still couldn't go as far as Kenny and say my family was cool, but they knew how to have a good time. I guess somewhere on the road to adulthood I had lost sight of that. Even looking at Gabe, who was grinning at me, I felt a dab of sentiment do a sticky drip over my heart. We'd had some good times. Maybe a dark, snowy night was a good time to bury the hatchet.

Of course, that didn't mean love would spring up where you buried it. I'd have to make sure Gabe understood that.

It went without saying there would be no burial service for that proverbial hatchet until I found out why he and Keira had broken up. Obviously, my sister wasn't going to volunteer the information, and I wasn't going to let her think it was

123

all that important to me to know. (Because it wasn't, really.) But I'd find a way to get the dirt before I left for New York.

"So, are we going house hunting tomorrow?" Gabe asked Keira while looking at me.

"I really want that one in Fairhaven," she said. Now she too looked at me. "But it wouldn't hurt to have a Plan B."

"You two go ahead," I said. "I'll be out with Mom and Aunt Chloe tomorrow."

"We won't be gone all day. You could go after we get back," Mom suggested. Good old Mom, Santa's helper.

But I was going to spend the afternoon getting ready for my big date. "That's okay," I said to Keira and Gabe. "You two go."

Gabe didn't look quite so interested in making a sale now, and Keira shrugged.

"We can do it the day after," she said.

"That's getting pretty close to Christmas," I said. "Maybe Gabe has plans."

"No plans," he said cheerfully.

I didn't have any either. At least not yet. I was hoping that would change after my date with James. "I'll let you know," I told them.

I said it nicely, but Gabe looked like I'd turned him down for a date. There were still plenty of women left in Carol. I was sure he could find a way to console himself somehow.

All the men finally trooped out into the night, leaving just us girls.

"Well," Mom said. "That was fun. In fact, that was the most fun I've had in a long time."

How sad, I thought, then realized it was the most fun I'd had in a long time too.

That was ridiculous. I was tired. My mind wasn't functioning well.

"I need to go to bed," I decided. A good night's sleep would bring a more balanced perspective.

"Oh, come on. Not yet. Let's watch a chick flick," Keira begged.

"Great idea," Mom said. "*Charade* with Audrey Hepburn."

"No, *Thirteen Going on Thirty.*"

The story of my sister's life as a grownup.

"How about one of those old Jane Austen movies?" I suggested.

"Okay. *Emma*," said Keira. "I'll start the popcorn."

So we sat in the family room curled up in blankets and watched Gwyneth Paltrow look beautiful and talk elegantly.

"Isn't it weird how the perfect man can be right under your nose and you don't even see it?" Keira said as the ending credits started to roll.

"I'm going to bed now," I announced, and left before my sister could hit me over the head with any more subtle remarks.

As I slipped under the covers I tried to decide which would be worse: being snowed in with my sister the matchmaker or having to do lunch with Gram the Inquisitor. I decided I preferred being snowed in with Keira. I could tell her to shut up.

I got into bed hoping that the snow would stick. But only until the afternoon. I didn't want to miss my date with James, which was looking like it would be the highlight of my visit.

*I see you have time in your schedule for making new friends. Maybe you could fit in dinner with an old one.* Gabe's words from the night of the concert had sneaked up on me out of nowhere.

I burrowed deeper under the covers. Why was he trying so hard? Why was he being so nice? *Who cared?* I told myself. It was a mystery I had no desire to solve.

By 10 the next morning, the tree boughs were dripping and the snow on the lawn was turning to a slushy mess. The street was almost clear. I was doomed to a day of torture. At least I had my date to look forward to.

Mom and I drove to Grandma's house on slushy streets, past white lawns with torn patches revealing lawn beneath. In some yards, lopsided snowmen stood sentinel over their melting kingdom, a reminder of winter fun enjoyed the evening before. I wished the snow had stayed longer, wished we could have gotten out and made a snowman and snow angels like we'd done when we were kids. Sometimes going back and being a kid again sounded really good. No bills to pay, no ignored e-mails (I'd sent off six that morning), no job to stress over, no one asking about your love life.

My mind jumped ahead to the ordeal before me. I knew my grandmother would give me the third degree on who I was dating. And if Mom had already told her I was leaving early, I was bound to get the inquisition on that too.

Maybe I could get Grandma talking about the decay of American society. That was one of her all-time favorite topics, and if I could steer her there I could avoid getting put under the grandmotherly microscope. I practiced my opening gambits. *Say, Grandma, what do you think of the fashions in the store this season?* I looked down at my jeans. Were they too tight? Would Gram have something to say about them? Maybe that wasn't the topic I wanted to use to distract her.

"Oh, I almost forgot, we need to stop at the store," Mom said. "Your grandmother wanted me to pick up some whipping cream for dessert."

Prune Whip, of course. Gram was a firm believer that whatever was good for her was good for the rest of the world.

"Let me pay for the whipping cream," I offered as Mom and I walked into the grocery store.

"Oh, you don't need to do that."

"I know, but I want to. Is there anything else you need while we're here?"

"We could use some bread," Mom said.

Bread. Why couldn't she have said milk or eggs? Prunes, even. I followed her to the bread aisle with leaden legs.

There it sat: Nutri Bread, my future, the one I was neglecting for tuna casserole and Prune Whip, and old boyfriends who stirred up all kinds of unwelcome memories. What was happening back at Image Makers? I should be there.

Mom grabbed a loaf. "You know, I've never tried this Nutri Bread."

Just what I needed sitting on Mom's kitchen counter, a visual reminder of my career swirling in the toilet. I grabbed a loaf of Wonder Bread. "Let's get this."

Mom looked at me, puzzled. "I didn't think you liked white bread."

"Ben does. Let's get it." I took the Nutri Bread from her unresisting hand and put it back on the shelf. "We'd better hurry or we'll be late."

I got her out of the store in record time, but I didn't succeed in getting away from wondering what was coming unglued back at the office while I was home, bonding with my family.

Nothing, I assured myself. I was getting back in time for the big meeting. Everything was cool. And sometimes e-mails got lost.

"I remember when this was all small farms and pastures," Mom said as we drove to the little brick rambler where my grandma lived.

The farmland had pretty much disappeared, but the city planners had held the business park invasion at bay, making sure all new businesses in the area either set up shop in the old farmhouses or erected buildings that matched the surrounding architecture. Ancient elms and maples and chestnut trees still occupied prime real estate, and you could even find an occasional residence and small cabbage patch dotted here and there among the lawyers' offices and the insurance companies. Gram's house was between the Vine Building, which housed a dentist and an orthodontist (handy, huh?), and Bernie's Berries, the one surviving berry farm. Bernie also had a tiny café that featured the best strawberry shortcake in three counties. Gram is good buds with Mrs. Bernie, so summers would find us visiting Gram in the afternoon a lot. In between lunch and dinner, we could be guaranteed a sample of strawberry shortcake left over from lunch.

Maybe I should have played Let's Make a Deal with Mom and offered to come home for a week in the summer, I thought as we walked in and the smell of tuna casserole greeted us. At least in summer I would have had shortcake. No holiday stress either. Just lazy days out at Lake Carol.

"Andrea, dear," my grandma greeted me. Gram was the only one who called me by my given name. She thought it was awful how everyone called me by a boy's name. I hated the name Andrea, but somehow I'd never quite worked up the nerve to tell my grandmother that. Maybe because, deep down, I knew it wouldn't do any good. She would still insist on doing exactly what she wanted.

"Hi, Gram," I said and gave her a kiss. "Have you lost weight?"

My grandmother is normally a little on the plump side, but she wasn't looking all that plump this day. She looked like the human equivalent of a feather pillow that had lost half its stuffing.

Gram shrugged. "Maybe. I haven't had much appetite. I haven't been feeling all that well lately."

Mom looked at me as if to say, "See? I told you."

"Nothing serious, I hope," I said.

"Heavens, no! I've got plenty of good years left in me," Gram assured me.

I cocked an eyebrow at Mom, who said, "I'll go whip this cream." Then she turned and retreated to the kitchen.

"Well, you still look great," I told Gram.

No lie. She was wearing gray wool slacks, a white turtleneck, and a red Christmas sweater appliquéd with snowmen and Christmas trees. Unlike Mom, who was Lady Clairol's best friend, Grandma didn't believe in lying about things people could figure out anyway. Her hair was Mrs. Santa Claus white, and she got it styled every week. I wasn't sure where she got it done, but now I wondered if it was at Chez Rory's. Probably not, I decided. Brittany was still alive.

"Thank you, dear. And, I must say, you look lovely. New York seems to agree with you."

That it did.

Gram linked her arm through mine and walked me into the living room. It was small, cozy with antiques and cluttered with knick-knacks. On the coffee table, she'd set up a tiny potted pine tree, decorated with odds and ends of Christmas ornaments, some of which I recognized from when I was a kid. The morning newspaper lay on the end-table next to the couch, open to the crossword puzzle. It looked like she had already finished the puzzle.

"We're just waiting for your Aunt Chloe, then we can eat," she said. "I hope she isn't too late. Otherwise the casserole will be ruined."

What a shame, I thought, listening to the whirr of beaters as Mom whipped cream.

"I hope you brought your appetite," said Gram.

I glanced to where her little dining table sat and saw it set with her best china and crystal (an interesting contrast with Aunt Chloe's thawing hamburger still-life hanging on the wall). The water glasses were already filled, and the teapot, muffled in a knitted blue tea cozy, sat next to Grandma's place at the head of the table. I eyed the bowl of what looked like her homemade oatmeal muffins, one of the few recipes Gram had that we all liked. If they were, it would make up for the tuna casserole. Sort of.

"I'm sure I'll have room for your oatmeal muffins," I said, latching onto the one thing I could say truthfully.

Mom joined us just as we heard the sound of wheels slushing up the street. I looked out the window to see Aunt Chloe's old LeBaron pulling up to the curb.

"Good," said Grandma. "We're all here. Now we can eat. Janelle, you can go pull out the casserole."

A moment later Aunt Chloe was in the room, stamping her feet. She was enveloped in a green knitted poncho today and had on a red knitted cap. She was wearing her black stretch pants and some gray moon boots leftover from the eighties. She looked like a model for a thrift store fashion show.

"That's some outfit," Mom observed from the table, where she was setting out the main dish.

"I just finished the hat," said Aunt Chloe. "I'm finding knitting very satisfying."

That didn't bode well for the rest of us. It meant next Christmas we would all get hats to match Aunt Chloe's. Maybe even ponchos.

Grandma was already to the table. "Come on, girls. We don't want this to get cold."

We don't want this at all, I thought, but I politely followed my mom and aunt to the table.

In addition to the casserole, Grandma had prepared a molded Jell-O salad with celery and cranberries. It was shaped like a Christmas tree. I took even less of that than I did the casserole.

Aunt Chloe was talking, so I temporarily relaxed. Maybe I wouldn't have to distract Gram with a discussion about the state of the world after all.

Aunt Chloe took a breath and Grandma rushed into the breach to ask me, "Aren't you hungry, dear?"

"Not really," I said. *At least not for this.* I took a muffin, something I knew I would actually like to eat. Aunt Chloe was talking again. I let down my guard, slathered the muffin with butter, and prepared to enjoy.

Sadly, Aunt Chloe now had her plate piled high and was abandoning talking for chewing. Grandma pounced. "So, I'm dying to hear how things are going in New York. Tell me who you're dating, Andrea."

The last of my appetite slipped away, and I set down the muffin. "I've been pretty busy working." I wondered if I could just insert a distracting sentence here. *And speaking of work, you should see what my friends wear to the office.* No, that sounded too forced.

Grandma looked disapproving. "You're not getting any younger, dear. The clock is ticking."

If it was, I hadn't heard it.

Mom rushed to my defense. "Girls don't get married as young as they used to."

Grandma nodded sagely. "And that's why they have problems getting pregnant. They wait too long. Their eggs get old. Then they have to use fertility pills and wind up with sextuplets."

In under a minute I'd gone from having a ticking clock to sextuplets. That had to be some sort of record.

"I think my eggs are probably fine," I said. How about slipping in my distraction here? *And speaking of eggs, you should see . . .* Hmmm.

"There you have it," said Aunt Chloe. "She's got great eggs." I was just about to feel grateful to her when she added, "Still you ought to find somebody, Andie. Restaurants in New York aren't cheap. It's the pits to always have to pick up the tab yourself."

That sounded even more pitiful than having old eggs.

"Don't be ridiculous, Chloe," Grandma said. "She ought to find someone. Period. You don't want to go through life alone, Andrea."

"Oh, Mother, please," snapped Mom. "If a woman gets married too young it won't last. Mike and I are proof of that."

Mom's rebuke ended the discussion of my love life. Rather awkwardly, but at least it ended.

"Well," said Grandma in a huff. "Some men just don't know when they've got a good thing. Andie, I have plenty of casserole. Eat up."

"Yes, put some meat on your bones," said Aunt Chloe. "I'll have some more, Mom."

I finished my casserole first. I sat back in my seat and tried to relax, but I couldn't get the vision of that loaf of Nutri Bread out of my mind. I shouldn't have taken time to come home right now. I should be back in New York, making myself indispensable.

"What are you playing, 'Little Drummer Boy'?" Mom asked.

"What?"

She nodded at my drumming fingers.

I pulled my hand off the table. "Bad habit."

"New habit," Mom observed. "Is your life in New York making you stressed?"

"No, no." My life with my family was making me stressed.

"Well, we'll have you relaxed and enjoying yourself in no time," Gram said. "Let's have dessert."

Gram agreed with Aunt Chloe that I needed more to eat, so she gave me an extra large serving of Prune Whip.

I steeled myself, then dug my spoon into the bowl.

I had just forced it into my mouth when Gram asked, "So, have you dated anyone at all since you got to New York?"

Boy, I thought, it doesn't get any better than this.

But I was wrong. After the Prune Whip inquisition, it was time to hit the mall for fun with Mom and Aunt Chloe. And the first stop was to be Gifts 'N' Gags, where we would admire the sight of Mom's Christmas mugs sitting on a shelf.

Santa's workshop was busy with a line of kids dressed up and squirming next to their moms as they waited to climb on his lap and pull his beard. I wished I could climb on his lap myself and ask him to clone me. Then my clone could go to Gifts 'N' Gags with Mom and Aunt Chloe and I could buy some spa goodies. I thought of the bath packet sitting in my suitcase. A soak in a tub of hot, gardenia-scented water was exactly what I needed right now.

Maybe I could stall. "Anyone for hitting that new Starbucks over by Penney's?" I suggested. The caffeine would fortify me. It would also get the taste of prunes out of my mouth.

"Let's do that after we stop at the shop," said Mom, and picked up her pace like a general leading a charge.

Aunt Chloe looked longingly in the direction of the Starbucks, but followed like a good soldier.

I didn't want to follow like a good soldier. I made a strike for independence. "I'll meet you there, then," I said. "I need coffee."

Mom surrendered. "Oh, all right," she said, her voice slightly pouty. "We'll do a caffeine fill-up first."

"Good idea," said Aunt Chloe, and I hid my gloating smile.

It seemed every store we walked past was playing a different Christmas song. Brass ensembles proclaiming "Joy to the World" blared against jazz versions of "The Christmas Song" and Elvis singing "Blue Christmas." The cacophony echoed the feelings bouncing around inside of me. Here I was in a small town, feeling more emotionally jostled than I had ever felt in one of the fastest and busiest cities in the world. "New York, New York," began to play in my head, making me want to scream, "Stop!" The Starbucks loomed like an oasis, and I picked up my pace.

"What's the hurry?" Aunt Chloe puffed behind me, and I slowed down.

She was right. A simple shot of coffee wasn't going to change my life. But it would make it more bearable.

Armed with a grande eggnog latte, I felt more able to face the gift shop expedition.

Clarice, the shop owner, was at the cash register ringing up a sale when we wandered into the store.

She bagged the purchase and sent the customer on her way, then greeted us. "Well, look who's here. Merry Christmas, darlings."

"Same to you," Mom said.

"I see your girl made it home. And she's just as pretty as you said." She smiled at me and introduced herself. "So you're the one who came up with the idea for the Valentine mug," she said after we'd finished the meet and greet.

I nodded.

"Brilliant."

"Thanks," I said and tried to look humble.

She turned to Mom. "And speaking of mugs, yours is still selling well."

"What did the woman who was just in here buy?" Aunt Chloe asked.

"Three of those lumps of coal for bad boys and girls."

"Lumps of coal?" I repeated.

Clarice left the register and went to an aisle. She picked up a little red tin with Santa on it, then held it up like Vanna White, displaying a prize on *Wheel of Fortune*. "It's got a lump of coal inside. Great gag gift or stocking stuffer. These things sell well every year. They're a gift classic."

"Like our mug is going to become," Aunt Chloe predicted.

"I wouldn't be surprised," said Clarice.

Two women wandered into the store. They looked about Mom's and Aunt Chloe's age and were dressed in Eddie Bauer casual. I could tell by their hair and nails that they didn't lack spending money. Next to me I could almost hear the little cash register in Aunt Chloe's head ringing. *Ka-ching.*

She broke away from us and casually wandered up an aisle. I sensed embarrassment waiting in the wings and moved in the opposite direction.

Now the two women were moving down her aisle. All three of them were out of sight, but I didn't need to see to know what was going on.

Sure enough, "Oh, Janelle, come look at this cute mug," called Aunt Chloe's disembodied voice.

"Oh, yeah?" Mom gave a great impression of a casual shopper.

Meanwhile, Aunt Chloe continued her shtick. "What a great present this would make. Say, do either of you gals know anyone who's going through a divorce? I bet this would give her a chuckle."

How embarrassing was this? Did my aunt lie awake nights thinking of new weird things to do? Maybe I'd just stroll to the CD shop next door and see what was new.

Before I could escape, Mom came up to me. "The mugs look really great the way Clarice has them displayed."

Here was where I was supposed to say, "Let's go have a look." But I really didn't want to watch Aunt Chloe doing her routine of a Rolex knock-off salesman.

"Oh, that is clever," said one of her victims. "I think I'll get one for my sister. She could use a laugh."

Mom gave me a look that said, "There you have it. We're a success."

She started toward the shelf where her Man Haters gingerbread mugs sat. I looked over my shoulder to make sure no new customers had entered the shop, then followed her. Hopefully, this holiday show-and-tell session would be fast.

We passed Aunt Chloe's suckers coming down the aisle. They were each holding a mug. Behind them, Aunt Chloe was grinning.

"I sold two," she whispered when we got to her. She pointed to the shelf. "Look, only two left."

Mom's smile was positively smug.

The store filled with more voices, and Aunt Chloe looked over my shoulder. Her eyes lit up, and she shoved a mug in my hand. "Say, look at this mug."

I stared at her in horror, and she nodded her head in a direction somewhere in back of me and off to the left. She reminded me of a horse trying to get its rider to loosen up on the reins.

"Cute, isn't it?" she said, prompting me.

I was sure her other victims could hear her. Would they notice she was like some figure in a ride at Disneyland, doing the same thing over and over?

"I don't know anyone who's getting divorced," I said, and tried to set it back on the shelf.

Aunt Chloe put up a hand and blocked my move. "Yes,

but you might know someone who's broken up with their boyfriend."

"It *is* clever," Mom said, picking up one, herself. "And reasonably priced."

"Oh, that is cute," said a woman behind me.

I found myself turning and handing her mine. "It would make a fun gift filled with candy. And it's affordable."

Oh, no. What was I saying? What was happening to me?

## Chapter Eleven

Whatever was happening to me, my mother and aunt approved. They both beamed on me like benevolent fairies. *Look. Princess Aurora has used her gift of baloney.*

The mug really wasn't all that bad, I reasoned. And it was kind of fun helping Mom and Aunt Chloe push their merchandise. (I know. How sick is that?) They did have lots of creative ideas. Maybe I could help direct their creativity.

"I should have had twice as many of these done up," Mom said as our satisfied customer departed with her new mug.

*Thank heaven you didn't,* I thought. Then we'd have been down here every day, hawking them, and it wasn't that much fun.

Aunt Chloe caught sight of new victims and went into her act again. "There's only one left of that cute mug. You should let me have it."

Mom held onto hers like it was treasure. "No, I saw it first."

From the corner of my eye I could see a woman approaching. She reminded me of a deer smelling bait in a trap and coming for a closer look.

"But I have the perfect person for it," Aunt Chloe protested, reaching for the mug.

Mom held it away from her. "Sorry."

It was like I'd been swept away into Lucy Ricardo Land. I couldn't help myself. I took the mug from Mom, saying, "There's only one way to settle this." I put on a smile and turned to face the deer, er, customer. "Are you looking for a stocking stuffer?"

Of course, she was dying of curiosity. She reached for the prize and I gave it to her. "Oh, that is funny," she said.

"Sorry, girls," I said to Mom and Aunt Chloe, who were doing a great job of looking like covetous customers.

"But I don't have anyone to give this to," the woman said and handed it back to me.

I felt deflated, insulted even. I shot a look at my co-conspirators. They were both frowning.

The woman moved on.

"No taste," muttered Aunt Chloe.

I suddenly thought of Camilla, whose skunk boyfriend had dumped her for an older woman with tons of money. I took the mug. "Actually, I know someone who would really appreciate this."

My aunt and mother stared at me. "There's no one coming," Aunt Chloe whispered.

"I know. I want it."

Mom looked as pleased as if I'd told her she was going to be a grandmother, and Aunt Chloe patted my arm. "You're a good daughter."

Yes, I was.

I purchased my mug and we went home. Aunt Chloe stayed for a cup of sugar plum tea, then went on her way, and I grabbed a packet of Crabtree and Evelyn from my suitcase and went to soak in the tub.

By 7 o'clock I was bathed, perfumed, and primped, and psyched for my date with James. I had on my favorite L.B.D. (little black dress), the one with the square neckline. I'd accented it with a simple gold necklace and small gold hoops in my ears. I looked very classy, very New York. I should have, considering how much those clothes had cost me. My shoes alone had cost a week's groceries. Not a very noble way to spend money when there are people starving in the world, but at the time I'd rationalized my spending by convincing myself they were an investment. You know, dress for success and all that.

I heard a knock, then my door opened and Mom poked her head around it.

"You look Special Delivery," she said. "I hope your date is picking you up in a taxi."

"Why's that?"

"He won't be able to take his eyes off you. He's sure to run right off the road if he's driving." She crossed her arms and leaned against the door jamb. "So, why didn't you tell your grandmother you had a date tonight?"

"You're joking, right?"

Mom's mouth lifted at the corners. "I wouldn't have let her come with you."

I pulled my lipstick out of my purse and turned to the mirror. "I'm just here for a visit, not to get involved with anyone. If she heard I was going out she might get ideas."

I leaned into the dresser mirror and concentrated on my lips. But I could still see Mom reflected in the doorway, studying me.

"You could be dating more than one man. Gabe's interested."

"Been there, done that. Anyway, don't you think the women in our family have given him enough chances?"

Mom shrugged. "Oh, I knew he and Keira weren't a match. She was bored, and he was trying to find a substitute you."

"Right."

"That boy's been in love with you since you were in high school."

"Which is why he latched onto someone else the minute we broke up."

"Wounded pride," said Dr. Mom.

"Well, he's had several years and several women to heal it."

"You think so?"

"I know so. Anyway, he's here and I'm on the east coast. It would hardly work."

"Things change, people move."

*Not me,* I thought.

"And you're here right now. It doesn't hurt to be open to possibilities. Who knows what the future holds?"

"Not me and Gabe together, that's for sure," I said. *And not me moving home either.*

The doorbell rang. "I'll get it," Mom offered and disappeared. I heard her voice, then a low, male voice. A moment later she called, "Andie, your date's here."

Instead of an image of James Fender, my mind flashed on Gabe Knightly. He was wearing a tux. I gave myself a mental shake to dislodge him and left my room before he could get back inside my brain.

James was dressed in jeans and a shirt and sweater with a leather jacket thrown over it. I suddenly felt humongously overdressed. I'd forgotten people rarely dressed up in the Northwest.

"Wow," he said when he saw me.

Well, okay. The L.B.D. had been a good choice after all. "Is that a good wow or a bad wow?" I teased.

"It's good." He looked down at his jeans. "I feel like a bum."

"You look like a musician," I told him.

I grabbed my coat out of the closet, and he took it and helped me into it. A gentleman musician. He hadn't learned those manners from my brother, I was sure of that.

"Have fun," Mom said.

"We will," James promised, smiling at me.

Oh, yes. This was going to be a great night. As we went out the door, I felt like Cinderella on her way to the ball.

Then I saw my coach. It was some kind of beater from the sixties, a gas hog special that was half turquoise and half gray primer paint.

"That's quite a car," I said, trying to sound open minded.

"It's a '67 Chevy Impala. Gonna be gorgeous when I get done fixing it up."

James opened the door for me, and I got in. The air freshener almost covered up the musty smell. I wondered if I'd smell like my perfume or car mold by the time I got out.

"I've had some problems with the windows," James explained after he got in. It leaks a little."

Which would explain the smell. He started the engine, and the radio roared to life. The system was first class. He'd obviously had no problem with the stereo.

"I've got reservations at Lulu's," he told me.

Looking at his unfinished car and knowing he was a musician, I had a moment's guilt. Could James afford Lulu's?

I know. It probably sounds like a hamburger joint. But it isn't. Lulu's is the closest thing we have to expensive in Carol. Billed as a Polynesian restaurant, it sports tiki lamps at the entrance and imitation Easter Islands wood carvings. The menu features lots of fish and rice and pineapple, and drinks served in hollowed out coconuts with little umbrellas in them.

We pulled up in front of the restaurant, and James surrendered his car to the valet.

"Whoa," said our valet. "Hot wheels." He hopped in and backed up the car like he was at the Indianapolis 500, then squealed off.

"Maybe we should have taken the bus," I said. "Is your car going to survive tonight?"

James shrugged, unconcerned. "That happens a lot. Guys love it."

Maybe that was because they didn't have to worry about their perfume getting overpowered by *eau de mold*.

Once inside the restaurant it was evident that even the Polynesians were celebrating Christmas here in Carol. A fake tree sat in the lobby, decorated with little hula girl dolls and lights shaped like pineapples. I could hear Burl Ives singing his Holly Jolly Christmas song softly in the background. The old guy sure got around.

"Do you have reservations?" asked the hostess.

"Fender," James said.

"Right this way," she said and started to weave through tables of happy couples.

I followed, with James bringing up the rear.

Then I stopped, tripped up by shock. I didn't mean to stop right there in the middle of the restaurant, making James nearly run into me. I couldn't help it. A million thoughts started ricocheting around my mind, leaving me wrapped in indecision and holding me paralyzed.

This was supposed to be a great evening. How was I going to be able to concentrate on James with my father and The Girlfriend just a few tables away? We had to walk right past them. What was I supposed to say? And what should I do if Dad asked us to join them? That would be awkward and embarrassing. I could suddenly remember I was allergic to pineapple and ask James to take me somewhere else. I was sure I must be allergic to something here. My skin suddenly felt like I had hives.

Maybe Dad wouldn't see us. Maybe I could pretend I hadn't seen them.

There was a plan. I could just sort of slip by, looking the other way. If the hostess seated us at a booth in the darkest corner of the restaurant I could hide behind my menu, sit with my back to them. She was already homing in on a table by the kitchen, completely unaware that she'd left us behind six tables ago.

I took a deep breath. Okay. All I had to do was sneak past my father's table and I'd be home free.

I was just about to sneak when one of Mom's favorite sayings popped into my head. *Honesty is the best policy.*

This isn't dishonest, I told myself. It's avoidance, which is different. *Now, get sneaking.*

Too late. James moved past me, veering off the escape route and approaching Dad's table. "Brittany?"

Great. He knew The Girlfriend.

And how did he know her? Had he gone to Brittany for a haircut and a shrink session?

She looked our way, and her smile melted off her face. "James?"

Dad turned around to see who Brittany was looking at, and his face lit up like a kid on Christmas morning. "Andie."

"You know him?" James asked me.

"Just a little," I said. "He's my dad.

## Chapter Twelve

"Your dad?" James stuttered in shock. Obviously James wasn't familiar with the term *trophy wife.*

Not that Brittany was going to become one of those, I rushed to assure myself. Right now she was just a trophy girlfriend.

"Andie! Come join us," said Dad.

I stood there, frozen like a snow-woman, watching my perfect evening slip away.

James wasn't suffering from any such immobility. He was already pulling out a chair. For himself. "You don't mind, do you, Andie?"

*Mind? Why should I mind? There is nothing I'd rather do than double-date with my dad.* Was this normal?

I sort of fell onto a chair while James and Dad shook hands.

By now the hostess realized we had dropped out of the parade. She came to the table, menus in hand, and Dad explained that we were joining him, effectively barring the door to escape.

She gave us a polite smile, left the menus, then went off

in search of someone more deserving of a nice, quiet corner by the kitchen.

Meanwhile, Dad was doing the introductions.

"Actually, Brittany and I know each other," James said.

"She cuts your hair too?" Dad guessed.

James gave Brittany The Look, the universal Once-You-Loved-Me-But-Then-You-Betrayed-Me look that one half of every broken up couple wears when they bump into each other socially. The half giving it is always the one who wants to turn back time and be a couple again.

My appetite deflated like a ruined soufflé and I wished I hadn't bothered with the L.B.D.

Brittany's expression toward me was decidedly less chummy than what she'd been doling out the day before. "So, you and James know each other."

I opened my mouth and James said, "We just met."

It looked like I was going to spend the evening as a well dressed ventriloquist's dummy. *Andie, tell us how it feels to be dumped on your first date for the guy's former girlfriend who just happens to be here with your dad. Okay, now tell us while James is drinking water. Wow, isn't that amazing? His mouth barely moves.*

I decided I was jumping to wild, unsubstantiated conclusions. Had to be.

"You're with Andie's dad now?" James asked Brittany.

It could be just an idle question, a way of making conversation, except for the fact that James was still wearing The Look.

"Yes." Brittany had been leaning against Dad when we first came in. Now she sat up and reached for her water glass, putting space between them. Body language said it all.

Okay, no jumping here. I barely had to move. In fact, the conclusions were jumping to me. James still wanted

Brittany, and Brittany was open to being wanted. That turned Dad and me into human leftovers. It was a disheartening moment, and I almost asked for a doggie bag for myself.

But then I remembered I was now a tough New York businesswoman. I knew how to fight for what I wanted. Brittany already had my dad. She wasn't going to get my date too.

"Small world," I said, and leaned close to James so he could get a whiff of my perfume. He needed something to remind him that there was another woman at the table.

The perfume worked. He turned and looked at me as if he was seeing me for the first time.

*Yes, it's me, Andie, your date.*

"Well," said Dad in a falsely cheerful voice, "Maybe we should think about ordering. Get whatever you want, kids. It's on me."

I was sure Dad had meant his remark to make him sound generous, but instead it made him sound old, like an amiable geezer rewarding us kids for being good at the dentist's with a trip to Dairy Queen.

I sneaked a look at James. He was frowning slightly. "I'll pay. It's the least I can do for Andie's dad."

James' offer sounded more competitive than kind, and it further cemented the fact in our minds that Dad was the father figure at the table.

Poor Dad. He looked like a chaperone at a teen party who had tried to join in the fun and games. I figured he was now wishing he'd hid behind his menu and pretended not to see us.

"That's really sweet of you," I said to James, just so he'd know I appreciated his generosity.

He smiled at me, then shot a glance Brittany's direction. And that irritated me. What was the point in shooting compliments if the person they were aimed at recycled them for another woman? How badly did I want to fight for this guy, anyway?

We opened our menus.

I scanned the selections. Normally I'd be considerate on a first date and choose something relatively inexpensive, like the Polynesian chicken. But with the way things were degenerating, I have to admit, I was not feeling my usual noble self. I went for the Lobster Lulu, the most expensive item on the menu.

"That sounds good," Dad said. "I think I'll have it too."

"Me too," Brittany decided.

James suddenly looked pale.

"What are you going to have?" I asked him. At this point, all he could probably afford was water.

"I think I'll try the Polynesian chicken."

"You can't go wrong with chicken," Dad said, but when the waiter came, he stuck to his Lobster Lulu order.

"So, James," Dad said, "what do you do?"

"I'm in the band with your son."

Dad nodded. "Oh, yeah. So, what else do you do?" I guess being a rock star in the making wasn't enough when it came to his daughter.

"I give bass and guitar lessons at the music store."

"You can make a living doing that?"

"Almost," James replied honestly.

Dad looked underwhelmed.

"Hopefully, the band will take off," James added.

Dad shook his head. "Bands these days, they lack style."

James stiffened next to me.

"I think Fish Without Legs has style," I said, then hoped Dad wouldn't ask me to back up my statement with proof. They were all cute. That should count for something, but probably not with Dad.

"Me, I like oldies," said Brittany. "Like ABBA."

"Abba doesn't qualify as oldies," Dad informed her. "Now, stuff by Sam the Sham and the Pharaohs, that's oldies. Or the Righteous Brothers."

"That's not old, that's ancient," James joked.

Dad's eyes narrowed to laser-shooting slits, zapping James' smile.

"Who is Sam the Sham and Pharaohs?" asked Brittany.

"You know." Dad began to sing a cheesy old song about Little Red Riding Hood, and I cringed. Brittany looked blankly at him. The generation gap at this table was getting wider than the Grand Canyon.

The food arrived and I waited in dread, hoping Dad wouldn't bring out one of his favorite restaurant cracks. Surely he wouldn't.

He did. "I'll give you a dollar if you eat this collie," he said to Brittany.

She'd obviously already heard it and just rolled her eyes.

Both James' eyebrows shot up.

"The movie, *Badlands*," Dad explained.

"Oh," James said and nodded the way you would to placate someone who might be dangerous.

"It was before we were born," Brittany explained, and James nodded again, this time with understanding. He left Dad rambling around, lost in the past and asked Brittany, "How've you been, Brit?"

"Fine. I went back to school."

"So, you finally took my advice," he said.

She nodded. "You were right."

"Of course I was. You have a lot to give."

So did I, but my date wasn't interested. I wanted to say, "Hello, I'm here," but I wasn't sure he'd even hear me. It was like he and Brittany were encased in some Plexiglas hut with unbreakable walls.

I shot a look over at Dad. He was pouting. He signaled a passing waiter. "I'll have another beer."

Now Dad was going to get plastered and make the whole evening even worse. Oh, boy.

My dream date was feeling more and more like a nightmare. How long until our dinner came, and how fast could I eat it and then scram? I started drumming my fingers on the table. My mother or grandmother, even my aunt, would have noticed this and observed that I was tense, would have showed some concern by suggesting I relax and enjoy my meal.

No one at the table even noticed my drumming fingers. I told myself to relax.

Our waiter showed up with the food. I looked down at my Lobster Lulu. It was drowning in thick sauce, lumpy with pineapple and peas. I scraped off the sauce and dug in. At least I would get a free meal out of the deal.

Brittany's smile was as syrupy as the sauce on my lobster, but it didn't match her eyes when she looked at me. She reminded me of a toy poodle guarding its favorite squeeze toy.

Take the squeeze toy already, I thought.

"How did you and James meet?" she asked.

"We met at the band concert," James the ventriloquist replied, putting fresh words in my mouth. He remembered me, his date, and donated a surplus smile.

"You have an amazing talent," I said. I don't know why I said that. It made me sound like a groupie. At the time, though, it seemed like the occasion called for it. I suppose I still had hopes that I would be able to flatter him away from the strong attraction of unrequited love.

I wondered what our conversation would have been like by now if it had been the two of us back at that nice, private corner table. Would we have been discussing favorite movies or books we'd read? Maybe we would have already progressed to sharing our dreams. Or maybe we would have been comparing bad first dates. Instead, here we were, having one. Boy, would I have a story to swap with the next guy I went out with. If I ever went out again. After this night, who knew?

James and Brittany included us two outsiders for a while, but it seemed they couldn't help drifting off to their own little conversational deserted island.

"You still renting that funky place over by the berry farm?" James asked her.

Oh, who cares? I thought.

She smiled and nodded.

Okay, I decided. Let the chick have him. Very noble of me, considering the fact that she'd had him since the moment we sat down at the table.

"Still cutting hair on the side in the kitchen?" he asked. Since his hair looked like it had been cut recently, I doubted he was asking because he wanted a makeover.

"No," she said.

"She wants time to spend with me," Dad said. It was a good try on his part, but it only felt like a bit of wedged-in verbiage.

"I'd give you a haircut, though," Brittany offered. Even an idiot could intercept the message behind that.

I studied my father, trying to decide if he knew he was about to lose his trophy girlfriend to a younger man and was putting a brave face on things, or if he really thought he and Brittany were a solid couple. He looked cheerful enough, but I was sure I detected panic deep in his eyes. I thought about all the Christmas presents he'd bought this ingrate. He'd spent a fortune on her. Poor Dad.

A new thought entered my mind. Poor Dad would be feeling very lonely without The Girlfriend. Maybe he'd want to stop by the house on Christmas Day and visit with his long-lost daughter. He'd be humbled after getting dumped by Brittany, and he'd show up on our doorstep with his eyes opened. He'd see Mom in a fresh light and realize he'd been a fool. He'd beg her forgiveness, ask her . . .

"Who wants dessert?"

My dad was being dumped over pineapple lobster and he was thinking about dessert? Well, that settled it. He didn't have a clue. Oh, poor, poor Dad. I clenched my hands together to prevent myself from reaching across the table and strangling the haircutting heartbreaker.

"None for me. I ate like a pig and I'm stuffed." Brittany patted her size-six midriff.

Yeah, yeah, I thought. Actually, I was stuffed too. I decided I'd already made James pay enough for his disloyalty. "I think I'll pass," I said.

James looked relieved.

"The Lulu on Fire is pretty good," Dad said, being generous with James' money.

"Go ahead, Mike," James said, but his tone was unconvincing.

Dad shook his head. "Nah. I'm fine."

But not as fine as James, who Brittany was looking at like he was a Lulu on Fire.

James called for the check, the waiter brought it, and Dad scooped it up. James argued half-heartedly, but Dad waved off his feeble protest, reminding him he was a starving musician.

So, Dad wound up paying for the dinner. And I knew, as surely as I always know who's going to win the Miss America pageant, that Dad would really be paying before the night was over. I could already picture him back at his lonely apartment, listening to Elvis sing "Blue Christmas."

As we walked out of the restaurant, Brittany managed to get near enough to James to say under her breath, "Call me," and he nodded.

They looked like a couple of conspirators planning to murder an inconvenient husband. I felt a surge of righteous anger. They deserved to be pelted with rotten pineapples. (I was sure I could find some in Lulu's back dumpster.) I resisted my uncivilized urge, telling myself to let it go. In the end these two would get exactly what they deserved, which was each other. Anyway, there was no sense creating a scene and embarrassing my father.

Outside the restaurant, the valets squealed back with our cars. Right before Brittany climbed into Dad's midlife crisis special, I saw her shoot James a look of longing. I sneaked a peek at him. He was reflecting it right back at her.

Well, that was the perfect ending to a perfect night. Now I felt like the warden, leading a poor prisoner of love off to solitary. Had I asked for this? I mean, who asked whom out?

James reminded me of Gabe Knightly, disloyal Gabe who feigned a broken heart, then went on to date every woman in Carol. Men, I concluded in disgust, they're all the same: disloyal and scummy. Well, except Dad, who was more stupid than scummy.

After James and I got in his car it was "Silent Night," and not the holy version.

Finally, he spoke, "Um, I guess you're wondering what the deal is with me and Brittany."

Did he think I was a moron? "No, I figured it out pretty fast." Under six seconds; that had to be a record.

"We went together for two years." He shook his head. "I'm still not sure what happened. We just sort of, I don't know. It all blew up one day about a year ago."

Now, there was a good explanation. I could tell he'd given this a lot of thought.

"I think she was jealous of the band," James decided. "We have to spend a lot of time practicing, and then there are the gigs. Other women would talk to me after the concerts, and she'd get jealous."

The psychology expert would get jealous because other women talked to her boyfriend after a concert. That made a lot of sense, almost as much sense as it made that he preferred Brittany, the psycho hair stylist, to a normal woman.

"Mmm," I said frostily.

He gave me a quick little sorry look. "I don't know what to say."

*Then maybe you should stop talking.* I shrugged. "Stuff like this happens." Mostly in movies, though. Unless you were a Hartwell. Then you could count on it happening to you in real life.

James kept talking all the way home, psychoanalyzing himself and Brittany. Fascinating stuff. I tuned it out.

I had my hand on the door handle as we pulled up in front of the house. As soon as the car stopped I opened the door. "Thanks for the dinner," I said. "I hope it works out for you and Brittany." No lie there. James and Brittany would make a perfect couple: Mr. and Mrs. Idiot. And Dad needed to be set free so he could see the light and come back to Mom.

James could hardly look me in the eye, but the quick contact I got showed relief. "Thanks," he said.

*Go and sin no more.* "See you in concert," I said. I got out and shut the door.

So James drove off, probably to see Brittany and set himself up for a future of free haircuts, always a good thing for a broke musician.

As for me, I went into the house, reminding myself that

things have a way of working out. Just not always the way you want.

Oh, well. My date had fizzled, but at least my father had been set free.

## Chapter Thirteen

I really didn't want to talk about my nondate with my mother, so I tried to slip in the house undetected. But Mom has superhuman hearing.

I was halfway down the hall to my bedroom when I heard her call, "Andie?"

Who did she think it was, the Ghost of Christmas Past? I sighed inwardly, then put on the fake but sincere-looking smile I always use in New York. I call it my Meet the Client smile. If I was lucky, it would also become my fool the mother smile. I turned to face her, my body language what I'd call casual-glad.

Actually, considering the fact that I'd just played a part in setting my father free from Miss Shampoo 'n' Shrink, I should have been ecstatic-glad, tidings-of-great-joy-glad. But I've got to admit, my pride was smarting.

"I'm just going to change into my jeans," I said.

"Your date's over already?" Mom sounded surprised. No, not surprised, shocked.

"We decided to call it a night," I answered vaguely.

"You've got a slim definition of night," Mom said in disgust. But then she smiled. "Oh, well. All the better for me. Now I get you all to myself. Want to play Anagrams?"

Anagrams is a word game, kind of like Scrabble only without the math. It had been my grandmother's, and she finally passed it on to us, complete with the old red Folgers can the letters had been kept in since I was a kid. We kids used to play with Mom and Grandma, and sometimes Aunt Chloe, who cheated by making up words right and left. Ben abandoned the game once he was old enough for little league, and Keira left when she got too busy turning herself into the socialite of Carol. So, after a while, it was just Mom and me, sorting the alphabet soup into words and stealing words from each other to make bigger and better words. I remembered how much I used to love to play Anagrams because it meant I got Mom all to myself. Mom can be fun when she wants to be.

"Get the can," I said.

As I changed into my jeans, I couldn't help thinking what an odd direction this night's events had gone. It was going to be my getaway from my family's craziness, my big night of romance. Instead, here I was spending the evening with my mom. Funny how things turn out sometimes.

And funny how the things you don't plan often turn out great, like a sentimental movie scene. Mom and I played Anagrams and ate pretzels. In the background, *It's a Wonderful Life* played on TV, and Jimmy Stewart ran up and down Main Street, hollering Merry Christmas at everyone. If I was reduced to something like this back in New York, I'd have considered the night a dismal failure. For some goofy reason, here it felt right.

Oh, boy. Was this how Alice began to feel after living in Wonderland for a while? Did weird start to become normal, fun even? Next I'd be suggesting Mom and I head on down to Gifts 'N' Gags and hawk mugs or asking Aunt Chloe to do a still-life painting that I could take home for my roommate Camilla. Or convincing myself that my family wasn't that crazy and wondering what my life would have been like if I'd stayed in Carol.

"Well, that was a close game," Mom said after she'd beaten me by one word. Want to play another?"

One more sentimental game with Mom and I'd be calling Gabe, begging him to show me houses. "No, I think I'll quit while you're ahead," I said.

I kissed her on the cheek and she reached up and patted my hand. "You're a good daughter. You know that?"

No sense disillusioning her. I simply smiled, then went to bed.

I read for a while, then tried to go to sleep. My old bed didn't feel right anymore. I tossed and turned, trying to get comfortable.

At last I conked, but I didn't get any visions of sugar plums. Instead, I suffered through a series of weird dreams. In one, I was getting chased by Frosty the Snowman, who wanted to double-date with Dad and Brittany. Frosty melted only to be replaced by Gabe Knightly in a Santa suit, ho-ho-ho-ing and telling me he knew exactly what I wanted for Christmas. And all the while, he kept stuffing a huge sack with Mom's gingerbread boy mugs. The topper came in the early morning hours, when I dreamed that Dad and Brittany got back together and Dad moved Brittany into Keira's dream house. Keira went over and set fire to it. Next thing I knew, my whole family was on the lawn in their jammies, giving Brittany the stink eye. She and Mom got into a hair-pulling fist fight and the cops came. I heard sirens. No, it was a ringing.

It was my cell phone. Camilla. "Did I wake you up?" she asked.

"Umm, yeah," I mumbled. "What time is it?"

"It's nine." She said it like of course I should be up by now.

"That means it's six in the morning here."

"Oh. Yeah. Sorry."

"No problem. Are you at work?"

"Actually, I've taken a few days off. You'll never guess who's here."

She was right. I wouldn't. "Who?"

"My cousins Tess and Wess. Oh, and Wess' friend Morris. They came down from Rhode Island to surprise me. How's that for sweet?"

"Sweet," I said.

"I gave Tess your room. I hope you don't mind."

I was barely gone and my roommate was already loaning out my bed? Without even asking me? "Yeah, as a matter of fact, I do," I said.

"But you're not here," Camilla reasoned.

"I just think my room should be off-limits," I said, "especially since I'm paying two-thirds of the rent."

"Geez, well okay," she said, making me feel like a selfish rat.

"We've got the sofa bed, and that blow-up mattress," I reminded her.

"The guys are using them."

"Well, I guess she can sleep with you. She's your cousin."

There was silence on the other end of the line, followed by a martyred sigh. "I guess that means she can't borrow that blue beaded dress of yours."

"What? She has no clothes?" First Camilla was loaning out my bed to strangers, and now my wardrobe. What next?

"It's just that we decided to go to this New Year's Eve party that Manuel at work is having and she really didn't bring anything that's going to work for it."

I rolled onto my stomach and propped myself up on my elbows. "Actually, I'm going to make it home for New Year's. I'm coming back early. I'll be there by next Wednesday."

Big silence. Finally Camilla said, "Oh." It wasn't the kind of *oh* you'd put in front of the word *great* or *wonderful*. It was the kind of *oh* you'd put in front of the word *no*.

Okay, I was in the social badlands and there was only one way out of them. I still wasn't sharing my bed, but I decided I could be generous with my dress, especially when I'd been planning on getting rid of it anyway.

"I guess she can wear my blue dress," I said. "I have another one I can wear to the party."

Another big silence.

"I am invited, right?" I'd just given up my dress. Surely that counted for something.

"We didn't know you were going to be in town."

"Well, now I am," I said, irritation bleeding into my voice.

"I'll see what I can do," Camilla promised.

"Camilla," I protested. "We had plans to do New Year's Eve."

"Then you left to see your family."

"That wasn't exactly my idea. Anyway, now I'm coming back and I want to go to the party." I knew I sounded bratty, but hey, fair is fair.

"Okay, I'm coming," she said to someone else in the room, probably Tess the bedbug. To me, she said, "Hey, I've got to go. See you when you get back. Have fun with your family."

She knew I never had fun with my family. I felt a stab of jealousy that Camilla was whooping it up back in New York while I was suffering the trials of Job here in Carol. And now it looked like I might not even get to do any whooping when

I returned because my roommate was going to a party with her cousins and my blue beaded dress. I said a grumpy good-bye and hung up, then I dropped my cell on the floor and buried my face in my pillow in search of a pity party.

Staying in bed all day sounded like a good option. I could just lie there and pretend my roommate was excited that I was coming home early, that the people in my new, important life cared about me, that my life in New York was perfect.

Maybe I should have said Camilla's cousin could use my bed. I wasn't sleeping in it. Why was I being so territorial, anyway?

Because I was paying for two-thirds of the territory, that was why. And, come to think of it, I'd been paying for more than my share of the groceries lately too. I punched my pillow and rolled over with a growl, irritated with both Camilla and myself.

I managed to drift back to sleep, but I only got more weird dreams. I walked in on Gabe Knightly kissing my roommate. He smiled when he saw me and said, "Welcome home, Andie." Then I was at that party with Camilla and her cousins. Tess looked great in my blue beaded dress. I, on the other hand, was wearing nothing. It seems my luggage had gotten lost en route to New York, and in my absence Camilla had given all my clothes to Goodwill.

I finally gave up, got up, and showered, reminding myself that dreams have nothing to do with reality. My clothes would still be there when I got home. All but the blue beaded dress.

As soon as I was dressed, I called Image Makers. The line was ringing when Keira came to my room, home from work early and ready to hound me about going house hunting.

I held up my hand to shut her up and concentrated on speaking to Iris.

"Beryl can't talk right now," she said. "But I'm glad you called because I was supposed to call you about the Nutri Bread meeting."

"You were? I already talked to you about the meeting," I said.

"This is a new development."

I suddenly got that feeling in the pit of my stomach that you get when a roller coaster first starts to drop. I'd known all along something bad was going to happen! "What's going on?" I demanded.

"I guess your client is really excited. They want to get a jump start, so Beryl and Mr. Phelps are accommodating them."

"A jump start," I repeated, and began to replan my Christmas vacation. If I left the day after Christmas I could be in the office by . . ."

Keira derailed my train of thought. "Why did you call back there, anyway? What do they want now?" She sounded like a nagging wife. Getting in practice for Spencer, I supposed.

I put my finger in my ear so I could hear better.

"The new meeting is scheduled for the twenty-fourth," Iris said.

The roller coaster in my stomach picked up speed. No, forget the roller coaster. Wile E. Coyote was in there, going off the cliff. "What?"

"What's going on?" Keira's decibel level was rising quickly.

I turned my back on her.

"In the morning," Iris said, "so everyone has time to get home for Christmas."

"Everyone but me. Does anyone remember I'm on the west coast, or is this some kind of sick joke?" I snapped. It wasn't very nice to take out my frustration on poor Iris. I'm not normally an angry person, but lately Image Makers was transforming me into one.

"Beryl did say she'd understand if you couldn't get here."

*Yeah, yeah.* *"Not to worry, my poppet."* I'd poppet *her.* Before this I'd only suspected it. Now I knew for sure. Beryl was trying to cut me out of the action, keep me in the background, rob me of any credit for this entire campaign. She was Ebenezer Scrooge, the chick version.

"Well, tell her don't worry. I'm a team player and I can make it back in time," I said between gritted teeth.

"Oh, no," Keira moaned in back of me. "Not again."

"Okay," said Iris. "And Andie?"

"Yeah?" I practically snarled.

"I'm sorry you're going to have to miss Christmas with your family."

I rubbed my aching head. "It's okay."

But it wasn't. I should have been glad that I was getting a chance to bug out on the Hartwell holiday insanity, but I didn't feel glad. Instead I felt like a traitor to my family, an unwilling traitor, forced into betrayal by the corporate greed of her superiors. I loved my job (except for the times when it made me angry and stressed), enjoyed the creativity, the excitement, the thrill of promoting cool products and seeing people start using them. And, up until now, I had loved the fact that the job gave me an excuse to keep a healthy distance between myself and my hometown. But suddenly, the job looked like a monster, trying to gobble my time, my life, my soul. This simply wasn't right.

I hung up and tossed the cell phone on my bed.

"You have to go back even sooner, don't you?" Keira said in a voice of doom.

"They want me to." How could I tell Mom? What kind of an ingrate daughter would I look like if I left?

"When do they want you back?" Keira asked.

"Christmas Eve day."

"Christmas Eve?" she exploded.

Great. Now the whole neighborhood knew. "Keep it down, will you?" I told her.

She half-lowered her voice. "Who works on Christmas Eve?"

"Lots of people," I informed her.

"Are you going?"

I could fly to New York for the meeting, then turn around and take a red-eye back. I'd still be here for Christmas. Well, sort of.

Keira got tired of waiting for an answer. "You know your job owns you?" she said in disgust, then flounced from the room.

"That's because I have a real job," I called after her.

Easy to take time off when all you did was make expensive coffee concoctions for people. I did real work. I wrote the ads for the expensive coffee.

I fell on the bed next to the cell phone and glared at it. *Look at all the trouble you've caused this morning.*

That last thought made me remember one of my mother's mommyisms: You shouldn't blame inanimate objects for your stupidity.

I had, indeed, been stupid. I should have turned off my cell the minute I got off the airplane. Then I'd have remained in happy ignorance of Beryl's plotting to shove me behind the curtain to work the levers while she did her Wizard of Oz act with the smoke and mirrors. And I wouldn't have had to choose between my career and my family.

*You're being overly dramatic,* I scolded myself. The family will understand when you sit down and logically, calmly explain the problem to them. These things happen.

I'd always have my family, no matter what. But my job

was a different story, and my future at Image Makers depend-
ed on whether or not I picked up that cell and changed my
flight.

I snatched the cell from my bed.

## Chapter Fourteen

I moved to shut the bedroom door while I waited for the next available operator at Great Bargain Airlines. The last thing I needed was eavesdroppers.

I could hear Mom's and Keira's voices floating down the hall from the kitchen. Good old Keira, going right to Mom to rat me out. I took a couple of steps and strained my ear so I could hear.

"What do you mean how bad do I want Andie here for Christmas?" Mom was saying.

"We could still have a good Christmas without her," Keira insisted.

*Thanks.*

"Keira, I don't know what you're getting at," said Mom.

I did. She was trying to get Mom to disown me. Or maybe she was figuring between the two of them they could weigh me down with so much guilt that my plane would never be able to take off.

That wouldn't be hard to do. I already had a pretty big load of it hanging on me like Marley's chains.

I'm just saying that if, for some reason, Andie had to leave you'd still have Ben and me."

*The good children.* I frowned.

"Your sister's not going anywhere," Mom said.

"But her job," Keira began.

"She doesn't have to be back until after Christmas. She wouldn't leave early, not when she knows how much it means to me for us to be together."

More guilt. Now the chain was down to my feet.

"It doesn't mean anything to Andie," Keira said. "I heard her making plans. She's going back. She's probably flying out tonight. You can ask her yourself." Then Keira hollered, "Andie, Mom wants to talk to you."

What a manipulative little brat! My cell phone still to my ear, I marched to the kitchen.

"You should have your tongue cut out," I told my tattletale sister.

Just then Aunt Chloe hollered from the front door, "Ho, ho, ho. Anybody home?"

"Out here," Mom called. She gave me one of those mother looks. You know, the kind that says, "What have you done? You'd better 'fess up now." "Your sister thinks you're not going to be around for Christmas."

A voice was on the phone now, saying, "Welcome to Great Bargain Airlines. This is Betty. How may I help you?"

It seemed I had been suddenly struck with laryngitis, because I stood there in the middle of the kitchen, unable to say anything, Mom's words from a minute ago echoing in my brain. *She knows how much it means to me for us all to be together, together, together.*

Meanwhile, Keira was glaring at me. Why had I bothered to bring home a present for her, anyway?

"What are you talking about?" Aunt Chloe demanded. "Why wouldn't Andie be here?"

"She has a meeting," said Keira.

*Important,* she forgot to say *important.*

"Hello?" repeated the voice.

"Go on," egged Keira. "Tell them how you have to get back to your big, important job."

Now she says it, I thought. Only my sister could manage to suck all the meaning out of a word, then use its limp carcass to completely distort a logical sentence.

Could you do that if it really were logical? I looked at my family. Keira was oozing scorn from every pore, Mom was gaping at me in unbelief, and Aunt Chloe was looking thoroughly confused. Was what I was about to do even remotely logical? Did I really need to be at that meeting? And how important was selling bread compared to keeping my promise to have Christmas with my family?

"Hello," the voice tried again. "May I help you?"

"No, never mind," I said and hung up.

"Andie, what is going on?" Mom demanded as I started on my second call.

"Nothing." Iris answered and I said, "It's Andie again. Tell Beryl I'm not going to be able to make it back for the meeting."

"Are you sure?" Iris asked. She might as well have added, "Are you out of your mind?" or "Want me to start cleaning out your desk?"

"I'm sure."

"All right. I have to admit, I thought it was unrealistic of Beryl to expect you to come back for that meeting. I mean, it's not much notice and it is Christmas."

Which was, of course, exactly why Beryl picked that particular date in the first place. She was determined to crowd me out and take all the glory for herself. She'd drained my brain of ideas and now she didn't need me any more.

"Tell her merry Christmas from the west coast," I said. *And I hope the British Grinch finds her stocking stuffed with lumps of coal.*

I said good-bye to Iris, then cut the connection and snapped my cell shut. Suddenly, I felt ashamed of my self-centered obsession with my life. Faced with a choice between my family and my job, I had almost chosen my job.

"You're missing a big meeting?" Mom asked. Her face was the picture of motherly guilt.

"It's okay," I said.

Like the last gasp of a bad dream I caught an image of myself modestly acknowledging thunderous Madison Avenue applause while I accepted a Communicator Award for my brilliant Nutri Bread advertising campaign. *Don't chuck this,* begged my ambitious self.

Then I saw my mother, seated alone at the dining room table, crying in her eggnog. *My daughter, Andrea Scrooge Hartwell, abandoned us on Christmas Eve. I'll never celebrate this holiday again.*

I shook my head to clear it of the terrible vision. Okay, I had definitely made the right choice.

My mom and aunt and sister were all smiling, instantly transformed into happy campers. It was a movie climax moment. The heroine does the right thing, tells her boss to take a hike, then marches off to a happy ending, accompanied by triumphal music.

I smiled too and tried to be happy that I'd just knocked myself off the ladder of success. I wished I could hear some triumphal music. Maybe it would have distracted me from the fact that I now felt slightly sick.

"I'm going to put away my cell phone," I said. Otherwise

I'd be tempted to call Iris right back and say, "Never mind. I'm coming."

"Good idea," Keira said sanctimoniously.

Someone once said that virtue is its own reward, but I began to have doubts about that as I went back down the hall. Even though I knew I'd done the right thing, it sure felt like a lose-lose situation. I'd not only shot my career in the foot, I'd also refused rescue from Hartwell holiday insanity.

*You made the right decision*, I told myself sternly. It seemed like I should have felt happier for someone who just made the right decision.

It felt like cutting off a hand, but I turned off my cell phone ringer, ending all contact with the outside world. Then I stuffed the phone at the bottom of my suitcase. *There.*

I looked at the suitcase. That had been a little extreme. What if I needed my cell for something? I dug it back out and put it on the charger.

What if Camilla had some sort of emergency back at the apartment and had to get a hold of me? I put the ringer back on. There was no need to get crazy.

Just as I went back to the kitchen the phone rang. Mom picked it up and said a cheery "Hello."

Her expression changed from joyful to shocked. "You're where?" Pause. "Oh, no. How?" She looked exasperated. "Oh, Michael. Yes, I'll tell the kids."

"Tell us what?" Keira asked. "What's wrong with Daddy?"

Mom just shook her head, forcing us all to wait in suspense. Then, "They'll want to come see you. We'll all come. Can you have visitors?"

"Visitors!" Keira echoed. "Where is he, in jail? What's wrong?" she demanded as Mom hung up the phone.

"Your father's in the hospital."

"What!" Keira and I chorused.

Aunt Chloe's face turned white. "Oh, no. What is it? Heart attack? Cancer? Prostate!"

"No, brain failure," Mom said. "He was out in that stupid sports car last night and wrapped himself around a tree. He's lucky he's alive."

Aunt Chloe put a hand to her heart. "Oh, my. Is he all right?"

"Well, he seems to be. He's talking," Mom said. She reached for her purse on the kitchen counter, muttering, "What a way to begin the morning."

"Are you going to see him?" Keira asked.

"Of course," Mom answered.

"Wait up," Keira said. "I'm coming too."

"Me too," I added.

"Me too," said Aunt Chloe.

While we drove to the hospital, Keira used her phone to call Ben at work.

"He's going to come as soon as he can get someone in to man the store," she said as she stuffed her phone back in her purse.

"What's wrong with him?" Aunt Chloe asked Mom. "Did he break anything?"

"I don't know," Mom said tersely.

"You didn't ask?"

"No, I didn't. I just know he's in the hospital."

"Hmmm," Aunt Chloe said. "That's a lot of panic for a man you don't care for anymore."

"Shut up," Mom told her.

Mom drove like an ambulance driver. All we were missing was the siren. I wondered if, before the day was over, we'd all be in the hospital. I could see it now, the Hartwell wing, with each of us occupying beds in adjoining rooms.

Keira put her hands over her face and whimpered, "Let me know when it's all over."

Aunt Chloe braced her hands on the dashboard as we fish tailed around a corner. "Will you slow down, Jannie? You're going to kill us all."

*Oh, Lord, please get us there in one piece,* I prayed.

Miraculously, we arrived unharmed. And then a second miracle occurred. We found a parking spot. Okay, so far so good. Now we just had to live through this visit.

Why was Mom doing this? I wondered. Somewhere, under all that anger, she had to still care. That was all I could figure. Her face was set in a stone scowl. It would be hard to blast through all that stone to find the love, and I doubted Dad had the strength to do it. I hoped he would survive this visit.

The hospital was decorated for Christmas, with a tree in the lobby almost as big as the one Ben had inflicted on us. They were serving visitors canned Christmas music, and as we walked toward the elevators, Burl Ives once again instructed us to have a Holly Jolly Christmas. Was no place safe from the ghost of Burl Ives? And what a song to be playing where people were grappling with illness and death! I supposed when that song finished, we'd be treated to "Grandma Got Run Over by a Reindeer."

Dad's floor smelled like antiseptic and worry. I began to feel anxious.

My heart was hammering by the time we found his room. We walked around a privacy curtain and there he was. His head was bandaged, his face was cut, and he had a black eye. One arm was in a cast. He looked old.

Next to me, Keira burst into tears. "Oh, Daddy!"

I bit my lip and followed her to the bedside. I took his good hand. "Poor Dad."

He smiled at us wanly. "My girls."

Mom moved to the other side of the bed. "Oh, look at

you," she said, and for just a moment her face softened. Then the stone scowl returned. "I told you not to get that car."

"It's not the car's fault the road was slick," Dad said. His voice sounded tired.

"What happened?" I asked.

"I think I hit some black ice."

"How fast were you going when you hit it?" Mom asked, not because she wanted to know, but because she wanted to insinuate Dad had been driving recklessly. It was a legitimate conclusion to jump to.

He glared at Mom. "Not that fast."

I looked him in his black-and-blue eye. "Were you drinking?"

Both eyes did a little shift. "I just wasn't paying attention. I'd gotten some bad news and I was mad. I guess I might have been going a little fast."

I'd been part of that dinner fiasco at Lulu's and I could guess what the bad news was, but I didn't embarrass him by guessing out loud.

"Speeding," Mom said. "I knew it. You're lucky to be alive. Were you wearing your seatbelt?"

"Of course," Dad said, sounding insulted.

"Poor Daddy," said Keira, patting his leg. "You look awful."

"Thanks, I feel awful. But the good news is, I'll be out in time for Christmas." He looked terribly despondent for a man with such good news. Probably because he was thinking about a lonely day stretching before him while his girlfriend rocked around the Christmas tree with someone else.

"What all is wrong with you?" Mom asked.

"Just a broken arm and some bruises and abrasions, and I've got a concussion."

"You can be glad you've still got a head," Mom informed him, and he frowned at her.

"We're glad you're not hurt worse," I translated for Mom.

"It looks like you're getting a second chance at life," said Aunt Chloe. She patted Dad's leg and plopped on the side of the bed, making it bounce and Dad moan, then started examining the contents of his food tray. "Are they feeding you well?"

"Yeah, Chloe," Dad said like he could care less.

"Aren't you going to eat your eggs?" she wanted to know. "The protein is good for your bones."

"I'm not hungry," Dad said weakly.

"There's no sense letting this go to waste," Aunt Chloe said and picked up the plate.

I touched his arm and asked, "Is there anything we can get you?" *Besides a new girlfriend.*

"I'm okay," he said and gave me a pitiful smile.

"Oh, look," said Aunt Chloe, pointing to the TV. "Here's something to inspire you. Where's the remote?" She leaned across Dad, making him snarl, "Do you mind, Chloe?" and grabbed the remote. Then she turned up the volume on *It's a Wonderful Life*. Jimmy Stewart was begging for a chance to live again.

"You could have killed yourself," Mom said to Dad. "That's why I didn't want you to have that car in the first place."

"We're not married anymore, Janelle, so you can quit nagging."

"I'm not nagging," Mom said sharply.

"How about just saying you're sorry I got hurt."

"Of course, I'm sorry you got hurt. You scared me half to death."

She softened her voice and a little bubble of hope rose in me. I knew it all along. Deep under that icy surface, Mom still had a spark of feeling for Dad.

"But I still don't understand how you could have . . ."

Dad cut her off. "I was going too fast, okay? I was mad and a I took a corner too fast."

"There's no need to bite my head off," Mom snapped.

"It's the only way I can get you to shut up," Dad snapped back.

"You haven't changed at all," she informed him.

"Neither have you," he said. "Why are you here, anyway?"

"Because you called."

"I wanted the girls to know."

"Well, next time be more specific who you do and don't want to know that you're an idiot. Like anyone can't guess without you telling them."

My stomach began to churn faster with each flying barb. Okay, so if my parents couldn't be together couldn't they at least act like mature adults and quit torturing everyone around them with secondhand misery?

I turned my back and tuned them out, concentrating on the TV. There was George Bailey and company running around Bedford Falls, making small-town life look so perfect. Well, that was the movies. This was reality, a reality that included my parents fighting while my dad lay in a hospital bed. Would they be doing this even if he were lying there dying?

I left the room. Neither of them noticed. A few minutes later Keira and Aunt Chloe came out. Mom followed them. She was looking teary-eyed.

*Merry Christmas,* I thought grumpily, and wished I hadn't been so noble earlier and canceled going back to New York. I could have been on a red-eye this very night.

We met Ben halfway down the hall. He was moving like a one-man train, the Panic Express. I wondered who was minding the store. Judging by the worried look on my brother's face, it was entirely possible that he'd run out and not even locked the door.

He looked at our dismal expressions and Mom's watery eyes and stopped in his tracks. "Is he dead?"

"He's been dead from the neck up for years," Mom growled and pushed on down the hall.

Aunt Chloe hurried to catch up with her. "It's all right, Jannie," I heard her say as she put an arm around Mom.

Ben watched them, eyes popped open wide. Then he turned back to Keira and me. "How is he?"

That set Keira off crying again.

"Concussion and a broken arm," I said. "He feels good enough to fight with Mom."

"I guess he'll be okay then," Ben said, visibly relaxing. He gave Keir a hug, and she sniffed and wiped at her eyes.

I shook my head. "I'm not sure why she came. For a minute there, I thought . . ." I let the sentence die, unfinished. Better to keep my thoughts to myself than get anyone's hopes up.

"Don't think," Ben advised. He gave me a playful punch in the arm and rumpled Keira's hair, then strode on down the hall to clear out the room with a fresh breath of testosterone.

Keira turned to me. "I wonder what the bad news was."

I shrugged, playing dumb. "Who knows?"

"I wish there was something we could do," she fretted.

Hmmm. Maybe there was.

Later I'd look back on that pivotal moment and wonder what I was thinking, but my little brain baby seemed like a good idea at the time.

"Come on, girls," Aunt Chloe called, her head poking out from the elevator.

Keira ran down the hall and I followed, getting in after her. Even though I have to ride in them at work, I'm not fond of elevators. Standing in one of those things, squished between strangers, always makes me a little claustrophobic. There were only four of us in this one as it started for the ground floor, but Mom's black mood filled it nearly to the point of suffocation. New music was playing, and it grated on my nerves even more than Burl Ives had done when we came in.

It took me a moment to recognize what was playing because it was an instrumental rendition. Sick, I thought as a chorus of wind instruments whistled "Grandma Got Run Over by a Reindeer."

Mom was pathetically quiet on the way home. Once in the house Aunt Chloe instructed her to sit down. "I'll make you a cup of tea. You'll feel better."

"Nothing's going to make me feel better," Mom wailed. She looked practically suicidal.

This was not my mother. I felt like a three-year-old watching the end of the world.

"He's going to be okay," I ventured.

"I don't care if he's never okay." Mom slapped a sofa cushion for emphasis. "That stupid child can have him."

"I don't think they're together anymore," I said. "I'm betting that's why he was driving around town like a maniac."

Mom suddenly didn't look so suicidal. "How do you know that?"

I really didn't want to go into an explanation right then, not with Keira in the room, waiting for a juicy morsel of gossip about my nondate the way a baby bird waits for a worm. "I saw them together in a restaurant when I was out with James." *Saw it first hand and close up.* "It was all over."

Mom still wasn't smiling yet, but at least she had gone from hysterical to morose. She leaned back against the sofa cushions and shut her eyes. "This is not turning out to be a very good Christmas."

"It's not even Christmas yet," I said to her. "Things will get better."

Mom smiled on me. I saw gratitude and approval in her

eyes and knew I'd done the right thing in staying. By the time I got back to New York I might be a failure, but here in Christmas Present I was a success.

Aunt Chloe returned with Mom's tea, and Keira went to the kitchen to forage for food. Me, I slipped away to my bedroom to make an important call.

## Chapter Fifteen

"Dad?" I spoke into the phone receiver in hushed tones, like some movie spy reporting in to her contact.

"Hi, Princess." His voice had that muffled slur of a patient on drugs. "Thanks for coming to see me."

"I'm just glad you're okay. Is Ben still there with you?"

"He had to get back to the store."

That was too bad. If Ben had still been with Dad, he could have seconded my invitation. I'd have had a partner in crime and Mom's wrath would be lessened by half. Oh, well.

"Looks like I kind of screwed up your Christmas visit," Dad was saying.

I wondered which he was referring to, our disastrous double nondate or his car accident. "I'm just glad you're all right," I said. What if Dad's accident had been fatal? What if he'd been crippled for life? I found myself suddenly thankful for the small inconveniences I'd experienced during my homecoming. I'd take those over the alternative any day.

"Brittany left me." Dad sounded like a broken man. "For James," he added. "I'm sorry, Princess."

Here my dad's heart was breaking and he was feeling

sorry for me. What a hero. "Don't be," I said. "It was only our first date. Anyway, I got a free meal out of the deal," I added, trying to inject some humor into the conversation.

Dad just grunted. "And here I thought that James fella might be an okay guy."

"He probably is," I said, giving James the benefit of the doubt.

Dad sighed. "I wish I'd picked a different restaurant."

Like that would have made Brittany forever faithful. "If she was going to . . ." I caught myself in time, snipping off the words "dump you" from the end of the sentence. "If you and Brittany were going to break up, it was probably better to have it happen sooner than later."

"Better for who?" Dad retorted bitterly.

This conversation wasn't quite going like I'd planned. "Dad, how about coming over to the house for Christmas Day? You can get a free turkey dinner and we'll all sign your cast."

"Is this your mother's idea?" he asked.

"We all want you to come," I answered evasively. My heart was hammering as if the little drummer boy was banging on it. This would either work out wonderfully, with Mom and Dad turning sentimental and us all having a great time or it would blow nuclear.

*Don't go there,* I told myself. Deep down, my parents still loved each other. I was sure of it. And someone had to help them see that. Ben was busy with his band, and Keira was preoccupied with houses. That left me.

"I don't know," Dad said.

"You don't want you to be by yourself on Christmas Day," I urged.

"I'll see how I feel."

I couldn't blame him for hedging. He was probably still trying to recover from Mom's visit to the hospital. Still, I hoped he'd come.

"What time are you eating?" he asked suddenly.

I felt as excited as a kid on Christmas morning. "I think the usual time. Two."

"I'll try to be there."

"Try hard, Dad," I said. "I haven't given you your present yet." I'd gotten both him and Ben New York Mets hats, which I knew they'd love.

"Just seeing you has been a present."

Good old Dad. He sure knew how to make a daughter feel special. "Thanks, Dad. You're the best."

We said our good-byes and I hung up, confident in the decisions I'd made that day. That shows how much I knew. Boy, where's the Ghost of Christmas Future when you need him?

I was in the kitchen, heating water for a cup of instant cocoa, when the doorbell rang. Mom was in the tub, recovering from her visit to Dad with some bubble therapy, and Keira had gone off to get her nails done, so it looked like I was on door patrol.

I opened the door and there stood Gabe Knightly. He was wearing jeans and a suede jacket with an imitation lambskin collar. Mr. J. Crew. The man could have been a model. Really.

Model or not, I wished he'd stop coming over like this. It was just one more thing to stress me out.

He smiled at me and started to come in.

"Keira's gone," I said.

"I didn't come to see Keira. I came to take you out for a latte."

"I was just making cocoa," I said.

The microwave beeped, and I went to the kitchen. Of course, he followed me.

He upped the ante. "A latte and a Christmas scone at Swenson's Bakery."

Carol had the best bakery in the entire county, and Mrs.

Swenson's Christmas scones were the one thing I'd actually missed during my holiday avoidance years. I wavered.

Gabe could see me wavering. "Come on," he urged. "It will get you away from your family for a while."

"But it won't get me away from you."

My verbal bullet bounced right off him. "Yeah, but you don't really want to get away from me."

"You're delusional," I said.

He took a step closer. His aftershave didn't mix well with the chemicals in my brain.

"Okay," I said. Of course I only said yes because my brain was scrambled. And because I really wanted a scone from the bakery.

I got my coat, then called through Mom's bathroom door that I was going out with Gabe.

"For lunch?"

"No. We're just going out for scones."

"Well, bring him back for lunch," she called.

I was glad he was nowhere within hearing distance. "See you later," I said, making no promises.

Outside, the air had a Christmas nip, but I wasn't feeling it. Getting around Gabe Knightly had a way of overheating me.

The car was warm and smelled like evergreens. A soft jazz version of "We Three Kings" serenaded us as we pulled away from the curb. I felt nervous and self-conscious. The little drummer boy started banging around in my chest again, and I was suddenly roasting. I pulled off my coat.

"I guess you'll be with your family on Christmas," I said, trying to make conversation.

"For Christmas Eve. Then we'll go to the service."

As I nodded politely, I flashed back to a Christmas Eve a few years ago and saw myself sitting with Gabe and his family in a candlelit church. Everything had felt so right, so perfect. I'd sat in that church pew and envisioned Gabe and me up at the altar someday, exchanging vows. He'd squeezed my hand and smiled at me as though he'd been reading my thoughts.

I jerked myself back to the present with a stern command to quit digging up these Gabe Knightly Kodak moments.

"Your mom tells me all the Hartwells are going to be at the service this year," Gabe said.

"We might not get Dad."

"What, is he on strike for more candy canes?"

"He's in the hospital."

Gabe almost veered off the road. "What?"

"Hey, watch it. I don't want to join him."

"What happened?"

"He was in a car accident, broke his arm, got a concussion."

Gabe shook his head. "Bad news. How'd it happen?"

"He took a corner too fast in his Jag."

"I always thought your dad was a pretty good driver," Gabe mused.

"Not when he's mad."

Gabe cocked an eyebrow.

I shrugged. "His girlfriend broke up with him."

Gabe sighed. "That's tough. I know how he feels."

You didn't have to be an Einstein to figure out what he was hinting at. I frowned. "I knew I should have stayed home."

"Naw, you shouldn't have," he said. He smiled at me. "You'll be glad you came. It'll feel like old times."

It was already starting to. We'd hung out a lot at the bakery, eating freshly made cookies and slurping Italian sodas. That was back in the days when I thought my life would be a never-ending feast of carbs and Gabe Knightly. I was just a kid then. What did I know?

"Come on, Andie, admit it," Gabe prodded. "You've missed me."

"Just like you've missed me," I said and gave him an I-don't-care smile.

He didn't smile back. "I have missed you. How come you never returned my calls?"

He had left messages for me in New York a couple of times, but what would have been the point in calling him back? I wasn't planning on coming home.

I shrugged. "My life in New York is . . ."

He cut me off. "Yeah, yeah, I know. Busy."

"Well, it is."

He pulled up in front of the bakery. It was starting to snow again—big, heavy flakes, too wet to stick but still pretty. I'd barely been in Carol and we'd already had more snow than I could remember in years. Even the weather was trying to lure me into a nostalgic numbness.

He reached over to the back seat and grabbed a bag. "Stay put," he ordered, then got out and went around and opened the door for me, something he'd never done when we were going together.

I gathered my coat and got out, looking at him in shock. "Hey, I'm impressed. When did you become a gentleman?"

"Since I grew up. It does happen you know. People change."

"You can usually see when people change," I shot at him.

"You haven't been around to see," he fired back and pushed the door shut. "And you've been walking around with your eyes closed ever since you got home."

"Oh, yeah?"

"Yeah."

I scowled at him. "Open the car door."

"I just did, a minute ago when you got out."

"Open it again. I'm getting in. I want to go home."

"I can see you've changed," he said as he jerked the door wide. "Same old Andie. When the going gets rough, run away."

That last remark made me so steaming hot mad, the glare

I leveled at him should have lasered him into oblivion. I plopped onto the seat and he gave the door a violent shove, probably wishing it was me. Then he stomped around and climbed back in behind the steering wheel, dropping the bag on the seat between us.

Part of me wanted to know what was in that bag, but of course I didn't ask. I crossed my arms over my chest and started counting the minutes till we'd be back home and I could get out of this car and away from Gabe.

But instead of starting the car, he turned and looked at me. "What happened to us, anyway? How did we go from being crazy-in-love teenagers to bickering adults?"

"Do I need to draw you a map?"

It suddenly struck me how like my parents we were acting. No, I corrected myself, we were nothing like my parents. They'd been married. At least Gabe and I had never done that.

"Maybe you do need to draw me a map," he said softly.

"Okay, fine," I snapped. "We broke up."

"You broke up," he corrected.

"It was either break up or get knocked up."

He looked wounded. "I would never have done that to you. I was always prepared."

What a Boy Scout. "And always pushing. You knew I wasn't ready, but you kept pushing anyway."

He sighed and looked out the window. "I know. What can I say? I was young and dumb and bananas over you. I couldn't get enough of you."

"Which is why you went running off to the prom with Ashleigh Horne."

He frowned. "I swear, Andie, there are elephants with shorter memories than you. How long ago did that happen? And, anyway, what was I supposed to do after you dumped me, go shoot myself? Sit around in sackcloth and ashes? Camp out on your front porch for months? Call you and beg you to take me back?"

"That last option would have been nice."

"Would you have?"

I looked out the window. The snowdrops were flying into the windshield, knocking themselves out and doing a wet slide down the glass. "I don't know," I said truthfully. "Probably not. I was scared."

"Of me?" He sounded incredulous. I don't know how he looked because I wasn't watching him. I was staring at those snowflakes, hurling themselves against the windshield.

"No. Of myself." There was a moment of insight. "I was afraid if I stayed with you I'd blow it and wind up pregnant at eighteen."

"If you did I would have married you. You had to know that."

"Married or not, I didn't want to risk having a kid that young. I didn't want to ruin my life."

I remembered the pile of little shoes in one of those houses we'd looked at. Would I have been so unhappy if my life had played out that way?

Gabe started the engine and moved the car into the street. "Well, you didn't. Instead you just ruined mine."

I felt like he'd slapped me. What a thing to say! And completely untrue. He'd gotten along just fine without me. Just fine. A sneaky little thought suggested maybe that had something to do with why I was so irritated with him now, but I pushed it away.

I looked at him, incensed. "That is such an unfair thing to say, especially since you dated half the women in Carol."

"Yeah, I did," he said. "But they weren't you. And that's why you're here in my car right now. I tried to find a substitute for you. I can't." He took his eyes off the road long enough to give me a look filled with such honesty and yearning it melted my bones.

I blinked. What kind of a sneaky, underhanded, romantic thing was that to say? "Am I really supposed to believe that?" I said in disgust. I hoped not. I had just gotten a life. I wasn't ready to tip it upside down, especially not for Gabe Knightly, the Casanova of Carol.

He shrugged. "Did you ever ask your sister why we broke up?"

"What's the point? It's all water under the bridge now."

"Ask her," he said. He turned on the radio and started surfing the channels.

Burl Ives came on. "Oh, no. Not him. I can't take it anymore." I reached over and turned it off.

So we drove home in silence. I looked out the window and asked myself what I was doing here in this car, in this town even. I had to have been insane to come back. The snow was already turning to drizzle, mocking my secret hope for a white Christmas. I don't know what I'd been thinking, anyway, since it almost never snows in Carol.

We pulled up in front of the house. "Stay put," Gabe ordered. He grabbed the mystery bag, then went around and opened the passenger door.

I got out and he helped me pull my coat back on. Then he pressed the bag into my hand. "Merry Christmas," he said softly, and before I could say anything, he grabbed me, pulled me to him, and kissed me. We stood there for a moment in the freezing rain, our lips superglued together and me zinging like crazy. I could almost hear bells.

Then he pulled away very slowly and looked down at me. "They say you can't go back, but I don't believe it. I think you *can* go back and make it better."

I gave a cynical snort and stepped away. "Which one of us are you trying to fool?"

"We're not seventeen anymore. People change. People grow up."

"And they grow apart," I added. Not that you would have noticed it with that kiss.

"Sometimes. Sometimes they're closer than they think. People mature. Love can too."

I thought of my parents bickering in the hospital. "Sometimes it simply dies."

Gabe's smile was mocking. "How dead did you feel just now?"

I didn't answer the question. I was still vibrating from head to toe, and the mushy, sentimental part of me was urging me to go ahead, tell him that another kiss like that could convince me I wanted to come back home.

Instead I said, "Merry Christmas, Gabe." Then I turned and ran for the house.

"You can run but you can't hide," he called after me, and that made me run all the faster.

Halfway across the lawn I slipped on the grass and went down in a very unsophisticated heap.

"Don't break my present," he called.

Ignoring him, I picked myself up and walked the rest of the way with as much dignity as I could manage.

By the time I got to the front door I realized the reason I had slipped. The Harrises' schnauzer, Fritz, had obviously left a present (the poor dog wouldn't dare do anything to wreck Mr. Harris' perfect lawn) and I'd found it. Oh, that had to be symbolic.

I removed my shoes at the front porch, taking care not to look back to where I knew Gabe was still standing by his car, probably snickering. Then I went inside.

I met Mom as I was on the way to my bedroom. She was coming down the hall in her favorite pink sweats.

"Did you forget something?" she asked.

"Just my sanity," I muttered.

She looked confused. "Where's Gabe?"

"He had to go. It's just us girls."

"Another short date. This is becoming a very strange habit." She saw my don't-go-there expression and cleared her throat. "Well, then. I've got corn chowder all thawed and ready to heat. You hungry?"

It seemed like all I'd been doing since I came home was eating. But it was now well into lunch time, and corn chowder was one of my favorites. Mom had pulled out all the stops for my visit.

"Sure," I said.

"Meet you in the kitchen," she said and kept on going.

Curiosity was burning a hole in me. As soon as I was in my room, I opened the bag. Inside I found a white gift box wrapped with red ribbon. I took it out, pulled off the ribbon, and removed the lid.

*A snow globe.* I love snow globes, always have. I lifted this one out and examined it. An angel stood inside it. She was holding a harp and her eyes were turned heavenward. I shook the globe, and a flurry of glittery snow swirled around her. It was also a music box. I turned the key and "Silent Night" began to play. *All is calm, all is bright.*

There was a tiny gift card inside the box, and on it Gabe had simply written "Think of Me."

I sat on the bed holding the snow globe and did just that. And I found myself wishing we had gone into the bakery. People change, Gabe had said. He'd obviously become a deep thinker since our high-school days.

Actually, he did seem different. Oh, he was still the same fun-loving, hunkalicious Gabe I'd known in high school, but I had to admit, he'd added some layers to his personality. So maybe he had changed. Maybe I was keeping him stuck like I remembered him in high school.

I looked at the little angel, forever frozen with her harp in her hand. Had I changed? For the better? I wasn't sure I wanted to look too closely for an answer. I put the globe on my dresser then went to join Mom in the kitchen, hoping all the way she wouldn't pump me about Gabe.

I hoped in vain. "What happened with you and Gabe?" she asked the minute my feet hit the vinyl.

I shrugged. "We changed our minds about going out."

"Did we?"

Nothing like a nice bowl of corn chowder sprinkled with sarcasm.

"Mom," I warned.

"Look, I know you were young when you broke up," she said, "but now you're older, maybe even wiser."

"What's that supposed to mean?"

I shouldn't have asked. She proceeded to tell me. "Gabe's the sweetest man in Carol. He's president of the Carol Rotary—a sure sign of success—and he likes your family. That's not always easy to find in a man," she added pointing her wooden spoon at me for emphasis.

*You could say that again,* I thought, especially in the case of my family.

"And he's generous," Mom continued. "I know of at least two occasions where he's given up his real estate commission to help a struggling family get into a house."

Saint Gabe. "Well, then. We should get back together. That way he can give up his commission and get Keira into her dream house," I cracked.

Mom frowned at me. "You ought to give him a chance."

"There are plenty of sweet men in New York too," I told her.

He frown got bigger. "Do you really want to spend your whole life in New York, far from your family and friends?"

No, Timbuktu might be a wiser choice. Farther away. "He dated my sister, for crying out loud."

"Not for long. The one he's always wanted was you. Anyone can see that."

"Mom, could we drop it? You're going to spoil my appetite, and I love your corn chowder."

Mom gave the chowder a stir and sighed heavily. It was her discouraged-mother sigh, one of many tricks in her arsenal of manipulation. "You're making a big mistake."

I came up next to her and sniffed the aroma from the pot. "I would think you'd tell me not to be in a hurry. Look at you and Dad."

She stiffened. "That was different. We got married way too young."

"Well, I'm too young too."

"I didn't say you had to get married tomorrow. I just said you should give Gabe a chance." She began singing to the tune of her favorite John Lennon song, "All I am saying is give Gabe a chance."

She finished with a playful nudge, and I rolled my eyes.

The front door opened. "I'm home," Keira called.

"Mom, let's drop it. Now," I said.

She shrugged and turned her attention back to the chowder.

Keira came into the kitchen and sniffed. "Oh, yuck. Corn chowder. Is there anything else to eat?"

"Leftovers," Mom said.

Keira made a face. "I think I'll run away from home, then come back for a visit. Maybe I'll get all my favorite food then."

"Don't be small, dear," Mom said, not the least ruffled.

We had just settled in with our meal, Mom and me with our corn chowder, Keira with tomato soup, when the doorbell rang.

"I'll get it," Keira said and jumped up. "It's probably Spencer."

But it wasn't Spencer. It was Mr. Winkler from across the

street. "Just thought I'd see how you're doing over here. Looks like they did a good job of replacing the window."

"That was so sweet of you to drop by," Mom told him. "Would you like some corn chowder?"

"It smells great. Don't mind if I do."

With Mr. Winkler at the table, we got a whole new dynamic. Keira sat smirking while Mom tried not to flirt in front of her. I sat there in disapproving silence. Here my father was lying in the hospital and Mom was flexing her flirting muscles with our bow-legged neighbor. Disgusting.

"Bill, I don't know what we'd have done without you the other day," Mom said.

He put on one of those fake modest looks. "Oh, it was nothing. Glad to help." He pointed his spoon at his empty bowl. "That was darned good, Janelle."

"Would you like some more?"

What was she thinking? Single men were like stray dogs. Once you fed them they never left.

"Don't mind if I do," said Mr. Winkler.

I normally don't do things like this. I mean, I'm a middle child, a peacemaker. Stirring up trouble is not my specialty. But I felt overcome by a need to protect Mom from herself.

"It was good timing that you came over, Mr. Winkler," I said. "Mom's had a pretty upsetting day."

I could almost see Mr. Winkler's ears perk up at the thought of being able to ride to Mom's rescue again. "Yeah?"

"Our dad's in the hospital." *She's upset over my dad. Get the connection?*

Mr. Winkler's eyebrows shot up. "The hospital! What happened?"

"He tried to kill himself," Keira said. "Could you pass me the French bread, please?"

Mr. Winkler gaped at her like she was nuts as he passed her the plate.

He looked to Mom. "Depressed, was he?"

"No, he was stupid. He got drunk and drove his car into a tree."

"Whoa, that's not good," said Mr. Winkler, the new king of understatement.

"He's got a broken arm and a concussion," Mom said. "He'll be fine. And I'm not upset," she added, glaring at me. My comment had gone right over Mr. Winkler's head, but Mom had definitely gotten the connection.

"Well, it was pretty upsetting seeing him lying there in that hospital bed," I said innocently.

"You went to see him?" Mr. Winkler made it sound like she'd just committed a crime.

She set his bowl in front of him. "I took the girls."

Mr. Winkler looked at her suspiciously.

"He is my ex, Bill. He called here wanting us to come see him."

"My ex went to the hospital with appendicitis. I repainted the house," said Mr. Winkler. He spooned chowder into his mouth and chewed it thoughtfully.

Keira and I exchanged looks. I turned back to see Mom giving me one of those one-more-word-and-you-die looks. I don't know what her problem was. I was only protecting her from herself. The last thing she needed was to start dating Mr. Winkler. He didn't have a funny bone in his body that I could see. He and Mom had nothing in common except loneliness.

He slurped down the last of his chowder and Mom asked, "How about some coffee, Bill?"

"I could go for a cup."

If you asked me, he could go. Period. No one asked me, though.

Mom got Wee Willie some coffee, then they retreated to the living room to look at the tree and probably talk about window repair.

"What a snore," Keira said as soon as they were gone.

I shook my head. "I don't know why she's encouraging him."

"I do. She wants to make sure she's still got it and someone wants it." Keira shook her head in disgust. "I'm not sure Winkler counts as a someone, though. It's weird who people will date."

I thought of her and Gabe. *Ask your sister why we broke up.*

"Yeah, it is," I said slowly. "Take you and Gabe, for instance."

Keira looked at me warily. "You're not going to drag that out, are you?"

"So, why did you date him? Some kind of sibling rivalry thing?"

Keira rolled her eyes. "Oh, please."

"Then why?"

"Because he happens to be a nice guy and the hottest one in Carol. Next to Spencer, of course," she quickly corrected herself.

"And because he was mine," I said. Suddenly I was as irritated as if it all just happened yesterday.

"He wasn't yours at the time. Geez, Andie, give it a rest."

"Why did you break up?" I demanded.

"Ask Gabe if you want to know," she said in a surly voice.

"He said to ask you. I know why you dated him, just to get back at me because that dweeb we met at the lake the summer before went for me instead of you."

"That's not true!" Keira cried, stung.

"It was really a petty thing to do, Keir," I said. I felt stuffed with emotion. I picked up my bowl and went to the sink. "I never deliberately dated someone to hurt you."

"Well, neither did I," she said and followed me. She set her bowl in the sink and I washed it and put it in the dishwasher along with mine.

"Right."

"And I thought you didn't care about him anymore."

"I didn't. I don't."

"Then why are you bringing this up?"

I turned and faced her. "Because I need to know. I'm sick of Gabe's man of mystery game and I want to know why you guys broke up."

She scowled. "Okay, fine. If you must know, I'll tell you. I broke up with him because I didn't need to be Shadow Girl."

"What's that supposed to mean?"

"What do you think it means? I didn't want to live in your shadow. That Christmas you came home when Gabe and I were dating? Well, guess whose name he said when he kissed me. I'll give you a hint. It wasn't Rumplestiltskin."

My jaw came unhinged. I had to be hearing wrong. "What?"

"Oh, don't play dumb. He kissed me and said your name. There, are you happy now?"

## Chapter Sixteen

I stared at my sister. I had to have heard wrong. "He what?"

"He's always wanted you. Why do you think he's still single?"

Her question threw me. I concentrated on shutting the dishwasher. "He's been busy with his career, just like me." *But he kissed my sister and said my name.* The thought sent a little wave of excitement rolling over me. I told myself to stop being so silly, but I could tell by my zippy heartbeat that I wasn't listening to me.

"A hunk like Gabe Knightly doesn't stay single just because he's building a career," Keira continued. "He hasn't had a steady relationship since you guys broke up. And I can see why," she added in a mutter. "Who wants to be called by some other woman's name when she's getting kissed? By the way, if you ever tell that to anyone I'll kill you."

I looked out the kitchen window at the drizzling rain, trying to make sense of what my sister was saying. It put Gabe's serial dating in a whole new light. If she was right.

"Oh, that's ridiculous," I decided, and commanded my heart to slow down.

"Well, you tell me why he hasn't gotten serious with anyone. And tell me why he keeps hanging around here, even when we're not looking at houses."

"So, whose idea was the team house hunting?"

Keira shrugged. "I told him you were coming home for Christmas and he suggested you might like to come house hunting with us."

"So, you hatched that little plan between the two of you. Is that what you're saying?"

"Well," she hedged.

"So much for the really wanting me to come with you line," I said in disgust.

"I did."

"You just wanted to play matchmaker."

"So, what's wrong with that?" She looked earnestly at me. "Gabe really is a sweet guy. Whatever you broke up over in high school, it was a long time ago. You should give him another chance."

I suddenly didn't know what to think. Gabe had never settled into a permanent relationship with anyone. Neither had I. And every time I saw him my estrogen level spiked.

Still. "What's the point? I'm in New York, he's out here."

"Lots of people have bicoastal relationships."

She had a point there.

"Although I don't know how they manage."

She had a point there too.

"It's hard enough to have a good relationship on the same coast, in the same town."

I suddenly got the impression we weren't talking about me and Gabe anymore. And that was a red-flag statement if ever I heard one. Not that I'm an expert on relationships, but counseling Camilla through three breakups in one year had given me some insight.

I turned to look at Keira. "Is everything okay with you and Spencer?"

She gave a little shake of the head. "Oh, yeah."

Interesting. Mismatched words and body language. "Yeah?" I pushed.

"Well, except for the fact that he refuses to make an offer on the one house I really want." She frowned. "That man can be so stubborn. And selfish."

Uh-oh. This didn't bode well for the new year. "Are you sure you guys are a match?" I asked.

"Of course we are. We like the same kind of music, the same kind of movies."

"And you have the same philosophy of life, the same goals for the future," I suggested.

"Of course we have the same goals. We're going to get married and get a house. If Spencer will let go of his wallet," she added. "He's so tight with money. I mean, what's he saving it for, his old age?"

"Possibly." My sister was a high-maintenance woman. Spencer was going to have a hard time maintaining her.

They obviously had different philosophies when it came to money. There might be all kinds of other areas where they weren't compatible. She really hadn't been going out with him all that long. Maybe they should slow down.

I laid a hand on her arm. "You don't have to marry him, you know."

She looked at me like I was nuts. "Why wouldn't I?"

"Because maybe you guys aren't really a match."

"Of course we are. I can't believe you just said that."

I couldn't either, but since I had I forced myself to plunge on. "You don't want to end up like Mom and Dad do you? If you're having any doubts you should slow down."

"I'm not having any doubts."

She didn't need to. I was having them for her. "It sounds to me like you are."

"Then I guess you need to get your hearing checked. Not all of us are paranoid when it comes to men, you know." She moved out of touching range. "Geez, Andie. I'm beginning to wonder why we all wanted you to come home for Christmas. You're a real pain," she added as a parting shot, then left me alone in the kitchen.

I grabbed a mug from the cupboard and filled it with water. "I am not the pain," I muttered as I stuck it in the microwave. "That definition would go to everyone around me."

Boy, if that wasn't the truth. My dad was trying to mow down trees with his sports car, Gabe was taking me out then bringing me home before we even had a date . . . or whatever that little car ride had been. My sister was passing out insults like candy canes. What was I doing here? I'd jumped off my career track for this?

The microwave beeped at me and I took out the mug and dunked a tea bag in it. Sugar plum tea. Sugar plum fairies. Visions of sugar plums. Ha! I should be so lucky. The only visions that would dance through my head tonight would be those of me and Gabe squabbling in front of his car, or Keira flouncing out of the kitchen after telling me how so not worth a plane ticket I was. *Merry Christmas, Andie.*

I took my cup of tea and went to my room to read. I was well into my mystery novel now, and at the moment reading about mayhem and dead bodies looked a whole lot better than dealing with my family. Whoever said truth is stranger than fiction must have plucked that pearl of wisdom from a branch of the Hartwell family tree.

Hang in there, I told myself, it's almost Christmas. Then you'll have done your family duty thing and you can leave, go back to NYC, and get your life back.

Spencer joined the family for dinner that night, giving me a chance to carefully observe him and Keira. They were not at their best. She was pouting over the house stalemate, and Spencer was dealing with it by ignoring her.

"Great pot roast, Janelle," he said to Mom.

It seemed funny to hear someone my age calling my mother by her first name. All of our friends had and still did call her Mrs. H. Spencer didn't quite strike me as a Mrs. H. kind of guy, though. And maybe he felt funny calling her Mom when he and Keira weren't married yet.

"Thank you, Spencer," Mom said. "How about some more potatoes?"

"Sure," he said, and took the bowl of mashed spuds.

Keira looked at him like a disapproving personal trainer. "Seconds on carbs? I thought you were trying to cut back."

Spencer did have a bit of belly hanging over his belt. Obviously, Keira hadn't gotten him to the gym yet.

"I don't want to insult your mother's cooking," he said and piled a mountain of mashed potatoes on his plate.

Keira looked on in disgust.

Mom, CEO of Man Haters, Inc., rushed to Spencer's defense. "Potatoes are good for you. They're high in potassium."

"That's the skins," Keira said, and there's no skin in these."

Mom shrugged. "I think these modern health experts are a little wacko. People have been eating potatoes for centuries."

"You're absolutely right, Janelle," said Spencer, and

plopped on another helping. "Anyway, it's the holidays." He patted his stomach. "I'll take this off in January."

"Disgusting how men can do that," Mom said.

"Well, I hope so," Keira told him. "You want to be able to fit in your tux."

He gave her a condescending smile. "That's a few months away, so I don't think it's going to be a problem."

Ah, what a pair of lovebirds.

"So, Spencer, are we going to see you Christmas day?" I asked.

"Oh, yeah. I'll spend Christmas Eve with my folks. Then I'll come here Christmas Day so Keira can count my carbs," he added.

"Cute," she said sourly.

I could already envision a real merry Christmas if Keira and Spencer didn't get this house thing resolved tonight. There we'd be, dodging bullets as we tried to pull our presents out from under the tree.

After dinner the happy couple left to drive around and look at Christmas lights.

"How did they ever get together?" I said to Mom.

She shrugged. "Hormones. It happens to the best of us."

Another shining testimonial for the holy state of matrimony.

I passed on Mom's offer of *First Wives Club* on DVD and went back to my book.

Christmas Eve was a quiet day, with no trauma, no scenes. As I helped Mom make stuffing and cranberry salad and ambrosia for our holiday feast the following day, I couldn't help feeling like someone in a Florida mobile home at hurricane season, just waiting for the wind to start whipping up. The calm before the storm.

I decided I was being paranoid. Even my family could only wreak so much havoc. Between Ben's window stunt followed by his street-sweeping tree incident, not to mention Dad's car crash, surely we'd sucked all the insanity out of the air that we possibly could. Still, I couldn't shake that feeling.

At 5, Keira went to pick up Grandma, who was joining us for dinner, then coming to the Christmas Eve service. Aunt Chloe blew in shortly after Keira took off.

I took one look at her and that uneasy feeling grew stronger. "How do I look?" she asked.

She looked scary. She had paired a flared Christmas red knit dress that half a dozen elves could camp under with clashing blood red boots. Even I, who was not an artist, understood how the color palette worked. Had my aunt been struck with blindness when she went into her closet? No, I decided. Madness. Only a crazy person would wear a hat like that in public.

Mom was staring at her in horror. "What is that on your head?"

Good question. I'd never seen anything like it, not even in a costume shop. The hat was a high, green felted cone with little plastic pears nestled in corsages of gold netting and feathers. A huge, white bird with a tail that swooped down to her shoulders sat halfway up it.

The thought of being seen in public with her made me feel queasy. If I ran into someone I knew how could I introduce her? *This is my aunt. She's adopted.*

"It's an original design," said Aunt Chloe. "I made this hat specially for Christmas."

"It looks like you made it for Halloween," said Mom, unafraid to speak what was on everyone's mind.

Aunt Chloe regarded her with disgust. "Really, Jannie, you have no imagination."

"I have plenty of imagination, and I'm already imagining what people will say when they see you in that thing."

"They'll say, 'Now, there's a woman who understands Christmas,'" Aunt Chloe retorted. "This hat is symbolic."

"Of what? A bad dream?"

Aunt Chloe raised her chin, making the bird wobble precariously. "This hat represents the Twelve Days of Christmas."

Mom stared at her.

"You know, a partridge in a pear tree."

"Heaven help us," Mom said and turned back toward the kitchen.

Aunt Chloe's smile suddenly lost its mooring and slipped away. She didn't say anything, but the look she gave me begged for approval.

What could I do? I came over and hugged her. "You look very festive."

She smiled at me. "Thank you, sweetie. I'm glad someone in this family understands art."

"Well, I don't know about that," I said.

"I just want to make a good impression on Ben's friends," she told me.

*You'll make an impression,* I thought, and a fresh dread crept over me. But a small voice seemed to whisper, "Look how much trouble she's gone to." Seeing things in that light how could I not love the bird? Well, okay, not the bird. The hat was still horrible. But I loved my aunt for her efforts to support Ben.

"It looks like you're balancing the leaning tower of Pisa on your head," Mom said from the kitchen. "It will probably fall off in the middle of the service and you'll embarrass Andie."

Finally, after all these years, someone in my family was acknowledging the Hartwell embarrassment factor? I could hardly believe my ears.

"I have twenty bobby pins holding this hat on," Aunt Chloe announced. "It's not going any place. And I'm certainly not going to embarrass Andie." She turned to me for approval. "Am I?"

Oh, boy. What to say? Honesty might get the hat off her head, but then her feelings would be hurt. I remembered the toxic spill I'd created in my insanity induced honesty over Mom's business and suddenly couldn't find my voice.

Mom saved me by speaking first. "Oh, do what you want. You will, anyway. The artichoke dip's out. Come try it."

The mention of food distracted Aunt Chloe and, with relief, I followed her out to the kitchen for a sample of dip.

We were setting out the crab salad and French bread, our traditional Christmas Eve fare, when Keira arrived with Gram. Gram stopped at the dining room table on her way to the kitchen like a general making an inspection.

Mom already had it set for Christmas with her good china and crystal. There was one extra setting for Wee Willie, who Mom claimed was a Christmas orphan this year, but no place setting for Dad yet. This was because Mom still didn't know he was coming. I had decided to wait until the last minute to give her the good news. You know, surprise her. (Okay, I admit it, I was a complete coward and I was procrastinating.)

"I'm glad to see you didn't break tradition," Gram said, giving a nod of approval to the presence of the centerpiece she had made forty years ago. The stuffed Santa going down a cardboard chimney was awfully cute, but every year he got more worn, and his chimney looked ratty and ready to crumble. It was probably time for this centerpiece to retire.

"I put him out this year for Andie," Mom said, "but next

year he gets exiled to the North Pole. I'm going to try that cylinder vase with the cranberries and floating candles."

"Cranberries and floating candles can't compete with tradition," Gram said. "I'll take Santa home tomorrow and give him a facelift."

I knew Mom wanted to say, "Take him home and keep him," but there are some things you just don't say to your mother.

Gram had entered the kitchen now. Aunt Chloe's hat stopped her in her tracks. "Are you wearing that thing on your head to the service?"

And that started the great hat controversy again, which raged until Ben walked through the door.

"All right, enough fashion discussion," Mom said as she set a veggie platter on the kitchen table. "Let's eat."

We settled around the table and dug in. Mom started to pour a healthy slug of eggnog for Ben, but he said, "No milk, Mom. Not when I'm singing."

"I can hardly wait to hear you," said Gram. "What are you singing?"

" 'O, Holy Night.' "

"Oh, I always loved that song, Gram said.

She cleared her throat and started to sing in an off-key, wavery voice. We, her fellow diners, began to squirm in our chairs. Well, all except Aunt Chloe, who closed her eyes and smiled.

Gram came to the chorus and launched into her crescendo. As she moved for a high note, somewhere outside a dog began howling. I moved my hand away from my crystal goblet.

Keira shot me a can-you-believe-this look, and Mom sat in her chair with her lips pursed in daughterly disgust. Aunt Chloe was now swaying to the song as if to some invisible beat, the partridge on her head swaying too, as he clung to his precarious perch.

Gram finally hit her high note. Nothing on the table shattered, although I feared for my eardrums.

At last she wound to a soft finish. Aunt Chloe burst into thunderous applause and we followed suit with a polite but short round of clapping.

"That was very dramatic, Mom," said Aunt Chloe.

"You get your musical talent from me," Gram informed Ben with a prim smile.

He just nodded.

I hoped Gram wouldn't get carried away by any sudden urges to join him when he sang at church. That on top of Aunt Chloe's hat would make a double whammy the members might never recover from.

I passed when Mom pulled out Spritz cookies and her home made almond roca. Gram's warmup for the big event had started my stomach turning somersaults.

Ben checked his watch. "We'd better get going."

"All right," said Mom, pushing away from the table. She picked up a couple of dessert plates. "Let's just load the last of these dishes."

With four women on K.P., the kitchen was set to rights in record time.

"Andie and Keir can come with me in my truck," Ben offered as we put on our coats.

"I hope you cleaned it since we were in it last," Keira said.

"Yeah, right. And I put a vase of flowers on the dash."

"We're right behind you," Mom said as we went out the door.

"Thanks for the warning," Ben joked. We walked toward the truck and he asked softly, "What's with that thing on Aunt Chloe's head?"

"She made it specially for tonight," I said.

Ben rolled his eyes. "Lucky us."

"Well, I'm not sitting next to her," said Keira.

"We'll stick her between Mom and Andie," Ben said.

"Oh, thanks. Why me?"

"I have to sing," Ben reminded me.

The church foyer was packed with people when we arrived. Some remembered me from when I'd hung around in high school and stopped to say hello. Most of them cast discreet glances at Aunt Chloe's hat, then looked quickly away, as if she had a horrible but fascinating disfigurement.

Aunt Chloe was oblivious, happily chatting with one and all and feeling right at home. That was a good thing, I told myself. It was nice someone was feeling comfortable.

"Andie!" cried Mrs. Bailey, coming up to me, arms outstretched. She gathered me into a hug. "I thought I saw you the other day."

"Hi, Mrs. Bailey," I said, and hugged her back, thankful she didn't mention me being in the truck with the dog-eating tree that almost took out her cockapoo.

"Your mother tells me you're very successful in New York so I suppose we'll never get you back to Carol," she said.

*Not as long as I'm breathing.* "I do like New York."

"Well, I hope you'll have time to stop by for a cup of tea before you leave."

"Absolutely." I could always make time for a sane person.

Right before we entered the sanctuary a skinny, stooped man with a beaky nose and a balding head sidled up to Aunt Chloe. "Hello, there. I haven't seen you here before."

The way my aunt always dressed, he'd have remembered.

"I'm Oscar Johnson," he said and shook her hand.

"I'm Chloe Percy. My nephew here is singing tonight."

Oscar nodded approvingly at Ben, then returned his attention to my aunt. "I'm a widower."

"Really?" The sudden glint in my aunt's eye made her

look like a woman who had just discovered a department store clearance rack.

"Let's get a seat," Ben said and started to herd us toward the sanctuary.

"Nice meeting you, Oscar," Aunt Chloe said and gave the old guy a little finger wave.

He stood straighter and waved back.

"You're shameless," I teased.

"Yes, and proud of it."

Teenagers had been stationed at the doors to the sanctuary, and were giving out candles which would get lit at some point in the service. "Maybe someone will set Aunt Chloe's hat on fire," Ben whispered to me as we walked in.

"Cute," I whispered back and wished I'd had the nerve to set it on fire before we left the house.

We filed into a pew and sat.

I did a quick check on the other women in my family. Gram was sitting serenely with her hands folded in her lap as if she'd done this all her life. Maybe she had and I never realized it. It dawned on me that there was much I didn't know about my grandmother. Sometime after I hit puberty, she got pushed to the sidelines, an extra in the play about the life of Andie. I'd never even thought to ask her if she missed Grandpa.

I vowed to change my wicked ways and be a better granddaughter. I could accomplish that even from New York, I decided. I'd send her lots of cards. No phone calls, though. She'd just pump me about my love life and remind me that my eggs were aging.

Keira was busy checking out the other worshippers, especially the good-looking male ones. Yes, here was a woman ready to get married. Mom was studying the candle in her hands like an actress getting into her part. She and Dad had never been big on church. I wondered if Gram had made her go when she was a kid.

Aunt Chloe was looking around her raptly. "Everything is so lovely," she whispered to me. "Someone here has wonderful artistic sensibilities."

The sanctuary did, indeed, look gorgeous. Cedar swags hung along the walls from big gold bows and filled the air with fragrance. Pink, purple, and white candles flickered inside an Advent wreath on the altar up at the front. An arrangement of pillar candles nestled in greens, glowed softly on the piano on stage.

I caught sight of Gabe and his family seated on the other side of the room. He turned his head as if he'd felt me looking at him, and smiled at me.

Gabe Knightly, secret torch bearer. Not wanting to encourage him or myself, I flashed him a quick smile, then looked away. But just because I'd moved my gaze didn't mean I wasn't still seeing him. I wondered what my life would have been like if I'd stayed here in Carol. Maybe Gabe and I would have worked things out and gotten married. Maybe we'd be sitting in a pew with two little kids wedged between us.

The last of the worshippers filed in and the service began with everyone singing "Oh, Come All Ye Faithful." Gram's own unique rendition of the song echoed out over the congregation, torturing every ear in the place. We finished the final chorus before Gram, who made sure she had the last word. Her voice hung on past the most determined singer, even past the musicians, who were trying to drown her out with an extended finale. She finally let go of the note, which also put an end to the only other sound remaining in the church: the howl of some neighborhood dog that floated in to us through the stained glass windows.

I closed my eyes as a couple of middle-schoolers in the row in back of us snickered.

It suddenly felt very hot. I looked down at my hand to see if the candle I was holding had melted yet. Amazingly, it hadn't. I sure wanted to.

We sang a couple more songs, then listened to a short sermon. And then came the main attraction, as least as far as the Hartwells were concerned: Ben's solo.

He walked up to the piano and stood behind the accompanist. I noticed he was limping slightly. He had probably reinjured his leg that night we were out playing in the snow, but if he did I knew he wouldn't admit it to any of us, especially Mom, who would be eager to say, "I told you so."

I sneaked a look her direction. She was doing the doting mother smile. Tonight Ben could do no wrong.

The accompanist started to play, and soft piano notes drifted out over the congregation like snowflakes. Ben began to sing. The boy can sing, and tonight he sounded like an angel.

As Ben sang, the lights dimmed and ushers with long taper candles moved down the aisles, lighting the candles of the persons on the end of each pew. Those persons held their candles to the person next to them, spreading the tiny, dancing dots of light throughout the darkness.

Mom pressed her candle to mine, setting it on fire, and whispered, "I love you, sweetie."

I don't know if it was Mom's words or all those glowing candles, but in that moment I felt old family ties reaching out and wrapping tenderly around me.

I turned to Aunt Chloe as Ben sang for us to fall on our knees and hear the angel voices. "I love you, Auntie," I whispered as our candles touched. It was the truth. I loved my crazy aunt, wild Christmas hat and all.

The dots of light swelled to a glowing sea as Ben finished.

The pianist began to softly play "Silent Night," and the minister motioned for us all to stand and sing.

It wasn't until we came to the end of the song that I realized Gram was quiet. I sneaked a look her direction. She held her candle in both hands. Her eyes were shut and she was smiling, the epitome of a contented woman. Her whole family with her in church, her grandson singing. I could understand how she felt. I was feeling pretty contented myself, especially now that Gram was quiet.

The pastor said a final prayer and announced that cookies and punch would be served in the fellowship hall. And with one final song we blew out our candles and filed out of the sanctuary.

Once in the fellowship hall Gram found another woman her age to chat with and Keira found a hunk to flirt with. I moved next to Mom.

She smiled at me and kissed my cheek. "That was lovely. I'm glad we came. And I'm glad you came home."

So was I. I felt a warmth spread through my chest.

"Andie," someone called. I turned and saw Gabe coming my way.

I suddenly felt nervous, tongue-tied, stupid.

He fought through the crowd like a salmon swimming upstream and finally broke through to stand next to me. Mom made herself scarce.

"Nice service, huh?" he said.

"It was lovely," I agreed. "And I thought Ben did a great job on his solo."

"I guess he takes after your grandma," Gabe teased, making me blush. Then he sobered. "Did you talk to your sister?"

Suddenly I couldn't look him in the eye. I fastened my gaze on one of his shirt buttons and nodded.

"We do a lot of dumb things when we're kids," he said, his voice lowered so only I could hear. "I know I've done my share. But we're not kids now, Andie. What do you say to starting over?"

Starting over with Gabe, kissing him and having him whisper *my* name. Oh, that sounded good. But, realistically, how often would that happen with him here and me on the east coast?

"We're not exactly neighbors anymore," I pointed out.

He shrugged. "A minor obstacle."

"Of a few thousand miles."

"I don't mind racking up some frequent flier miles."

All I needed to complicate my life right now was to fall in love with Gabe. Again. "Let's think on it," I said.

"I have been," he pushed.

"Well, I haven't. I need some time."

"You've had years."

"That was years of you dating other women."

"Only trying to find another you. There isn't one."

"Stop already," I said half-heartedly. "You sound like something out of a book."

"One with a happy ending?"

I rolled my eyes. "Time to change the subject."

"Okay. So, what sights should we go see when I visit you in New York?"

"That is not changing the subject."

"Show me how it's done then."

"All right," I said. "Are you going back to your parents' to open presents?"

"Oh, yeah. The big Christmas Eve tradition." He nodded to where Mom and Ben stood talking with Mrs. Bailey. "Maybe you guys are starting a new tradition tonight. You've got the whole gang here and so far so good. Nothing weird going on."

I suddenly felt jinxed. I scanned the crowd, doing a quick check on my relatives. Gram was still talking with the same woman. Mom seemed to be enjoying her conversation with Ben and Mrs. Bailey, and Keira had found another cute guy. Aunt Chloe and her new admirer had drifted over to the refreshment table.

Now she was leaning over a plate of cookies. The bird on her hat was leaning too, precariously near the branch of candles at the center of the table.

I sure hoped all that netting and feathers were made of inflammable material. Of course, I reasoned, they had to be. Everything was fireproof these days.

Wait a minute. Was I seeing smoke?

## Chapter Seventeen

They say where there's smoke there's fire. Aunt Chloe gave us living proof of that. Before I could say "Smokey Bear," her hat burst into flames.

A woman next to her let out a screech while another pulled her away from the cookie plate, crying, "Your hat is on fire!"

One hundred and fifty people (not counting children) stopped their conversation and turned to see what was going on.

Someone cried, "Aunt Chloe!" I realized it was me. I pulled my gloves from my pocket and began pushing at the herd of shoulders in front of me in an effort to reach her.

Meanwhile, back at the eats table, Aunt Chloe's admirer had grabbed the punch bowl. His grasp on the thing looked anything but secure, and he teetered with it like a weight lifter competing for the world's record. The punch sloshed back and forth, spattering the people on either side of him. He finally balanced himself enough to give a mighty heave-ho. A stream of red punch went flying. So did the punch bowl. It bounced off the table and fell to the floor with a glassy crunch. For all his effort, Oscar completely missed his target, spilling the punch down Aunt Chloe's dress while her pear tree continued to burn. She barely noticed the drenching. She was completely hysterical, flapping at her hat, while shrieking and dancing in a circle.

A man rushed past me, calling, "I'll get the fire extinguisher."

Aunt Chloe's hat had a real blaze going now. She looked like a giant pillar candle with legs or an escaped extra from Disney's *Beauty and the Beast.*

If her hair caught, it was all over. I had my gloves on by the time I got to her. If I pulled the hat off fast enough, neither of us would get burned. I tried to get it, but she was still dancing around and kept moving out of range.

"Hold still, Auntie," I cried.

Ben had reached us now. He'd ripped off his shirt and wadded it up. Using it like an oven mitt, he grabbed the flaming hat and ripped it off Aunt Chloe's head. Along with about half her hair.

She let out a howl of pain as he pulled the hat off and threw it on the floor. He began stomping on it and she joined in, still shrieking and doing her own version of the Mexican hat dance.

The man returned with the fire extinguisher and, although the flames were already out, aimed the thing and squirted a chemical stream at the dying hat, making it jump.

Mom got to us just as the volunteer fireman emptied his last round. "Oh, dear," she said, looking at the mess at her feet. In back of us, two women knelt, picking up pieces of the broken punch bowl with paper towels.

Aunt Chloe's new friend hovered anxiously. "Are you all right, Chloe?"

"My hat," she sobbed.

Ben bent and gingerly picked his shirt away, and we all

stared at the pear tree corpse. The bird was charred and black, the pears had melted, and the whole thing lay in a puddle of fire extinguisher gook.

"No loss," I heard some kid mutter.

"Who is that woman, anyway?" someone asked in a loud whisper.

I felt like turning around and saying, "An angel in disguise, running a kindness test, and you just flunked, turkey," but I settled for giving the offender a dirty look.

Gram was on the scene now. "Chloe, are you all right?" she asked. "You're not in shock, are you?"

Aunt Chloe didn't answer. She just stood there, staring at the remains of her hat.

The foyer reeked of smoke and chemicals, and people were wrinkling their noses, speaking with muted voices as they moved away from the cookies. Or maybe it was us they were trying to get away from.

The pastor came up to us and asked if Aunt Chloe was all right.

She was trembling now. She wrapped her arms around herself and whimpered, "Everyone told me not to wear the hat."

"Well, we're glad you're not hurt," he said, wisely avoiding any discussion of my aunt's fashion decision. "The Lord was surely watching over you."

And speaking of watching, I could feel everyone's eyes on us. The Hartwells were already infamous in the neighborhood. Now we had left our mark on one of Carol's local churches. My whole face flamed with something no fire extinguisher could put out. Even though I was thankful my poor aunt was unhurt (and even more thankful her hat was dead), I found myself wishing I could rewind the evening and take everyone to some other church's Christmas Eve service, someplace in another town where no one knew me.

"Maybe we'd better go home," Mom suggested.

I was all over that. I led Aunt Chloe toward the door. People parted before us like the Red Sea. Actually, it was more like we were lepers and they were avoiding contamination. "Don't worry," I wanted to say, "you can't catch Hartwell craziness from physical contact."

Aunt Chloe's new friend was behind us now. He tapped her on the shoulder and said, "Come back again, Chloe. We don't have candles every week."

"Thank you, Oscar," she said. "That's very kind of you."

Out of the corner of my eye I saw Keira skirting around the edge of the crowd, trying to pretend she didn't know us. I couldn't blame her. If I wasn't busy trying to keep my aunt calm I'd have skirted too.

"I'm so glad you're all right," Mrs. Bailey said to Aunt Chloe right before we reached the door. "You be sure and come back again."

Aunt Chloe gave her a wobbly smile and nodded.

After Mrs. Bailey left, Aunt Chloe turned to me, teary-eyed. "I ruined everyone's evening."

"You didn't ruin mine," I told her and hoped my nose wouldn't grow like Pinocchio's.

But then I realized it was no lie. Aunt Chloe hadn't really wrecked my evening. Yes, I have to admit I had been embarrassed after the fact by her performance. But my embarrassment had been overshadowed by relief that my aunt hadn't torched herself completely. With my family's proclivities toward fire, I could be thankful the church building was still standing. It had survived the Hartwells.

"I'll bring the car around," Mom said once we had all reached the door. "You don't want to go out in the cold all wet," she told Aunt Chloe.

Aunt Chloe stopped suddenly. "My coat!"

"I'll get it," Ben offered.

"I left it over there on the seat," she said, pointing.

"I'll take Gram out to the car," Keira offered, using our grandmother as cover for a quick escape.

It was just my aunt and me standing together now. I felt like I needed to say something. "I'm sorry you lost your hat," I ventured.

She shrugged. "It was just one of those things. It probably could have happened to anyone."

I wasn't sure about that. In fact, I thought this was probably some kind of first for the church. I suspected next year the refreshment table would be devoid of candles.

We ran Gram home, then went back to the house. Keira took off practically the minute we got in the door, saying, "I told Spencer I'd meet him at his parents' after we were done with church." She gave Mom and Aunt Chloe each a quick kiss on the cheek, then she was gone. Merry Christmas to all, and to all a good night.

Ben came in and plopped down on the living room couch. "So, what's to eat?"

Was that all he thought about? "You can't be hungry," I said to him even as Mom went to the kitchen to find goodies.

"I didn't say I was," he replied. "I just asked what's to eat. I didn't get any cookies at church."

"Thanks to me," said Aunt Chloe. She looked like she was going to cry again. *Way to go, Ben. Let's revisit the whole burning hat experience.*

"You couldn't help it if your bird took a dive into the candles," Ben told her. He slumped against the couch cushions and stretched his legs out in front of him. "Man, this has been a real personal injury Christmas."

"Which reminds me," Mom called from the kitchen. "How's your leg? It looked like you were limping tonight."

"It's fine," he called back.

Mom returned with a platter of cookies. At the rate we

were going through those things we'd all be round as cookie jars by the time she was done with us.

All except my brother, who never gained weight. The rat. He grabbed two and stuffed one in his mouth. "So, what time does the party start tomorrow?" he asked, his words muffled by cookie crumbs.

Mom looked at me. "I don't know. What time should we open presents?"

"Whenever Keira gets up, I guess." Keira was the closest thing we had to a child, and she was always the first one out of bed. When we heard the Christmas music start playing on the radio we knew Keir already had the tree lights on. If no one came out within ten minutes, she started banging on doors.

"Why don't we plan to open presents around ten?" Mom suggested.

"Think Keir can wait that long?" Ben asked.

Mom grinned. "She can play with the things in her Christmas stocking until the grownups are ready to open presents."

An old Mom and Dad ploy from when we were young. It could still work, though, since Mom had never stopped giving us stockings.

We sat around for an hour and reminisced about Christmases past. I was careful not to mention Dad as we talked.

Aunt Chloe was a different story. "Well, I think the most memorable Christmas was when Michael started that chimney fire," she said, making Mom frown.

"Which one?" Ben joked, just as obtuse as Aunt Chloe.

"If you're going to talk about your father, then I'm going to bed," Mom threatened.

So we all shut up. The silence hung there in the middle of the room like a no-man's land no one dared cross.

Ben looked at his watch. "Well, I'd better shove off."

"Already?" asked Mom the wet blanket.

"Yeah. I have to go see . . ." He stuttered to a stop. "Gotta make a stop on the way home."

It didn't take an ace detective to figure out he was going to go see Dad. Mom made a face like she'd bitten into a rotten nut.

Oh, boy. If she looked like this now, just hearing about one of her kids going to see Dad on Christmas Eve, how was she going to react when he walked through the door on Christmas day? Maybe inviting him hadn't been such a good idea after all.

"I guess I'll head home too," said Aunt Chloe.

Five minutes later they were gone, and it was just Mom and me and my misgivings.

"Well," Mom said cheerily. "What shall we do?"

Eat a whole bunch of chocolate and pray that tomorrow never comes, I thought.

## Chapter Eighteen

I was dreaming that Gabe and I were in a winter wonderland, sledding down a fast hill. We had started in the middle of the street, but halfway down the sled went crooked, taking us onto the sidewalk. Now we were hurtling toward someone's front yard and a huge maple tree.

"Look out for the tree!" I cried.

I heard the sound before we hit. My eyes popped open and I jerked upright in bed, my heart thudding. I heard more banging, and it was coming from the direction of my bedroom door. I wasn't dead or crippled. Whew!

"Come on, get up," Keira called and thumped the door again. "Coffee's ready."

Then she was down the hall, hammering on Mom's door.

I took several deep, calming breaths. Okay, back to reality. Christmas Day with the Hartwells. I looked at the clock. It was only seven thirty. I let out a moan and flopped back down, shutting my eyes and throwing an arm over them for good measure. Maybe I could still find my way back to Sleepy Land.

And a careening sled with Gabe Knightly. What would Freud say about a dream like that?

I turned my head and peered out from under my arm at my angel snow globe on the bed stand. The inscription on Gabe's card wavered at the back of my brain. *Think of me.*

"I'd rather not, thank you," I muttered.

I reached out and picked up the globe and shook it, ushering in a glittery storm. My little angel stood with her face transfixed heavenward, unmoved by the stuff swirling around her. *That would be me today,* I decided, calm and immune to whatever my family chose to swirl around me.

Oh, that it would only be glitter.

My door flew open, and Keira leaned her head in. "Are you getting up any time before next Christmas?" she demanded.

I set the snow globe back and threw off the covers. "Did you run out of things to play with in your Christmas stocking?"

"Only old people sleep in on Christmas Day," she informed me and left.

"Old people and grownups," I called after her. I don't know why I bothered. I would never win the battle for more sleep. The baby of the family was awake and ready to play. That meant the rest of us had to be too.

I took a shower and put on some jeans and a black sweater, then told myself I was ready to face the day. The smell of coffee beckoned me down the hall, and Christmas music greeted me as I entered the living room—both courtesy of my sister. A whiff of bayberry and vanilla caught my attention, and I saw Keira had lit Mom's candles. The tree lights were already on, giving the room a soft glow. Keira was a big believer in setting the stage for Christmas morning, and I had to admit, she'd set it well. Looking at the tree with all the presents, smelling the old, familiar smells, I could almost believe I was ten years old again.

Keira was already parked on a kitchen stool, dressed for

the day in jeans and a white blouse that showed off a large tear drop of glimmering, blue gemstone.

I moved in for a closer look. "Is that a blue topaz?"

She nodded, and that was when I noticed matching drops dangling from her ears. First an engagement ring the size of a small country and now this. I got a sudden flash of insight into how that matter of Cain and Abel came about. *Don't be petty,* I told myself, trying to rinse the green out of my eyes.

"Spencer gave it to me," said Keir.

Well, there was a surprise. Maybe we could clone Spencer. I'd like to have a man to buy expensive jewelry for me.

*Hey, you got a snow globe,* came the thought. Considering the way I'd been treating Gabe, a snow globe was pretty generous.

Mom joined us now, looking comfy in her bathrobe. "That is quite the set," she said, her own eyes looking a little green.

Keira held up the pendant dangling over her chest and examined it. "It's a bribe."

Mom stared at Keir like her body had been taken over by aliens. "What?"

"He's hoping I'll compromise on the house."

"If you sold all the jewelry he's given you, you could buy the house outright," Mom cracked.

My sister had lost her sense of humor since the last time I saw her. "Funny, Mom," she said grumpily and took a sip of coffee.

"So, what did you get him?" I asked.

Her enthusiasm returned. "Oh, this is so fun. There's this company called Hollywood Is Calling, and for practically nothing you can get a celebrity to call and deliver a message to someone."

"A celebrity? Like who?" Mom asked.

"Like someone from one of those old seventies TV shows. They've got the guy who was the principal on *Saved by the Bell*."

"That's who you got?" I asked. She'd gotten blue topaz and Spencer had gotten Mr. Belding?

"No, I got the Professor from *Gilligan's Island*." She held up her hand and snapped her fingers. "Snaps for me."

"Something for you," I muttered.

"Hey, Spencer loved it. The Professor called him at his parents' when I was over there last night and wished Spencer a Merry Christmas from the island."

"If he had a phone he should have used it to make a call and get off the island," Mom said in disgust.

"He was going to make that call next," Keir said with a grin."

So, Keira received an expensive necklace and earring set and Spencer got a two-minute call from the Professor. Somebody got a bargain.

"I need more coffee," Mom said.

It was pushing nine and she was still in her bathrobe, visiting with us and guzzling java, when the doorbell rang. "Oh, my gosh, I'm not even dressed!" she cried. "Somebody get the door."

I remembered the days when Mom would sit around all day in her bathrobe. Of course, she was married then so had no motivation to spruce up.

I sighed. I wished she hadn't invited Mr. Winkler over.

Keira went for the door, so I stayed parked at the kitchen counter and poured more coffee down my throat.

"Hi, Gram," I heard my sister say. "Mom," she hollered, "Ben and Gram are here."

As they moved toward the kitchen I heard Gram telling Keira, "I hope you haven't made breakfast yet. I've got my homemade cinnamon rolls."

Hockey-puck cinnamon rolls, right up there with Gram's Prune Whip. I quickly grabbed for the cereal. If I were already eating, I'd have an excuse not to eat the hockey pucks.

"Ben, you can put those presents under the tree for me," Gram added. And then she was in the kitchen, catching me right in the middle of pouring cereal into a bowl.

"Hello, everyone," she sang. "Oh, Andie. You don't want cereal, not on Christmas morning." She plucked the box from my hand. "Not when we have homemade cinnamon rolls."

Behind her Keira was smirking. She could well afford to. She'd probably wolfed down something while I was showering.

My grandma was holding the plate out to me now. I was trapped.

"Thanks," I murmured and took the smallest one. Which isn't saying much, considering they were all the size of bricks. Just as heavy too.

She looked at me expectantly. I smiled and bit down and almost broke a tooth.

"I think I'll get some more coffee to go with this," I said. Maybe if it sat in coffee for an hour . . .

"We need more than cinnamon rolls," said Ben. "Clear the kitchen. I'm making omelets."

*Thank you, bro,* I thought.

"That'll clear the kitchen," Keira cracked.

"Hey, I can make omelets," he said, sounding insulted.

"I don't know why you need a big heavy breakfast when we're going to have dinner in the middle of the day," Gram grumbled.

Ben sneaked a conspiratorial wink my way. We did.

Keira didn't give us long to eat breakfast. As soon as Aunt Chloe came through the door she said, "Come on, guys. You can eat anytime. We're all here now. Let's open our presents."

"Like you need anything on top of what Spencer gave you?" Ben teased.

Keira fingered the topaz. "Just sitting here talking is boring."

"We talked about you half the time," Ben pointed out.

"And we talked about you the other half."

"Okay, enough," Mom said. "Let's go open presents."

"That sounds good to me," Aunt Chloe said, plunking a cinnamon roll on her plate. Now, there was desperation.

We went into the living room, a small parade marching to "Jingle Bells" playing on the radio.

The number of presents under the tree had been steadily growing since we put it up, and now we had enough there to take care of the entire town of Carol. I knew we would find at least a couple presents for each of us just from Mom, who went completely nuts every year.

One present under the tree might as well have had a spotlight shining on it. It was painting size—large, impossible-to-hide painting size—and wrapped in red foil with silver ribbon. Aunt Chloe's portrait of me. I tried not to shudder and began rehearsing my lines. *Oh, wow. Now, this is quite a piece of . . . Hmmm . . . art! That was so sweet of you.*

"Okay, who's going to play Santa?" Mom asked.

"I did it last year," Keira said, plopping onto the couch and tucking one leg under her. She was wearing multicolored striped socks with each toe a different color, an interesting fashion complement to her expensive jewelry.

"I'll do it," Ben volunteered and settled himself at the foot of the tree. "Hey, here's one for Mom from Andie."

"Be careful, it's fragile," I cautioned.

"No problem," said Ben, then pretended to drop it, almost giving me a heart attack.

I'd hauled those tulip plates from the Metropolitan Museum of Art home in my carry-on, praying all the way they wouldn't break. "You are so not funny," I told him.

He snickered as he set it in Mom's lap, then dug under the tree again.

"Give Andie mine," said Aunt Chloe.

*Well, might as well get the torture over with.* I braced myself and put on a smile. My aunt eagerly watched as I unwrapped her masterpiece.

And there I was, at least I think it was me. This version of me had a nose twice as wide as mine and a lower lip that looked like someone had plugged me into the collagen pump then gone away and forgotten me, and my skin was the color of something from the supermarket's seafood department. But at least I wasn't in the bathroom. She had put me in a field of multicolored dots that I think were meant to be wild flowers. I was wearing something resembling a Greek toga and had margarine-colored hair that reminded me of Medusa. I guess that went with the toga.

Aunt Chloe was watching me expectantly. Time to deliver my line. "Wow, this is quite a piece of art!" Quite a piece of something, that was for sure.

"Do you like it?" asked Aunt Chloe eagerly.

Oh, dear. I hadn't rehearsed any response for that question. I didn't want to lie. *Think fast, Andie. Think like Madison Avenue.*

"How could I not like it, considering you made it for me?"

It was true. As paintings went, the thing was abysmal, but the fact that my aunt had labored over it in love gave it value. At least enough value that I would take it back to New York. Where on earth was I going to hide it? And if Aunt Chloe ever came to visit, where would I hang it? I thought of my grandma, maybe doing penance for past motherly sins, hanging that thawing hamburger masterpiece in her dining room. I hadn't been a bad niece. I shouldn't have to suffer. Maybe I could talk the apartment manager into letting me hang this in the laundry room.

"Andie, these are lovely!" Mom cried as she pulled out a plate from the box. She smiled lovingly at me. "You shouldn't have. They must have cost you an arm and a leg."

They had. "Only an arm," I said, trying to sound humble.

"Hey, cool," Ben said, displaying the New York Mets baseball cap I'd gotten him. He put it on. "How do I look?"

"Like a dweeb," teased Keira. "Give Andie my present."

Ben obliged and I opened it. Coffee. There was a surprise. But hey, I like coffee. And the mug she had picked to go with it was really cute too. It had a stylized picture of a trendy-looking woman sitting at a café table, writing in a journal.

"That's you being sophisticated in New York," Keira said.

"I like it. Thanks."

The presents kept coming. From Mom, a check for Ben and clothes for Keira. For me, pretty stationery and stamps. (Subtle as always, Mom). But she didn't stop there. I opened a smaller package to find a pendant with a small ruby, my birthstone. Where was my mother getting all this money? Surely not from selling mugs and tacky jackets. "Mom, you shouldn't have done this," I said.

"Of course I should have," she said and smiled.

As if that weren't enough, she'd also gotten me a bunch of scrapbooking supplies. "So you can keep track of your adventures in New York," she told me.

She hated having me gone, wanted me home, yet here she was, being supportive anyway. I felt all choked up. "Oh, Mom."

Gram gave me a set of hand-embroidered kitchen towels that I knew I'd never use. Not because they were an embarrassment, but because they were lovely and irreplaceable, and I didn't want to get them stained. Gram couldn't cook, but her handwork was true art. Maybe I'd have them framed and hang them in my kitchen.

Keira loved the scarf I'd found at the Columbus Avenue flea market, and the little kitchen knickknack I'd bought at another flea market for Gram went over well too.

"Okay, sis, open mine," Ben said and handed me a fat plastic bag sealed with duct tape. My brother, Mr. Martha Stewart.

I wrestled the bag free of the tape and pulled out a black sweatshirt with I LOVE NEW YORK emblazoned across it.

"I got it online," he said. "Like it?"

Now I could look like a tourist in my own town. "I do," I said. My brother had put a lot of thought into that present. In fact, it seemed my whole family had done nothing but think of me this Christmas. I hugged him and tried not to cry.

Mom opened Gram's gift, pulling out quilted pillow shams. More beautiful handwork. "Oh, Mom. These are fabulous."

"They'll match the quilt I gave you," Gram said.

"You're right. They will."

"Get the quilt and let's see how they look," Gram suggested.

"Good idea," Mom said and disappeared down the hall.

And that was the last we saw of her. At least until the presents were almost all opened and Gram called, "Did you find it?"

"Not yet," Mom called back.

Now Aunt Chloe was tearing into my present. "An art book! Thank you, Andie." She hugged the book to her. "This must have cost you a fortune."

"Not really," I said. I'd gotten it at a used book store. On a budget like mine, you've got to be creative.

"Hey, here's one more for Andie from Mom," Ben said.

It looked like clothes. I was suddenly clutched by a prophetic sense of dread. I held my breath as I pulled off the ribbon and paper and opened the box. Inside lay a pink jacket. Oh, no. Not the Man Hater one Mom had been wearing at the airport. I pulled it out.

"That's from the spring line," Aunt Chloe said proudly. "You're the first person to have one."

Lucky me, I thought miserably. I turned it around and read the back. I'VE DONE CAROL (THE TOWN).

"Those are going to sell like hotcakes," Aunt Chloe predicted.

Maybe someone would like to buy this one. I nodded and put it back in the box, praying Mom wouldn't expect me to wear it to the airport when I left.

She came back down the hall, looking perplexed. "It's not there."

"What do you mean it's not there?" Gram's sweet little old lady smile was beginning to dissolve into something not so sweet.

"Where could it have gone?" Mom wondered. "It was right in that room and . . ." She looked at Aunt Chloe. "Wait a minute. Did you?"

Aunt Chloe was already looking defensive. "What?"

"You took that quilt to the emergency room."

Gram looked ready to send Aunt Chloe away without any dinner. "Why were you taking my quilt to the hospital?"

Now Aunt Chloe looked like Eve with a mouthful of apple. "It was when Ben hurt his foot," she explained. "He was in shock."

"Well, where is it now?" Gram demanded.

Mom frowned. "I think we left it there."

"You left the quilt that took me six months to make at the hospital?" Gram looked like she was going to have to go to the hospital herself. Did she take high blood pressure medicine? I wondered. If so, she needed some now.

"I'm sure it's still there somewhere," I said, hoping to avert World War Three. "Maybe in the lost and found."

"A handmade quilt? I doubt it," Gram said scornfully. "Really, Chloe," she snapped. "How could you?"

"It's not like I did it on purpose, Mom," said Aunt Chloe. She suddenly sounded twelve years old.

"Hey, Gram, it's okay," put in Ben. "It'll probably turn up."

Gram looked like she could hurl lightning bolts from her fingertips now. "It'll turn up all right. On some homeless person."

"We don't have any homeless people in Carol," Keira said.

Gram talked right over her. "You might as well take the shams to the hospital too. Then whoever stole the quilt can have a matching set."

"I'm sorry," Aunt Chloe wailed, and began to cry.

"Honestly, Chloe," Gram said in disgust. "Why don't you think before you act? I can never reproduce that quilt."

A new song was playing on the radio, a choir singing how there's no place like home for the holidays. Boy, that was an understatement.

"Hey, who'd like some eggnog?" offered Ben.

Gram looked at him in disgust. "Eggnog! At a time like this?"

And then the doorbell rang. I hoped it wasn't Dad coming early. This would not be the best time for him to arrive on the doorstep.

Mom opened the door and there stood Mr. Winkler, decked out in slacks and a green plaid shirt, holding a gift platter of dried fruit. "Merry Christmas," he said, handing it to Mom. "Hope I'm not too early."

Only about two hours, I thought. Was this man an android? Didn't he have any family, any other living human being who would like to see him and his dried fruit?

"Not at all. Come on in," said Mom.

"What's he doing here already?" Keira whispered to me.

"Peace negotiations," I whispered back.

It was no exaggeration. Having a stranger in our midst forced us to close ranks. Aunt Chloe sniffed up her tears and, although she was still glowering like the Grinch, Gram at least shut up.

"Mom, you remember our neighbor, Bill Winkler," Mom said to Gram.

"How do you do, Bill," Gram said and gave him a regal nod.

"Nice to meet you," he said, giving her a friendly head bob in return. No need for him to say how he did. He was doing fine. He had a place to camp all day and a free meal. If you asked me, we were more than paying for that window he mended. Of course, no one asked me.

"Hey, Mr. Winkler, how's it goin'?" Ben greeted him.

"Not bad," said Mr. Winkler as they shook hands. Sparkling conversationalist, our Mr. Winkler.

"Would you like some eggnog?" Mom offered.

"If it's not too much trouble," he said politely. "Say, I'm not interrupting you folks' present opening, am I?"

"No, we're pretty much done," Mom assured him.

A few presents still lingered under the tree, but nobody contradicted her. Maybe that was because we all needed a break from the stress of gift giving.

Mr. Winkler made himself at home in Dad's easy chair, and he and Ben started talking football. It was an unsettling sight seeing another man sitting in my father's chair. I turned away and set to work cleaning up the wrapping paper mess. As I worked, I got to wondering why Dad didn't get to take his chair when he left.

Spencer arrived, wearing perfectly creased, gray wool slacks and a new red sweater. He looked like a freshly minted model looking for a place to pose.

Good looking, well off, generous—the guy was a prize. You'd think Keira would have showed a little more enthusiasm over him. Instead she gave him a ho-hum greeting as he came through the door. As for the way she kissed him, I've seen women kiss their brothers with more enthusiasm. May as well make a R.I.P. tombstone for this relationship. It was doomed.

"I'm getting some coffee," she told him. "Want some?" She turned and started for the kitchen without waiting for an answer.

"Sure," he said to her back.

"Hi, Spencer," I said, trying to put enough warmth into my voice to compensate for Keira's lack of it.

He gave me a grateful smile and joined me at the wrapping paper bag. "So, have you been enjoying your visit home?"

Actually, I had enjoyed much of it—something I had not expected when Mom first issued her invitation. "Yes, I have. I'm glad I came back." Amazing, to hear myself say those words.

He nodded, then picked up a piece of paper and stuffed it in my bag.

"That's some present you gave my sister," I said.

He shrugged. "I thought she'd like it."

"She does," I assured him.

"Well, it's not a house."

"You'll get your house."

"Yeah, but I won't get hers, and that's a problem." He suddenly looked sad.

"I'm sure you guys will be able to work things out," I told him. False assurance. Shame on me.

"Are you?"

"Actually, I'm just trying to be nice and make you feel better," I admitted.

"You don't seem to have to try too hard. You've got that 'being nice' thing down pretty good." He looked at me gratefully.

His gratitude made me nervous. Grateful looks and kind words could be easily misinterpreted.

I was suddenly aware of Keira standing behind us and felt a guilty burn on my face.

"Here's your coffee," she said to Spencer. She sounded like a prison warden. *Here's your last meal. Scum.*

She glared at me like Spencer's behavior was my fault, then took his arm and pulled, a subtle hint that he was now to get up and get away from me. He rose like a puppet who had just had his strings jerked, took his mug of coffee, and followed her to the couch, seating himself on the end next to where Mr. Winkler sat in Dad's chair.

"How's it going?" Mr. Winkler greeted him.

Not so good, I thought. Oh, boy. The Hartwell living room was turning into an emotional mine field, and Dad hadn't even gotten here yet.

I gathered up the wrapping paper mess and took it to the kitchen to feed the garbage. (We didn't burn wrapping paper in the fireplace anymore.)

Keira followed me. I felt like a little kid who was about to get a spanking.

Sure enough. "What was that about out there?" she growled as she filled her own mug.

How unfair. How grossly unfair! "What? You mean me

trying to encourage your fiancé not to run screaming into the night?"

"Maybe you're trying to encourage him to run screaming to you," she hissed.

"Oh, please." Had my sister always been insane, or was this an adult onset thing? Adult? Who was I kidding! Keira was the world's oldest thirteen-year-old.

She put her hands on her hips. "That's it, isn't it? You're trying to steal him. You're out for petty revenge. It isn't enough that I told you Gabe didn't really want me. You have to ruin my life. Out of spite!"

I threw up my hands. "You're right. I came home to ruin your life."

She saw no humor in my remark. Instead, she crossed her arms over her chest and scowled at me.

"Listen to you. How paranoid do you sound?"

She suddenly got busy with picking a crumb off the counter. "Okay, maybe I am being a little paranoid. Things have been kind of strained between Spencer and me lately."

And whose fault was that? I decided this was the perfect moment for some sisterly advice. "You'd better quit being so self-centered or you're going to lose this guy."

The sisterly advice thing was a bad idea. "Where do you get off?" Keira snapped. "Who asked you to come home and tell us all our faults?"

Her words stung. "You did." Wait a minute. That didn't sound quite right. "I didn't come home to do that," I corrected myself. "I'm just trying to help you."

"Well, stop it. Okay?"

I took a step back and held up my hands. If I'd had a crucifix I'd have used it. "Okay."

That cooled her down a little. "I don't need your help," she added.

"All right." *You're on your own. Feel free to mess up your life as much as you want.*

My backing off did the trick. Hurricane Keira downgraded herself to a tropical storm and blew back out to the living room.

As she exited Mom came in to check on the turkey. "Well," she said as she shut it back in the oven, "I think our bird is going to be done earlier than I thought. We should be able to eat at one thirty."

One thirty. That was half an hour earlier than I'd told Dad. "Let's wait till two," I said.

"Why would we want to do that?"

"Tradition. We always eat Christmas dinner at two."

Mom cocked a suspicious eyebrow.

I opened my eyes wide, trying to appear intensely innocent.

She pointed her turkey baster at me. "That look. I know that look."

"What look?" I forced my eyes wider.

She wagged the baster. "The one you're wearing now. Andrea Rose Hartwell, you're up to something." Her eyes narrowed. "Andie, you didn't . . ."

I didn't let her finish. "Whatever bad thing you're thinking I did, I didn't do it," I said evasively. Then I escaped from the kitchen before she could question me further. I hadn't lied. Inviting Dad over for dinner was not a bad thing, at least not in my estimation.

The doorbell heralded new company. It was still too early for Dad. So that left only one other person.

"I'll get it," I called and hurried for the door.

Sure enough, there stood Gabe in jeans and that suede jacket, open to reveal a Christmas-red sweater.

He smiled at me. The man could do toothpaste ads. "Merry Christmas, Andie."

My heart went into an overdrive version of the dance of the sugar plum fairy as I stepped back to let him in.

"Hope you don't mind my stopping by."

"Boring at your house, huh?"

"You're not there." Gabe Knightly had always been quick with a smart answer.

Even as various members of my family called out their greetings, part of me screamed, "Get him out of here, Andie. Why are you doing this to yourself, anyway?"

I answered myself. *Because we're both older, wiser. We're grownups now.*

Which meant maybe we could start over. Maybe I'd been wrong to stall Gabe at eighteen in my mind, never giving him a chance to show me he'd changed. I thought of the angel sealed in my snow globe. That was Gabe.

Although he'd been no angel, I reminded myself.

He wasn't now either. He was a man, and a good one at that.

"Let me take your coat," I offered.

"Take my heart too," he urged softly, making my cheeks sizzle. "It's already yours, anyway."

"Don't push," I cautioned. I didn't care what Gabe or the crazy part of my brain said. A woman doesn't kick over past neuroses in a few days any more than she falls back in love with a guy. Well, at least this woman doesn't.

He smiled like a man who knew he'd won anyway and could afford to be generous. I hung up his coat, and he sauntered into the living room to join the gang.

While the turkey sent out tantalizing smells from the kitchen, we all sat around and visited. The presence of outsiders kept the female Hartwells on a verbal leash, but every once in a while someone would look at someone else like they wished they had a gun handy. Then the grandfather clock bonged half past one.

"I think our turkey's done," Mom announced.

"Great. I'm starving," said Aunt Chloe.

"Gosh, I'm still so full from Gram's cinnamon rolls and all that eggnog," I lied.

"I could go for some turkey," said Mr. Winkler. Who asked him, anyway?

"Gabe, you're staying. Right?" Mom asked.

"Sure," he said.

"Keira, set another place for Gabe," Mom said. She went to the kitchen, and Keira followed to help her.

Oh, boy. The train had left the track. There was no way I could stop it. Dinner was going to get set out on the table right now unless I said something. Then Dad would arrive too late. He'd feel awkward and leave, and I'd have wound up making his Christmas even worse than if I'd left him alone with only Elvis for company.

I steeled myself to make my confession. No, that was the wrong terminology. *To spring my surprise.*

I hurried after them to the kitchen. "Mom, can't we wait a little longer?"

"Everything's ready, dear," Mom said. The turkey was now on the stovetop, and she was digging stuffing out of it.

"If we could just wait another half-hour."

She looked at me expectantly. "Why?"

"I have a surprise coming."

"I love surprises!" gushed Keira. "One of those singing telegrams?"

"Not exactly."

Mom's eyes narrowed. "What, exactly? Does it have something to do with that look we were talking about a minute ago?"

I bit my lip.

"Andrea Rose Hartwell, what have you done?" Mom demanded.

The doorbell rang again.

"I. . . ." Oh, dear. How to explain this so Mom would see it as a good thing?

"I'll get it," called Aunt Chloe.

Mom was looking at me with dawning horror. "Oh, Andie, tell me you didn't."

"Michael?" Aunt Chloe's surprised voice drifted out to us from the living room.

## Chapter Nineteen

"Daddy!" Keira cried and flew out of the kitchen, leaving me alone and unprotected with Mom.

I felt suddenly thankful my mother had a spoon in her hand and not a knife.

"I can't believe you did this." She plunged her spoon into the turkey with so much force, I was surprised it didn't come out the other end.

"He didn't have anyplace to go."

"I'll tell him where to go," Mom growled.

"Mom, please," I begged.

"You're ruining our Christmas bringing him here."

"He's only here for dinner. How can that ruin our Christmas?"

"Your father will find a way, believe me."

"Come on, Mom. Peace on Earth, goodwill toward men."

"Any man but your father."

"Please. Can't you do it for my sake? For your kids' sake?"

"What about your mother's sake, or doesn't that matter?" She was near tears now, and it was my fault.

But I was doing this for all of us. I put an arm around her and hugged her. "Of course, it matters, but it's Christmas."

She gave a snort of disgust. "He's been with another woman."

"Not until after you kicked him out."

"I don't care," she said stubbornly.

I had a flashback. Mom and me talking in the this very same kitchen. It was my senior year, and Gabe had asked someone else to the prom.

"You dumped him," Mom had said.

"I don't care," I'd cried. "He shouldn't . . ."

"Have a life?" My mother had supplied.

I guess that's how we expect it to work for our men. We dump on them, we kick them out, and they are supposed to live out the rest of their days in limbo, waiting for the moment we deign to take them back.

I returned to the present. "Mom, for all our sakes, can't you two try to get along?" I pleaded. "We love both of you. This shouldn't be a war. We shouldn't have to choose."

Her lip began to tremble. "I always knew you loved your father more."

I tightened my hug. "I don't. I just want us all to be together, if not as a family at least as friends, as people who have a history together. Can't we do that? Just this year, for old times' sake?"

Another snort. "Auld Lange Syne?"

"Something like that. He doesn't have anyone now, Mom. And you do," I added. There. If she wouldn't let him stay out of pity, petty revenge would motivate her.

She took a deep breath. "All right. He can stay if it means that much to you."

"It does. Thanks," I said and kissed her.

She shook her head. "But mark my words, we'll all be sorry."

Mom had barely finished her prediction when Dad came into the kitchen, frowning. He nodded back toward the living room. "What's he doing here?"

*Oh, boy.* I suddenly felt like Dr. Frankenstein. What had I created?

"He who?" Mom said.

"You know who. Winkler."

"I invited him. What are you doing here?"

"Andie invited me. I'm her father. What's his excuse?"

"He's my friend."

"He's in my chair."

"It's not your chair anymore."

"It should be."

*Well, if you two will excuse me, I, your invisible child, will just go on out to the dining room to avoid flying shrapnel.* I grabbed the bowl of stuffing and scrammed. But once in the dining room I kept shamelessly eavesdropping.

"Doesn't that guy have some other place to go?" Dad complained.

"No. Like you, he's alone. And he's a nice man."

"What, and I'm not?"

"You want an honest answer? Look how you're behaving."

"Can you blame me? Here I am in what used to be my house, with my family, and you've brought in another guy."

"You're a fine one to talk. You with that . . . child for a girlfriend."

No need to strain to hear what they were saying now. Their voices were rising, and I was sure everyone in the living room could tune in to them.

Gram confirmed that when she said to Keira, "I'm very fond of this version of 'Silent Night,' dear. Can you turn it up?"

"Gladly," said Keira.

So "Silent Night" blasted through the house along with Gram's obligato while in the kitchen my parents argued on.

"You're lucky to be here at all, Michael. You don't live here anymore."

"Yeah, well, whose idea was that?"

Suddenly there was silence. Well, from the kitchen at least. Oh, dear. Had Dad just strangled Mom . . . or vice versa? I sneaked closer to the doorway and peeked in.

Dad was standing kissing-close to her now. "I never wanted us to break up, babe."

He said it so softly I could barely hear him. I leaned in closer.

"We could have worked things out."

"No, we couldn't," Mom snapped.

"We still could."

Whoa. He had her trapped against the stove now. I almost giggled. Dad was making a move on Mom. Any second I'd be humming, "I Saw Mommy Kissing Santa Claus."

That had been overly optimistic. Mom gave Dad a shove. "Back off, Michael. You're making me sweat." Good old Mom. Such a romantic.

I sighed and went back in the kitchen. Forget Mommy kissing Santa Claus. I'd have to settle for her not killing him. "What else can I take out?"

Mom glared at me. "Yourself. Both of you, beat it. I'll call you if I need you."

*Okay.* We scrammed before the wrath of Mom could scorch either of us further.

Dad was looking like a little kid who'd just gotten sent to his room. I understood how he felt. I felt the same way.

But at least he was here. We were together as a family again. Sort of. "I'm glad you came," I told him and squeezed his hand.

"Thanks, Princess." He looked to where Mr. Winkler sat in his chair. "I don't even have a place to sit."

Dad sounded so forlorn. I wished I could think of something to say to comfort him, but I couldn't. And that made me feel even worse.

The forlorn attitude didn't last long. Dad hiked up his pants with his good arm and went to stand by where Mr. Winkler sat, drinking eggnog.

"How's it going, Winkler?"

His question sounded innocent. If he'd asked it of any other person in the room, I'd have heaved a sigh of relief. I felt dread start swirling in my stomach. This was not going to turn into anything pretty. I backed away and took refuge by the dining room table, adding another place setting for Dad. Mom had been right. This had been a bad, bad idea.

"Going fine," said Mr. Winkler. "How do you like your new place?"

"I don't."

Mr. Winkler just nodded. "Too bad."

"Got no place to go today?" Dad asked.

"Well, look at that," Aunt Chloe said. "It's beginning to snow. Looks like we're going to have a white Christmas. I can't remember the last time it snowed on Christmas Day."

The two people she was most hoping to distract ignored her. Mr. Winkler stood up slowly. Now he and Dad were facing each other like gunslingers playing double-dog-dare. "I had someplace to go. Here. I was invited."

"Yeah? Well, so was I. Nice of you to get out of my chair," Dad said, and sat down in it.

"We still have some presents under the tree," Gram said quickly. "This might be a good time to open them."

"Good idea," said Keira. "Here, Daddy. Here's one for you from Andie."

"Bring it to me," Dad said, unwilling to risk losing his chair to Winkler the claim-jumper.

I let out my breath. Things would settle down now that Dad had been distracted.

"Andie, come help me," Mom commanded from the kitchen.

I went into the kitchen where she was violently hurling mashed potatoes into a bowl. "This is what comes of asking your father over. I told you nothing good would come of it. You need to find a way to get him out of here."

"They're okay now," I assured her. "They're opening presents."

"They're not going to be okay. I've got a present under there for Bill."

"Oh." Now I really felt sick. We might as well have put a lit stick of dynamite under the tree. "Maybe it will be all right," I said hopefully. "After all, Dad wouldn't be expecting a present from you."

"That doesn't matter. He won't want to see me giving one to Bill. Andie, when I invited you home for the holidays, this was not what I had in mind."

"I'm sorry, Mom. I was just trying to help."

Male voices started to rise in the living room.

"I didn't ask you home to help. All this meddling—if you weren't grown up I'd send you to your room, you ungrateful child." She slammed the last spoonful of potatoes into the bowl. "Here. Take these to the table."

I did. Anything to escape. I couldn't remember the last time my mother had spoken to me so harshly. What happened to "It's a treat to have you home"?

I supposed she couldn't realistically say that, not with the way she was feeling about Dad's unexpected presence in the house. I had been out of line to invite him without asking her. And there in the living room was living proof of how dumb I'd been.

From the dining room table, where I stood blinking back tears of hurt and anger, I got a bird's-eye view of the whole disaster. A can of cashews lay discarded on the floor. My brother was in the process of removing the tulip plates I gave Mom from harm's way. Spencer was out of his chair and hovering, unsure of what to do, while Dad and Mr. Winkler stood in the middle of the room, engaged in a shoving match.

"Why don't you just get out," Mr. Winkler said, laying his hands on Dad's chest and trying to bulldoze him toward the door.

"Why don't you mind your own business?" Dad shoved him back hard with his good arm, and Mr. Winkler tottered dangerously near the tree.

"I don't want to hurt you," warned Winkler.

"I'd like to see you try." Dad moved in on him and gave him another shove. Now they were practically on top of the tree.

Ben tried to step between them. "Hey, guys. This is not the time."

"Stand back, son," Dad commanded and took a swing at Mr. Winkler. Winkler danced out of range and crushed the box that held my pink jacket.

Ben tried again, pulling on Dad's good arm. "Knock it off, Dad, before someone gets hurt."

"Someone needs to get hurt," Dad said and bore down on Mr. Winkler.

At this point Mom rushed past me, muttering, "I'm going to kill him." She stormed up to Dad. "Michael, if you don't stop right now I'm calling the police."

Both men ignored her. She whirled around and headed for the kitchen wearing her stone scowl.

Oh, no. Surely she wouldn't. I looked into the kitchen. She had the phone receiver in her hand.

Meanwhile, back in the living room Aunt Chloe had joined the combatants. "Stop!" she cried, jumping up. "You're going to trample the painting."

Gabe stepped in, trying to help Ben haul the two men apart, but they were going at it in earnest, and Aunt Chloe's presence didn't make the task easier.

It looked like a mini mosh pit with all of them wrestling in front of our oversized tree, bumping elbows, and in Aunt Chloe's case, hips against the boughs. "Rockin' Around the Christmas Tree" started blasting through the room.

"Look out," warned Gram. "You're going to knock over the tree."

The noise level had risen so high I was sure Mom wasn't the only one who had called the cops. Mr. Harris was probably on the line with Carol's finest right now. We were going to make the police blotter again. Even worse, someone was going to end up in the hospital. Dad would probably break his other arm.

"Dinner's ready," I called desperately. Of course, no one even heard me.

Too late, anyway. Before you could say "God bless us, everyone," Aunt Chloe lost her balance. She crashed into Dad and Mr. Winkler like a bowling ball taking down pins, and the three of them toppled into the tree.

Down it went, right into the window. It looked like a Three Stooges movie. Riding the tree, they pushed through the glass and shattered the window. Or maybe it was Aunt Chloe's scream that did it as she landed on top of Dad, who landed on top of Mr. Winkler.

I stood there in the dining room, staring in horror at the Christmas monster I'd created, a many-legged, moaning mess. I hoped Mr. Winkler wouldn't sue us. All I could see of him was an arm and a couple of feet.

"Chloe, get off me," Dad moaned. "You're suffocating me."

"This is what comes of inviting your father over for Christmas," Mom said at my elbow. Then she left me and went to scold Dad for getting territorial over territory he no longer owned.

Blue lights began to flash over the scene, announcing the arrival of the police. Another memorable Hartwell Christmas. Okay, so I'd been wrong to invite Dad over, but surely any civilized family could have managed to get through a couple of hours without trying to kill each other, certainly without putting their Christmas tree through the window.

And to think I'd almost convinced myself I was glad to be back. Well, I wasn't glad anymore. I'd put up with ridiculous scenes, insults from my sister, and a blistering scold from my mom. And now this. Enough was enough.

I looked in disgust at the pandemonium taking place around the Christmas tree. It looked like a scene from some old Peter Sellers movie. Aunt Chloe staggered up with the help of Ben and put her foot through the painting. That brought such loud wails out of her that if the cops hadn't already arrived they'd have come, sirens blaring. Dad came up holding his broken arm with his good one and swearing, and Mr. Winkler was sitting among the squashed presents and broken tree boughs like a fighter who couldn't rise to finish the round. Gram was hovering and tut-tutting, and Mom was yelling at Dad. Spencer was moving presents out of the way so we could heave-ho the tree back into the house, while Gabe just stood next to Ben, looking like he couldn't believe what he was seeing.

I was mortified. This was by far the worst Hartwell Christmas ever. And Gabe had been here to witness it first-hand. Any second now he'd be asking for his coat back. And his heart. And who could blame him? Not me.

Ben gave me a shrug as he went to to the door to let in the cops. "Good to be home, huh?" he teased.

But I didn't think it was funny.

"I'll get the first aid kit," Keira offered. She rushed by me. "Don't just stand there. Do something."

Good suggestion. I'd started my visit with a broken window. That was where I was going to end it. If I stayed even a minute longer, my head would explode. I hurried to my room to pack. I'd catch a red-eye, go stand-by, camp out at the airport, anything but stay in this madhouse a minute longer.

With all the pandemonium in the living room, I wasn't even missed. I grabbed my cell—thank God I'd kept it charged—and called a cab. Then I hauled my suitcase out of the closet and threw it on the bed. Working at warp speed, I gathered my clothes and toiletries and shoved them in any which way. The last thing I packed was my snow globe. The little angel looked so peaceful in there. I wished I could climb in with her.

My cell rang. I couldn't imagine who on earth would call me on Christmas Day. If it was Santa, checking to see if I was being a good girl, he was too late.

Amazingly, it was Beryl. "Are you having a lovely Christmas, my poppet?" she sang.

Where did she get off being so merry, anyway? She was probably at some quiet, swank gathering, nibbling hors d'oeuvres and listening to chamber music.

"I'm done," I said.

"Good," she said crisply, "because I truly need you here day after tomorrow."

"Not a problem," I assured her. "I'm actually packing for the airport as we speak. What's up?" *Why are you calling me on Christmas after squeezing me out on Christmas Eve?*

"Our dear Mr. Margolin was feeling a little peaked yesterday, so we postponed our meeting until day after tomorrow. It will be him and his people and you, me, and Mr. Phelps."

Me and my ideas in the same room with Mr. Big and Mr. Nutri Bread. Something was going right? I could hardly believe my ears. And the timing was perfect. Even if I couldn't get a flight out until the next day, I'd still make it back in time.

"Of course, I've been singing your praises like a little canary," Beryl continued, "and Mr. Margolin is dying to meet you, my poppet."

"Me?"

"Your ideas, darling."

Beryl wasn't taking credit for everything? Could this really be possible? If it was, I'd sure misjudged her.

"I'll be there," I promised, and snapped my suitcase shut.

"Smashing," Beryl said approvingly. "The meeting is at ten. Come to my office at nine and we'll rally the forces."

"Right-o," I said, sounding like a Beryl Junior.

We said our good-byes, and I disconnected and put the phone in my purse. Then I did a quick visual check to make sure I wasn't forgetting anything.

*Only your manners,* whispered my conscience. I told it to shut up and started for the door.

Wait a minute. The last thing I wanted to do was go past my family. That left me only the emergency exit: the window. I threw up the sash, then tossed out my suitcase and my carry-on.

Okay, I'll admit it was a chicken-livered thing to do, but I'd really had all the scenes I could stand.

I had one leg over the sill when Keira opened my door. "Mom needs . . ." She broke off. "What are you doing?"

I felt suddenly stupid, and tried to cover it up with attitude. "What does it look like I'm doing?"

"It looks like you're running out on us."

"Well, you won the final *Jeopardy* question. You can come back next show." I swung my other leg out.

"I can't believe you're sneaking out. You started this mess."

She was right, of course, but I was up to my nostrils in anger and frustration, so there was no room left for humility.

"Don't worry. You'll find a way to make another one without any help from me," I snarled. "I've got a plane to catch." *Hopefully.*

Keira looked at me in disgust. "Fine. Stay around just long enough to act like you're better than the rest of us, then, when we really need you, run out. You are such a complete hypocrite, I can't believe it."

"Well, we can't all be perfect like you, can we?"

Obviously, the truth hurt. At first she looked like she was going to cry. Then she glared at me and turned and slammed the door.

*Have the last tantrum. What do I care?* I jumped off the window sill, picked up my luggage, and marched across the lawn.

The cops were helping Ben, Mr. Winkler, and Gabe push the tree back through the window and into the house. I could see Dad and Spencer inside the house, each hauling a branch. *How many men does it take to put a Christmas tree back up?* Who cared?

The lights of the patrol cars were still flashing, turning the falling snow pastel blue. No one was yelling anymore, and the sounds of "Joy to the World" drifted out from the broken window.

I took my cell phone out of my purse for one final call. Of course, nobody answered.

I waited for the voicemail to click in, then said, "Mom, I just got a call and I have to get back to New York. You were, um, too busy to tell when I got the call about the big emergency, so . . ." I stumbled to a stop and bit my lip. "Sorry," I added. Then I pressed End, turned off the ringer, and put away my phone.

My cab pulled up to the curb, and I got in. "To the airport, please. As quick as possible."

## Chapter Twenty

I was surprised at how few people were at the airport. Of course, I reminded myself, most travelers had reached their destinations by now and were snug by the fire with family and loved ones.

My stomach rumbled. I wondered if my family was eating dinner yet. Maybe they were still putting up plastic on the broken window. Maybe Dad and Mr. Winkler were fighting over who would be the one to put it up. For all I knew, things could have escalated from a broken window to broken furniture and broken heads. It certainly wouldn't surprise me if they had.

The woman at the check-in counter assured me I could get on the red-eye to New York, for a price.

I paid it gladly.

Then I checked my luggage, bought a paperback mystery, and wandered to my gate. A smattering of people sat in the waiting area, anticipating boarding a flight to Denver that took off in an hour. A tired woman watched with glazed eyes as her two small kids ran in circles, while a grandmotherly type knitted and looked on benevolently. A woman who looked about in her forties was watching the kids too, with barely concealed distaste. She was pencil-thin, dressed in expensive casual, a Luis Vuitton bag by her feet. Successful career woman, traveling alone. I wondered if she was on her way to be with family or fleeing from them, like me. Would that be me someday, a middle-aged woman alone in the airport?

Hopefully, if my family was kind enough to disown me.

I opened my book and stared at the first page. *The body of poor Emily Emerson was found floating in the Thames this morning at 6 a.m.*

What if my plane crashed on the way home? I should have said good-bye. I should have taken the mashed painting. But then I'd have had to take the pink jacket too. Everyone would have known I was going, and they'd have taken me prisoner, never letting me escape.

The whole Christmas fiasco started playing again in my mind. Just thinking about it started my pulse racing, stressing me out. I directed my wandering attention back to the book. *The body of poor Emily Emerson was found floating in the Thames . . .*

I started free-associating. *Floating. Water. Tears.* Ugh. Poor Aunt Chloe was probably crying enough to fill a punch bowl. Mom probably had enough smoke coming out of her ears to set off every detector in the neighborhood. She would never speak to me again. I knew it. None of my family would ever speak to me again.

My sister wouldn't for sure. Calling me a hypocrite. A hypocrite! Just because I ran away from my own family on Christmas Day.

Guilt swamped me. I tried to paddle my way out by telling myself that my family would try the patience of Mother Teresa herself.

One of the kids let out a squeal of delight. I looked up and saw it was because his mom was blowing kisses on his neck. That would probably be Keira someday, if she ever grew up. She'd be Mother of the Year. I'd be . . . I sneaked a look at the career woman. She was poking at her palm pilot, oblivious to the sweet scene in front of her. At the rate I was going, that would be me. Alone, no family.

And where was the problem with that?

Meanwhile, back at page one. *The body of poor Emily Emerson was found* . . .

Oh, who cared? I shut the book and went to the nearest Starbucks stand to get coffee.

"Merry Christmas," said the barista as she handed over my double mocha.

Right. I had just lived through the remake of the National Lampoon's Christmas movie, and now I was alone at the airport, waiting to fly home to an apartment full of strangers. There were many words you could use to describe my Christmas, but "merry" wasn't one of them.

"Thanks," I mumbled and dragged myself back to my gate. This was pitiful. I was pitiful. What was I doing?

I told myself to snap out of it. Anyone in my shoes would have done the same. I'd find a new family in New York to adopt me. Maybe Beryl would like a daughter. I was already her poppet. Poppet, puppet, hmmm. I'd never noticed the similarity between those two words before. Was poppet British for puppet?

I sighed and finished my mocha. I pulled out my nonringing cell and checked messages. Two calls from the Hartwell house. I went back for another mocha.

By the time my plane left at 10:10, I'd downed three. Needless to say, I didn't sleep. I wasn't sure I would have, even without the caffeine, not the way I kept replaying my part in the Hartwell Christmas disaster over and over in my mind. By the time we landed at Kennedy, my eyes were gritty and my heart was heavy.

Hurried passengers jostled me as I retrieved my baggage. The taxi line stretched halfway to Texas. I sighed.

A nice-looking man with silver hair, wearing a business suit and carrying a briefcase, offered to share a cab with me.

"Thank you so much," I said to him after we'd given the driver our directions. "I just got off a red-eye from the west coast, and I'm dying to get home and get some sleep."

He nodded. "You looked like you could use a good turn."

A polite way for saying I looked like a wreck. Well, I felt like a wreck too.

My companion, on the other hand, looked completely unmussed. And he smelled good. More men should buy whatever aftershave he was wearing. The fragrance was hard to identify, but it made me think of the wise men with their frankincense and myrrh. One wise man in a business suit. Another solitary Christmas traveler. Why was a together-looking guy like this all alone?

"A lot of people are in hurry to get back from their family holidays," he observed. He had the most intense blue eyes, and the way he was looking at me, like he knew why I'd been flying home in such hurry, made me squirm. Of course, I was imagining things. It wasn't like I had a big, scarlet D for *deserter* on my chest.

I looked out the cab window. The streets were gray. I caught a quick glance at my own face, reflected in the window. I looked haggard, like an escaped criminal on the run.

Okay, so I ran out. But my family honestly couldn't have expected me to voluntarily remain in that madhouse.

Of course, they could have, because no one in my family realized they were crazy.

They're not really crazy, I corrected myself, just eccentric. And, for the most part, lovable. Which would explain why, loving person that I am, I was now on the other side of the country instead of sitting at my mom's kitchen table, laughing over the flying tree act. Probably nobody was laughing today about anything, not with the stink bomb I'd dropped when I left.

"So, you made a dash home for Christmas?" asked the stranger.

I nodded.

He nodded too. "Home. There's a word with a lot of powerful associations."

He could say that again.

"I'm on my way home to see my kids," he confided. "Haven't seen them in years." He shook his head. "Funny how time slips away."

In my case it couldn't slip fast enough. The sooner I had distance from this day, the better. I nodded politely.

"One minute your kids are little, then they're all grown up." The man fell quiet a moment, obviously thinking about his children. Then he sighed. "Funny how you can let things get to you, stop you from connecting with the most important people in your life. Little stuff, really, but, somehow, you let it grow into big stuff. You stay away, you lose track of what you had together. Next thing you know, you've got nothing. No, worse than that, you've got these gigantic walls between you, and you're a stranger, standing on the outside alone, wondering what happened." He shook his head ruefully. "Wish I'd torn down those walls when they were small and not so sturdy, instead of waiting all these years. I'm going to have a hard time kicking them down."

Now he looked a little embarrassed. "Well, you don't

want to listen to a stranger rambling on. How about your family? Are you close?"

"I'm afraid we live on different coasts." Different coasts? Try different planets.

"The world's become a small place."

"Yes, it has," I agreed. And talk about small places, with all the talk about family this cab was shrinking smaller by the minute, closing in on me.

The cab driver pulled up in front of my apartment. "Looks like you're home," said the businessman.

Home. I looked at my slightly run-down apartment building. It was just a building. When I thought of home, I thought of the house in Carol on the corner of First and Noel.

Guilt-induced sentiment, I told myself. I shook off the feeling and paid the cab driver, then waved at the stranger inside. As the cab swooshed off on wet streets, I realized I'd never even asked his name. Mr. Good Deed.

I gathered my bags and headed for my apartment. *Bed,* I thought, *just get me in bed.* After a good sleep everything would look better.

But I'd forgotten that people on vacation didn't have to wake up early. There was no place for a good sleep. Two male bodies were laid out in the living room, one on the couch and one taking up what little floor space our Christmas tree and several piles of discarded wrapping paper didn't occupy. Oh, yes. Wess and Morris. And I knew, like the three bears, I'd enter my bedroom to find someone sleeping in my bed: Tess.

Sure enough, there she was. Tears of self-pity sprang to my eyes. Home from the tortures of Job, and there was no place for me to lay my weary head. I retrieved a blanket from the closet and shuffled to the bathroom. Then I locked the door, took my blankie, and climbed into the tub.

It seemed I was barely asleep when someone banged on the bathroom door. "Hey, who's in there? I need to use the can."

I climbed out of the tub, rubbing my hurting neck.

The banging started again. "Hurry up, man."

I opened the door to find a blond-haired guy, shirtless and in jeans, waiting none too patiently. He wasn't even half as cute as Gabe.

"Thanks," he said and pushed past me, shutting the door on a corner of my blanket.

Interesting. He didn't even ask who I was or how I got in. A man on a mission.

I left the trapped blanket and stumbled out to our tiny living room, where the couch was now vacant. I stepped past the empty potato chip bag and the glasses scattered in my path, and sat on the couch. It would be more comfortable to lie on it, I decided, and let myself fall over. The guy in the bathroom had warmed it all up. I took over his pillow and blanket and shut my eyes. *Today the couch, tonight my bed.*

"Hey, excuse me." A hand shook my shoulder, and I cracked open an eye.

It was Mr. No Shirt. "Who are you? I was sleeping there."

"I'm Andie. This is my apartment, and now I'm sleeping here. You can have the bathtub."

He glared at me and stomped off, and I shut my eye again.

The next time someone woke me, it was Camilla. "Andie, you're home."

I knew I couldn't have slept for long, because this time when I opened my eyes they were still as gritty as ever and I felt that slightly woozy feeling you get from lack of sleep.

"Where's Wess?" Camilla asked.

"In the tub," I mumbled.

"Oh. Taking a bath?"

"No, I sent him there to sleep. I just got in on a red-eye, but I didn't have a bed to sleep in."

Camilla's face turned red. "She wanted her own bed."

"Yeah, well, that makes two of us," I growled. "Tonight she can have the bathtub." I said and rolled over.

Pretty soon other voices woke me.

"This is my roommate, Andie," Camilla said to the people lounging around my living room, drinking coffee.

Everyone murmured hi and looked at me like I was some unusual specimen on display in a science class. Mr. No Shirt regarded me as if I were a hostile alien.

"You can have your bed back," said the strawberry blonde who was occupying the best chair in the apartment. She was already dressed in very expensive-looking jeans and a blue cashmere sweater. She was dangling one leg over the chair and eating cereal from one of my bowls. My favorite bowl, in fact.

"Gee, thanks," I said.

"We're going to hit the after-Christmas sales," Camilla explained.

No "Andie, would you like to go?" But, of course, they wouldn't ask me. They knew I needed to sleep.

I nodded and got off the couch. Mr. No Shirt flopped down and took my place. Maybe they'd taken a vote on whether or not I could come, and he'd cast the deciding vote. Voted off the shopping island.

"Have fun," I said, not really meaning it, and started down the hall.

Nobody answered. Nobody even heard me. They were already talking about their plans for the day.

*Great to be home,* I thought, and crashed on the bed.

The apartment was silent when I finally got up. I felt like the last living person on the planet, abandoned and hopeless. I got myself a cup of coffee. What to do for the day? I could check my e-mail, but I was afraid of what I'd find.

I opted for a bath. On my second, more alert visit to the bathroom, I noticed that it was a mess: wet towels on the floor instead of in the hamper, toiletries strewn everywhere, and someone had been using my favorite body wash.

I picked up the mess, then got cleaned up myself. Then I hid my body wash. There. That was better.

In the kitchen I found the sink piled with dishes, and there were more dishes scattered around the counter. Camilla tended to leave dirty dishes around, but never anything like this. If the four little pigs thought I was going to clean up after them, they could think again. I got my purse and went shopping myself.

While I was out, I decided to be a good sport and make dinner for our guests. They hadn't exactly seen me at my best yet. Some homemade butternut bisque (my specialty) would make a good impression. I did stop for a minute to ask myself why I was bothering to make a good impression on people who obviously didn't care about making one on me, but I decided I didn't want to answer. Then I'd have to start asking myself all over again why I was here with people who didn't care about me instead of home with ones who did.

Back with my squash, I called Camilla on her cell. "Hey, I've got dinner covered. When do you think you guys are coming home?"

"Oh, don't worry about dinner," Camilla said breezily. "We're going out for pizza. Wess is paying."

"Pizza sounds great. Where are you going?"

"Uh, we're already there."

*And you're not invited.* "Oh," I said. "Okay."

"Don't wait up for us," said Camilla. "And don't worry about your bed. Tess said she'd share mine."

Which she was supposed to have been doing in the first place. "Thanks," I said.

My sarcasm was lost on Camilla. "No problem. See ya."

And I'd rushed home for this, could hardly wait to leave my crazy family for the world of sane people. I grabbed a carving knife from the wood block on the counter and put it through the squash, telling myself I needed a quiet evening at home, anyway. I had to get prepared for my big meeting the next day.

After my solitary meal (I cleaned up after myself and left the rest of the mess for Camilla and the snob-slobs), I made a half-hearted attempt to finish my mystery novel. But I found I simply couldn't get fired up over who had done in Emily Emerson, not with the mess the life of Andie Hartwell was in.

Our phone rang, and I checked the caller I.D. It was Mom. I didn't have the courage to pick up. What could I say to her? *Sorry I made you nuts and ran away.* That was exactly what I needed to say, but the words were lodged in my throat, probably caught there under other, less noble words. *You made me come back and I didn't want to. If you'd have just let me stay in New York where I was happy, this would never have happened.* Yeah, it was all Mom's fault I'd been a Grinch.

Our vintage answering machine clicked on. "Andie, it's Mom. Are you there? I guess not. Sweetheart, we need to talk. Please call me."

I half got up to grab the receiver as she spoke, then fell back in my chair. I couldn't pick up. Not now, not yet. Maybe not ever. I went to bed and pulled the blankets over my head.

I tossed and turned that night, thinking about my family, my future, who I was, and what I wanted to be. I tried desperately to put the words of the stranger from the cab out of my mind. But I couldn't. I just kept playing them over and over. All that talk about walls. Someone else had been talking about walls recently. Who . . . ?

*Oh, my.* The guy in the emergency room. Two men talking about the same thing. To me. What were the chances? And, come to think of it, those two men had looked a lot alike. I started remembering all the movies I'd seen with . . .

Oh, don't be ridiculous, I told myself. Next I'd be seeing Scrooge's ghosts.

I left the bedroom and tip-toed past the sleeping bodies in the living room to nuke myself a cup of instant cocoa. Then, steaming mug in hand, I stood, looking out the window at a sky tinged with predawn light and began a do-it-yourself shrink session, starting with acknowledging some important home truths I'd been denying.

Like, if I were going to be honest with myself, I had to admit I'd built up some walls. Hiding behind them, I could distance myself from the craziness, the squabbles, the over-the-top behavior of my family. From a distance, I could tell myself how much I loved my family while completely avoiding them. I could check out and skip happily down my own, self-centered path. Boy, I put on a good face: Andie the perfect, Andie the problem-free.

Andie the distant, Andie the hypocrite.

Keira was right. I liked to pretend I was superior, but when my superiority was tested by my family's imperfections, I flunked. Oh, I was an expert wall builder.

And grudges? I could hold a grudge tighter than Scrooge could pinch a penny, especially against poor Gabe.

I squeezed my eyes shut in an attempt to block out all the scenes pressing in on me: my embarrassment over my mom's business, giving the brush-off to an old friend, changing my departure date, my rudeness to Gabe on our near-bakery trip, and my undignified climb out the bedroom window. Oh, that was the worst, the most pathetic of all. Even though I'd tried to find one, there was no excuse for what I'd done.

I hadn't exactly been at my best since I'd been back either. I don't like me in New York, I thought.

I felt hollow inside, the kind of hollow that couldn't be filled by a simple cup of cocoa.

The sun was rising now, opening a blazing curtain of color on a new day, my big day at work. And all I could think about was fixing the mess with my family. What was I going to do?

## Chapter Twenty-one

Image Makers was the same buzzing hive of activity I had left only a few days ago, with busy co-workers shooting casual hellos at me. No one asked about my Christmas. *Welcome back to the Big Apple. Take a number. And don't expect anyone to call it.*

"You look awful," said Iris, but she never asked me what was wrong. Had everyone here always been this uncaring, and if the answer to that was yes, why hadn't I ever noticed?

I went to my office and checked my e-mail, not the smartest thing to do right before a big meeting, I concluded. My mailbox was overflowing with mail from my family.

From Keira: "Mom cried all day. I hope you're happy with yourself."

I felt sick. I deleted the message, unanswered.

From Ben: "Hey, Bruno, what gives? How come you ran out on us?"

If he'd asked me that a few hours earlier, I could have told him exactly why, and the reasons would have all left my self-made halo of perfection in place. Now? I didn't answer his either.

From Keira again: "Gram thinks you're a spoiled brat. I am now her favorite. You're probably out of the will."

I deserved to be.

I opened the next e-mail from my sister, this one with the subject heading of "Aunt Chloe."

"Aunt Chloe is still crying," Keira informed me. "We think she's having a nervous breakdown."

I moved on to the next Keira blast, titled "the wedding."

"FORGET BEING MY MAID OF HONOR," she typed in upper case anger. "I'LL FIND SOMEONE WHO CARES!!"

Who could blame her? By now I had a lump in my throat the size of a baseball, and more e-mails with which to torture myself.

From Dad: "Why did you run away, Princess? The only reason I came over was to see you."

I could imagine him typing out his disappointment with his one good hand. I sniffed.

From Mom: "Andie, I'm so sorry I yelled at you. We can't leave things like this."

Tears stung my eyes as I typed an answer to her: "Mom, I'm a jerk. You should disown me."

I left the rest of the e-mails (six more from Keira and one from Aunt Chloe) unopened and unanswered, hoping I would eventually find the right words to say to everyone. I wished I were someone else, anyone else.

As I went to Beryl's office for our premeeting meeting, I tried to leave behind all thoughts of my family problems. But they trailed after me like so much toilet paper stuck to my shoe.

"My goodness," Beryl said. "You don't look very rested, poppet. When did you get in?"

"Yesterday."

She was looking at me like I was yesterday's garbage.

"I've got concealer in my purse," I offered, and she nodded.

"Well, let's make sure we're on the same page, shall we?" she said briskly, and we sat down at her desk. She pulled a folder to her and opened it and began to talk.

I tried to track, I really did. But my mind kept wandering. Even as I was here with Beryl my cell phone was probably bloating up with angry text messages from my sister and more pleading voice messages from my mom.

I was in advertising. Maybe I should take out an ad in the *Carol Clarion: Andie Hartwell has the best family in Carol.*

I rejected the idea. After what I'd done, it sounded insincere.

I should at least call Mom before the meeting with Mr. Margolin, tell her I was sorry. Keira I could e-mail. I'd send Aunt Chloe chocolates . . .

"Andie? Andie."

Beryl's sharp voice cut through my thoughts. I realized my gaze had drifted, and I hauled it back and anchored it on her.

"Where were you just now?" she demanded.

"I'm sorry. I guess my thoughts just wandered."

She laid down the papers she was holding and looked at me sternly. "We have a very important meeting and your thoughts wandered?"

"It won't happen again," I assured her.

"I should think not. You're being given a very great opportunity here. I hope you appreciate that."

I nodded. "I do."

I forced myself to at least look like I was paying attention to everything Beryl said, but she saw through the façade, probably because she had to ask me the same question twice before getting an answer.

"Andie, I don't know what is going on in your personal life, but you had better set it aside right now," she said sternly.

"I'm sorry. It's just that there's this problem with my family. . . ."

She cut me off. "You are not with your family anymore. You are at work. And we are about to go into a meeting with a client who represents a very large amount of money for this agency."

I bit my lip and nodded. This was my career, my future. I had to get a grip.

But all I could think about was the mess I'd left behind in Carol.

Beryl stood. "All right. I suggest you pull yourself together quickly. We're in the conference room in ten minutes."

I nodded and hurried to the bathroom to try and hide my worries with makeup.

I didn't look much better when I was done, but I gave up and sped down the hall to the conference room. Everyone else was already there.

"Ah," sang Beryl, "Here's my assistant now."

Mr. Margolin, Mr. Nutri Bread himself, was a man in his late fifties who looked like he ate too much of his own product. He rose from his chair to shake my hand. "Wonderful campaign," he said. "We're very excited."

"We're all very excited," said Mr. Phelps, smiling benevolently on me.

Oh, if I were in a happier frame of mind, what a perfect day this would be!

"Well," Phelps said briskly, "let's get started."

As we pulled up our chairs and began the meeting, I was wishing I'd talked with Mom the night before, wishing I could have heard her say, "I forgive you, Andie." Then maybe I could have forgiven myself. If only I'd taken a minute to call her when I first got to work and tell her I loved her and how sorry I was that I'd messed up Christmas.

There was a knock on the conference room door, then Iris

poked her head around. She looked apologetically at Beryl and said, "I have a call for Andie."

"Tell whoever it is that she's in a meeting," Beryl said for me.

"I did. She says it's very important."

"Who is it?" I asked.

"Your mother."

I started to get up, but Beryl put a hand on my arm.

"I'm sure your mother won't mind waiting for just a little bit." Beryl smiled at me as she spoke, but only with her mouth. Her eyes said, "Move and I'll run you through the paper shredder." To Iris, she said, "Please tell Andie's mother that Andie will return her call as soon as possible."

"Okay," Iris said, and shut the door.

"I really think I'd better take that call," I said.

"We're in the middle of an important meeting," Beryl said. Like she needed to remind me.

"I'll only be a minute," I assured her. "Family emergency," I added for the benefit of our client as I slid my chair back.

Mr. Nutri Bread raised an eyebrow at Mr. Phelps as if to ask, "What kind of a loose ship are you running?"

I hurried from the conference room before Mr. Phelps could prove what a tight ship he ran and command me to stay put. As I slipped out the door I heard Mr. Phelps say, "She's just the assistant. Beryl can carry on."

Carry on. How British! How depressing.

I was too late to take the call, of course. Iris had already cut Mom loose. I scurried to my office and dialed home, but all I got was a busy signal. I waited a minute, then tried again. Still busy. Mom was probably on the phone with Gram, telling her all about the ingrate daughter who wouldn't even take calls at work from her own mother.

I waited another minute and tried one last time. Still busy. I gave up and returned to the meeting.

Beryl was now holding forth, while behind her flashes of future magazine ads blazed from a screen. They looked great. The ideas—mine—were brilliant. Who cared?

After we had finished, Mr. Nutri Bread shook Beryl's hand, then mine. "Great stuff," he said to Beryl, "great stuff." If I'd stayed in the conference room he might have been looking at me when he said that.

"Your company is in good hands with Image Makers," Mr. Phelps assured him, then he clapped a hand on Mr. Nutri Bread's shoulder and led him from the room.

I started to follow. "A moment, please, Andie," said Beryl from behind me.

I stopped and the door shut after the two men, leaving us alone in the room. I turned slowly, bracing myself for the lecture that lay ahead.

"Andie, I don't know what is going on these days." I opened my mouth to tell her, but she didn't pause long enough to let me. "And I don't care. What I do care about is your performance here today."

"It won't happen again. I just needed to get some things straightened out."

She went on as if I hadn't spoken. "Busy as we were, I let you go home for Christmas. You had a nice vacation."

Nice? Compared to what, prison time?

"And once you came back, I expected the job to receive your full attention. That has not happened. If you cannot commit to this agency, I need to know now, because if you can't commit, we have to go on without you. That's nothing personal, my dear, it's just business."

Just business. No one here cared about me or my problems. That was how business worked. I understood that. But what about my friends? Back at the apartment my best friend was treating me like we were in high school and I was the unpopular geek trying to fit in. Nothing was right, here.

"Andie!"

I jerked my attention back to Beryl. Now she looked like an angry school teacher. "Sorry," I said.

She looked both disgusted and resigned all at the same time. "Not half as sorry as I am. I get the distinct impression that you don't care about this account or your position with this agency."

It wasn't that I didn't care, I realized, it was that I didn't care enough. Did I really want to stay here in New York with people to whom I had only a slender connection?

"I think you'd better carefully consider your priorities," Beryl said.

I nodded and fled to my office to carefully consider my priorities. At lunch I went home sick.

Camilla and company were all out sightseeing, so I had the place to myself. I looked out the apartment window at the stretch of gray sky, of sidewalks dotted with trees struggling for existence and buildings that packed people in like ants in an ant farm, and thought about Carol, with its abundance of space and greenery. Was this really where I wanted to spend the rest of my life? What was it here that was so important to me?

I thought of my family with all their faults, and a bubble of feeling swelled in my heart. It wasn't something I'd ever expected to feel, so it took me a few minutes to recognize that I was homesick. I replayed in my mind all those sentimental scenes: the Christmas tree outing with Ben and Keira, the snowball fight, playing Anagrams with Mom, that special moment with Aunt Chloe at the Christmas Eve service. Gabe's kiss.

I wanted to kiss Gabe again. And I wanted to go to my grandmother's for lunch and choke down Prune Whip, and maybe get a little place of my own in Carol and hang Aunt Chloe's portrait of me. Maybe in the laundry room.

I grabbed the phone and called home. Mom answered on the first ring with an anxious hello.

"Mom, I'm so sorry." It was all I could say before I started crying.

Mom started crying too. "Oh, Andie, this was the most horrible Christmas we've ever had." Considering past Christmas, that was saying something.

"Please forgive me," I begged. "I shouldn't have run away. I'll try to make it up to you somehow."

"I love you, Andie. We all do."

And there it was in a nutshell, the reason I belonged in Carol instead of New York.

After a few more teary protestations of love, I told Mom I had some important things I needed to do. We said goodbye, and I sat down at my computer and typed a fond farewell to Beryl.

Then I called Great Bargain Airlines.

"Heepy Nee Yeer," said a familiar voice. "Hee mee Eee heelp ee?"

*Geet mee heem where I belong.*

## Chapter Twenty-two

It was after 10, and Keira's New Year's Eve party was in full swing when my cab pulled up outside Spencer's place. It had started to snow, and soft flakes danced around me as I looked at the people moving around behind the living room window.

My heart rate picked up speed. Mom was the only one I'd gotten up my nerve to talk to so far, and I was a little unsure of my welcome, especially from Keira. One thing I did know. It was cold standing out here, and it looked warm in the house. I picked up my suitcase and walked up the front walk.

I remembered Ben's crack about me being a prodigal, and my finger hovered over the doorbell. I hadn't been a prodigal on my first return, but this time I truly was one, a woman who had scorned all that her family had given her. I thought of the messy apartment in New York. I'd even slept with pigs.

This party had originally been planned for me, but now I could as easily see my sister telling me to get out. And I deserved it. I wished I'd sent flowers on ahead of me, or one of those singing telegrams people used to send. Something. Anything.

*Stop stalling, Andie.*

I rang the doorbell and held my breath.

My sister answered, wreathed in holiday smiles. She looked at me and her face froze. "Andie?"

I gave a half shrug. "I'm afraid so. Is it too late to come to the party?"

The door slammed in my face.

I guess it was.

From the other side, though, I could hear my sister calling, "Oh, my gosh, it's Andie!"

"No kidding? Well, let her in, idiot." My brother's voice.

The door swung wide and Ben hauled me in. "Bruno! About time you got here."

"I knew you'd be back," Keira informed me as he fetched my luggage from the porch. "You *so* owe everybody."

She was so right. I looked past my siblings, into a living room full of staring people, all casually dressed and wearing shiny New Year's hats. A few I didn't know and assumed were friends of Spencer and Keira.

Great. I was going to have an audience.

I began to feel squeamish as my gaze darted around the room. Gram sat enthroned in the easy chair. The way she was frowning at me, I half-expected her to command, "Off with her head." Spencer stood gawking by the punch bowl, his cup halfway to his mouth. Aunt Chloe was frozen by the canapés, and her new friend, Oscar, stood next to her. From the way he was checking me out, I was sure he'd heard all about me by now. April was there with her accountant boyfriend and Mom and Mr. Winkler. Even Dad. Amazingly, with both Winkler and Dad in the room, Spencer's tree was still intact. And there, next to it, stood Gabe Knightly. He smiled approvingly, and saluted me with his punch cup.

The action made my heart flip-flop. It also gave me courage. I cleared my throat. "I guess you're all wondering, well, those of you who know me, why I'm here after running out on you on Christmas day."

No one said a word, not even Keira, who always had something to say about everything. They just kept staring at me.

"I came to say how sorry I am. I have no excuse." I bit my lip and lifted an apologetic shoulder. "Except maybe Christmas cookie overload," I added, trying to lighten the moment. Nobody laughed. I plunged on. "I hope you can forgive me. And take me back," I added.

That was all I could get out. My throat constricted, and my eyes filled with tears.

"Oh, Andie, dear," Mom said. She came toward me, arms outstretched, and I ran into them and started crying.

That opened the floodgates. Everyone rushed me, talking at once, telling me that it was okay and that they loved me and were glad to have me back. Aunt Chloe fastened a party hat on me, snapping my chin with the elastic strap in the process.

"Here," said Dad from behind me, "let her take off her coat."

The coat came off, revealing the sweatshirt I'd had specially made with an old picture of all of us from a previous Christmas, gathered around a tippy-looking tree. Underneath it bright letters proclaimed *Happy Hartwell Holidays . . . There's No Place Like Home.*

"Look at that!" cried Aunt Chloe. "Oh, Andie. It's adorable. Jannie, wouldn't this make a cute Man Haters item?"

Mom was beaming approvingly at me.

I smiled at her and said, "I mean it."

"I never doubted it," she told me.

"I hate to break things up," said Spencer, "but if we're going to get downtown in time for the fireworks, we should get going."

That started a flurry of action. "Who's got room in their

car for Andie?" Keira asked, looking at Gabe. Subtle as always.

"I'll take her," he said.

"Well, I'm going to go home," Gram announced from her chair. "All that standing around in the cold is too much for my old bones. Come here and kiss me good-bye, Andrea," she commanded.

I came and knelt in front of her, and she caught my chin in her hand. "You're a good girl. I always knew you'd do the right thing." Then she nodded Gabe's direction. "You could do worse than that one. Don't let him slip through your hands again. Your eggs are getting old."

Oh, yes, it was good to be home.

"I have to swing by the house," I told Gabe as we filed out.

He was carrying my suitcases. "Need to drop these off?"

"And pick something up," I said, then turned to Mom to find out where she'd squirreled it.

"You're not serious, are you?" Gabe asked after we'd gotten in his car.

"Penance," I said.

He shook his head. "That's not penance, that's purgatory."

Nonetheless, when we got to the house I dug out Mom's present and put it on.

"How do I look?" I asked Gabe.

He grinned. "Like a Hartwell."

I have to admit, I felt a little silly visiting the various food and craft booths on Main Street in my silver paper hat, which matched what the rest of my family were wearing. But the hat was nothing compared to that pink jacket. Here I was, a walking billboard for my hometown, announcing that I'd done Carol. But wearing Mom's present was the least I could do to show my family I loved them and make up for my bad behavior.

At eleven thirty we all stood together on a snow carpeted sidewalk under bursts of color shooting into the sky. The fireworks made the falling snowflakes glow like specks of glitter. *So this is what it's like to live in a snow globe,* I thought, and smiled at Gabe. He smiled back and squeezed my hand.

"Can I reapply for the position of maid of honor?" I asked Keira at one point.

She smiled at me. "Yeah, I guess. By the way, we signed papers on the house."

"The one you wanted?"

Keira was practically bouncing as she nodded. "Of course, I'll have to work for a couple of years to pay for it."

A couple of years, I thought. Very smart of Spencer to speak in generalities.

"And I'll have to quit the coffee shop and get a real job," she continued. "I'm sure I won't have trouble finding something."

Maybe not, I thought, but keeping something might be another story. I tried to imagine my sister in an office and failed. Her boss, whoever that turned out to be, had my sympathies.

As the minutes marched toward midnight I saw lots of people I knew in the crowd. The Harrises strolled by. I smiled at Mr. Harris, but he pretended he didn't see. And there were the Baileys on the other side of Main Street. Mrs. Bailey waved at me, and I waved back. I saw James and Brittany too. James gave me an apologetic smile. Brittany saw and tightened her grip on his arm. She could keep him.

The herd of people shifted, and I caught sight of someone sitting on a wrought-iron bench in front of the bakery. I knew that face by now. It looked like the businessman at the airport, who looked suspiciously like the homeless man from the emergency room. This time he was in jeans and a suede coat, his face muffled by a thick, white scarf, his hair covered by a matching knitted cap. But he couldn't hide those eyes. Of course, I gawked.

He gave me a thumbs up sign right before two couples joined the crowd, hiding him from view. I took a step and craned my neck, bringing the bench back into view.

Now he was gone, and there was nothing on the bench but a folded blanket. A very colorful, neatly folded blanket that looked familiar. Gram's quilt!

I ran through the crowd, Gabe chasing me and calling, "Andie, where are you going? The countdown's about to start."

I picked up the quilt. It smelled like Christmas. When I brought it to Mom, she decided that whoever had taken it from the emergency room had suffered an attack of guilty conscience and left it on the bench for a more deserving soul. Maybe by coming back I'd proved myself deserving.

The celebrants started the countdown to midnight, and Dad and Mr. Winkler both moved closer to Mom. They looked like the human equivalent of an Oreo cookie, with both of them pressing against her, lips ready for action. It was anyone's guess who she'd end up with in the new year.

As for me, my coming year was full of questions too. One thing I knew for sure, I was going to be leaving my judgmental attitude and my grudges in the past.

And then it was midnight and people went into action, blowing noise makers and kissing each other, and yelling, "Happy New Year."

I went into action too. I grabbed Gabe by the coat lapels and kissed him. And what a lip-lock it was!

"Whoa. Does that mean what I hope it does?" he asked.

"It is a new year," I said, and he smiled and kissed me.

As we watched the last firework pinwheel sprinkle itself into a shower of golden dust, I envisioned myself moving home and starting an ad agency of my own right here in Carol.

Yeah, it was a big step for me, risky even, but it was the right one. Anyway, I knew I'd have at least one steady customer: Man Haters, Inc.